W9-CCE-635

THE SOUR CHERRY SURPRISE

THE
SOUR CHERRY
SURPRISE

DAVID
HANDLER

THOMAS DUNNE BOOKS
ST. MARTIN'S MINOTAUR
NEW YORK

THOMAS DUNNE BOOKS.
An Imprint of St. Martin's Press.

www.thomasdunnebooks.com
www.minotaurbooks.com

Library of Congress Cataloging-in-Publication Data

Handler, David, 1952–
    The sour cherry surprise : a Berger and Mitry mystery / David Handler.
        p.   cm.
    ISBN-13: 978-0-312-37669-7
    ISBN-10: 0-312-37669-3
    1. Mitry, Desiree (Fictitious character)—Fiction.   2. African American police—Fiction.   3. Policewomen—Fiction.   4. Berger, Mitch (Fictitious character)—Fiction.   5. Film critics—Fiction.   6. Drug dealers—Fiction.   7. City and town life—Fiction.   8. Connecticut—Fiction.   I. Title.
    PS3558.A4637S68 2008
    813'.54—dc22

                                                                        2008013625

First Edition: July 2008

10   9   8   7   6   5   4   3   2   1

FOR BERT NEWMAN, THE LAST ANGRY MAN,
WHO HAS ALWAYS BEEN THERE FOR ME

THE SOUR CHERRY SURPRISE

PROLOGUE

AND NOW MOLLY PROCTER dribbles the ball downcourt with eleven seconds left on the clock. The UConn Lady Huskies trailing Tennessee by one, 65–64 . . . ten seconds . . . nine. The fans are on their feet. . . . Coach Geno Auriemma has the ball in the hands of UConn's best clutch scorer since Diana Taurasi. And with the national championship on the line in . . . seven seconds, there's no one he trusts more than the southpaw from Dorset with the droopy socks. . . . Five seconds . . . This is it, folks. Geno's Huskies against Pat Summitt's Lady Vols for all of the marbles. . . . Three . . . Procter's at the top of the key. Quick swing pass to Montgomery, who ball fakes to Houston, then swings it back to Procter with the championship on the line. . . . One . . . Procter lets it fly from eighteen feet and . . . she . . . SCORES! UConn wins! UConn wins! Her teammates are mobbing Molly! She disappears under the pile of blue and white Husky jerseys. Oh, my, this has to be the most exciting game I have ever . . .

Molly Procter, age nine and three quarters, faked left, dribbled right, and heaved the ball to the portable basketball hoop in the driveway, tongue stuck out of the side of her mouth. Nothing but net. She pumped her fist in the air as Jen Beckwith pulled into the driveway in her red Saab convertible. It was Jen's driveway. Jen's hoop. Jen lived in the little cottage right across Sour Cherry Lane from Molly's and was starting point guard on the Dorset High Fighting Pilgrims. Really nice and not at all stuck up even though she was a star athlete, straight A student, gorgeous, and her grandmother was the richest woman in town. Jen and her mom weren't rich themselves. Jen's dad died a few years back, and her mom had to work day and night at a chiropractor's office. Jen was working full-time herself that summer at the bakery in The Works. Just home from work now in her bright green employee's T-shirt.

"Okay, squirt, show me what you've got." Jen positioned herself to defend Molly one-on-one.

Molly ran a hand through her head of unruly gold ringlets. She was a gangly, freckle-faced girl with a rabbity pink nose. Her wire-rimmed glasses were slightly bent out of shape. Her T-shirt and gym shorts hung loose on her frame. Baggy white socks drooped down to her scuffed sneakers. "You're on. Prepare to be dazzled." She gave Jen her awesome head fake, then dribbled right and—

Jen promptly slapped the ball away. "You still telegraph when you're going to the hoop."

"Do not."

"Do too. You stick your tongue out."

"So did Michael Jordon."

"Guess what? You're not M. J."

"Duh, I know. I'm M. *P.*"

"Tell me, M. *P.*, when was the last time you tried combing that hair? And what is *up* with those dorky socks?"

"They're my trademark. When I turn pro, Nike is going to pay me a fortune for them."

"I see. . . ."

"That's what *you* need. A trademark."

"So that's my problem," Jen sighed, turning gloomy on her.

"Hey, are you okay?"

Jen mustered a faint smile. "Sure, you bet."

"Just because I don't have breasts doesn't mean I can't keep secrets, you know."

"I know."

"Is this about that party you threw when your mom was gone?"

"Work on your head fake, squirt," Jen growled. "And dinner's in about an hour if you want some." Then she headed for the house and went inside.

Molly had been spending more and more of her time over at Jen's ever since her own mom had taken up with Clay. Molly had zero interest in letting Clay be her new dad. She already had a dad. Besides, she'd hated Clay ever since that first morning three weeks back when he came slouching out of her mom's bedroom with no shirt on and his jeans slung low; a wiry, rough-looking stranger with a lit cigarette between his lips. Molly was sitting at the kitchen table, tapping away on her mom's computer.

Clay popped open a can of beer first thing and drank deeply from it, watching her. The very first words he said to her were, "Don't you have somewhere else to be?"

Molly said, "I live here."

And he said, "Well, so do I from now on. And I don't like lippy little girls."

"I'm *not* a little girl."

Then Clay ordered her to stay out of the root cellar underneath the kitchen from now on. "You're never to go down there, understand? There are snakes down there."

"I'm not afraid of snakes," she snorted. "And *you* can't tell me what to do."

"Girl, don't ever talk back to me again," Clay shot back, smacking her in the ear with his open hand so hard that it rang for a whole day.

And so she had stayed away from the root cellar.

Molly used to have a happy life. Her mom was beautiful and talented and sweet. Author of a really cool series of kids' books about a Kerry blue terrier named Molly (in honor of guess who) that solved mysteries on a farm. All of the characters in her books were animals. The farm was based on Aunt Meggie's place up in Blue Hill, Maine, where they usually spent every August. Molly's dad was a historian at Wesleyan and just a really wise person. He knew the Latin words for things, and loved to work with his hands. He'd made their kitchen table himself out of oak. He'd put in French doors to brighten up the kitchen and built a raised teak deck outside it where they could eat supper at another table he'd built. Molly helped him do everything. She was his Designated Measurer. Always, no matter how busy he was, her dad made time for her. Taught her how to use her mom's computer when she was really little so she could communicate with him by e-mail when he was at the university.

But Molly's parents weren't the same people anymore. Her mom wasn't lively and bright-eyed, wasn't *there*. In her place there was a glassy-eyed stranger who scarcely seemed to notice that Molly was even alive. She'd stopped writing—Clay even dismantled her computer and stashed it in a closet. She didn't go out to the grocery store or anywhere else. Some days, she never came out of her room. Just stayed in there with Clay. Or with Hector, the Mexican man who worked for Clay. Once, she was in there with both men at the same time and Molly could hear her moaning real loud. After that, Molly took to sleeping in the tree house that she and her dad had made together in the old sugar maple. She had a sleeping bag up there and a flashlight so she could read. She was plenty comfy unless it rained. Then she'd tap on Jen's window and Jen would let her sleep with her.

Molly wanted her dad to come home. She wasn't sure why he'd left, except that her mom had made him. He'd told Molly he'd be staying with a friend for a few days. But a few days turned into a few weeks. And then her mom started going out to the Indian casinos after dinner and stumbling home late, drunk, and sometimes not alone. Clay was the third man she'd brought home, and the first who'd stayed. Molly sure wished her dad would kick him out and everything would be like it used to be.

But it wasn't.

Now that school was out for summer she either worked on her game in Jen's driveway or headed out to her own job on Big Sister Island, which was close to Sour Cherry. The footpath through the woods at the end of the lane led right into the Peck's Point Nature Preserve. The wooden causeway out to the island was just across a meadow from there. Molly's friend Mitch used to live on Big Sister until he went away. Mitch watched movies for a living and had the hugest collection of DVDs Molly had ever seen. He was real cool about loaning them to her. Real cool period, even though he was a Knicks fan and everyone knew the Knicks sucked and the Celtics ruled. Molly missed him a lot. Although the old lady who'd moved into his house, Bella, was okay. Bella rescued stray kitties—eighteen of them at last count. She kept them in Mitch's barn while she tried to find homes for them. She paid Molly five dollars a day to feed them and clean up after them. Some of the kitties liked to be petted. Others, the feral ones, would hiss at Molly and try to rake her.

Big Sister was where Molly took her dad the night he did try to come home. It had been a total disaster. Clay went chest-to-chest with him out in the driveway. Told him he didn't live there anymore, then proceeded to beat the snot out of him. Molly watched it all in horror from her tree house. Clay flailing away at him with his fists, kicking him in the ribs after he was down. By the time Molly had scrambled down and screamed at Clay to stop, her dad was lying on the ground in a bloody, sobbing heap. Clay told Molly if he ever saw her dad anywhere near the house again he'd "cut" him.

Molly had taken her dad by the hand and led him through the woods out to the island. He didn't respond when Molly talked to him. Just kept sobbing. He needed her to take care of him and so she had. There was an ancient, tattered sofa out in the barn. She got him settled on it, found a few tarps to cover him with, and told him he'd be safe there. In the morning, she cleaned his face and gave him some food from Bella's refrigerator after Bella left to run errands. Bella had no idea Molly's dad was out there. Mustn't know. She might not like the idea.

Every morning at dawn, Molly would sneak out there and hide her dad somewhere on the island for the day. In the boathouse. Or a nice sheltered area of beach, where he'd nibble at whatever food Molly had pilfered from Bella. He was incredibly sad. Cried a lot. Hardly ever spoke.

The only words he ever said to her were: "They won't let me back in."

"I know, Daddy. Are you okay?"

"They won't let me back in."

Evenings, Molly would tuck him back in the barn for the night. She didn't know how else to help him. She loved her dad. She wanted to be a good daughter.

On her way home through the woods one night, Molly stumbled upon a man who was crouched there in the darkness with a pair of binoculars.

"Hey, quit that!" she protested when he shined a flashlight in her eyes.

He immediately shushed her.

So she whispered, "What are you doing here, mister?"

"I'm a biologist with the D.E.P. We're trying to track down a fisher that's been spotted in these woods."

"What's a fisher?"

"It's a carnivorous predator. Sort of like a bobcat. Lets out a god-awful shriek. Eats small dogs, cats . . ."

"Next you're going to tell me it eats little girls," Molly scoffed.

"I'm perfectly serious. They wander down from Canada. Speaking of which, where did *you* wander from?"

"Prunus Cerebus."

"Prunus Cerebus? Which planet is that?"

"It's not a planet, you dope. That's Latin for Sour Cherry."

"Oh, I get it. You live on Sour Cherry Lane. What's your name?"

She told him.

"What are you doing out here this time of night, Molly?"

"Exploring."

"Well, you'd better get on home."

Which she had, though she thought he was full of it. There were no fishers in the woods anywhere near Dorset. If there were, her dad would have told her. Besides, if that man really were a biologist with the Department of Environmental Protection he'd know that Prunus Cerebus wasn't a planet.

No question about it, Molly's life was turning strange.

And then it went from strange to just totally sucky.

Somehow, Bella got wind that Molly's dad was staying out there. She called in that mean trooper lady, who sent him away to the hospital. Then the trooper lady tracked Molly down when Molly was trying to shoot hoops over at Jen's. He was going to be okay, she promised Molly before she started asking her a whole bunch of questions about Clay and her mom. Acting like she wanted to be Molly's friend.

Her dad really did start to feel better. He even found a place to stay that was right nearby. His first night back, as Molly lay there in her tree house reading a library book by flashlight, she allowed herself to hope that maybe everything would be okay again. Clay and Hector would go away soon. Her dad would move back in and her mom would smile and be herself again. Everyone would be happy.

It was a warm night. Somewhere down below her a skunk was marking its turf, the stink wafting its way up to Molly's nostrils. Scarcely a breeze stirred the leaves around her. All was quiet.

Until she heard rapid footsteps somewhere down the lane. And a fierce struggle of some kind. Someone groaning. Then a horrifying shriek that pierced the still of the night. It was a sound unlike anything Molly Procter had ever heard before. And it was not any fisher. Molly knew exactly what it was.

It was a man dying.

Two Days Earlier

CHAPTER 1

IT WAS A CRISP, beautiful fall afternoon. They'd thrown their mountain bikes into the back of Mitch's plum-colored Studebaker pickup and driven out to Bluff Point with its miles of bike trails that meandered their way alongside the cliffs overlooking Long Island Sound. Mitch pedaled along next to her, his pudgy cheeks flushed. There was no one else out there. Just the cormorants and them. And lord, was that man pedaling hard. He was even pulling away from her.

"Come on, stretch!" he called to her over his shoulder. "I'm putting you to shame."

"Doughboy, you have a vivid imagination!"

They arrived at a scenic outcropping with an unobstructed view of the whole coastline and climbed down off of their bikes, chests heaving.

She had sandwiches and water in her day pack. "Want something to eat?"

"No, I want to kiss you."

And so he did, the two of them standing out there on that rocky ledge with the water lapping beneath them. And there was no one else, nothing else. Just them and their love and desire. His hands found their way up under her T-shirt to her breasts. She let out a soft gasp. And now he was whispering something in her ear. Not words exactly. More like a buzzing. Or a ringing, ringing . . .

And with a start Des was awake. She dove for the phone, the sleeping lump beside her in bed not so much as stirring. The illuminated dial on the alarm clock told her it was just past one A.M.

"Resident Trooper Mitry," she said softly, rubbing the sleep from her eyes as she listened to the Troop F dispatcher. Her fore-head felt damp. The night had turned warm and humid. The bedroom curtains hung limp. "Fine. I'll be right there."

Naked, Des got out of bed. Fumbled in her closet for a summer-weight uniform, in her dresser for a sports bra and thong. She padded silently into the bathroom and showered quickly. She was just starting to towel dry her lean six-foot one-inch frame when she felt another dizzy spell coming on. The bathroom was spinning. Her heart racing faster and faster. She slumped to the edge of the tub with her head between her knees, praying she wouldn't black out like she had the other evening, when she'd hit the kitchen floor with a thud and been out for something like five minutes. Thank God he hadn't gotten home yet. Breathing slowly in and out, Des steadied herself. Felt okay enough to finish drying off and get dressed. She ran a comb through her short, nubby hair. Put on her heavy horn-rimmed glasses. Des wore no makeup. She needed none.

His nightstand lamp was on now. He was sitting up in bed, bare-chested, his impossibly broad shoulders tapering down to an even more impossibly narrow waist. Pecs and abs rippled. Dark skin glowed in the lamplight. Truly, he was the most beautiful black man she had ever seen. All she wanted to do right now was tear her uniform off and stretch her naked self out against all seventy-eight inches of him.

"Desi, where are you going at this time of night?" he yawned, running a hand over his stubbly jaw.

"Drug overdose at a party. Teenagers, apparently."

He let out a laugh. "In Dorset? Get out."

"It happens here, Brandon." She perched on the edge of the bed and slipped on her socks. Stepped into her shiny black bro-gans, tied the laces. "It all happens here."

"Okay, but why do they always have to call you?"

"Because it's always my job, silly man."

"Then it's time to get you a new one. You ought to put in for a transfer. Get back on Major Crimes. Lord knows you've paid your penance."

"And *you* ought to go back to sleep," responded Des, who didn't like him or anyone else trying to run her career.

"Will you at least answer me this . . . ?" His rich burgundy voice was a purr now. "How does a woman in uniform look so beautiful at one o'clock in the morning?"

"You, sir, are still asleep and dreaming."

"No, ma'am, I'm wide awake and looking." He smiled at her. The smile that instantly turned her back into a bashful, knock-kneed giraffe of a high school girl with insides of melted caramel. "And that's not all I'm doing."

"Don't start anything you can't finish."

"Try me." He reached for her playfully.

She darted for the door. "Baby, I am gone. Get back to sleep. That's an order."

"Whatever you say, master sergeant."

Des got the coffee going in the kitchen, which opened out into the dining room and living room to form one airy space. When she'd redone her little house overlooking Uncas Lake she'd wanted to take maximum advantage of the view and the light. Back when she shared the place with her friend Bella Tillis, the living room had served as Des's studio. Here, she'd created her passionate, horrifying depictions of the murder victims she'd encountered on the job. Capturing their hollowed eye sockets and congealed brain matter on paper had been her way of dealing. But now that Brandon was back in her life, the living room was a proper living room with sleek black leather sofa, matching armchairs and glass coffee table. Her easel and 18 × 24 Strathmore 400 drawing pad now resided down in the garage, formerly known as Cats Landing. But their gang of rescued strays had moved out when Bella had. Brandon hated cats. It was mutual.

Brandon's very first night back Kid Rock peed in his $1,200 Il Bisonte briefcase.

The damp, windowless garage wasn't nearly as desirable a studio space. But that wasn't a big problem because Des had felt zero desire to draw lately.

Her Sig-Sauer was in the hall closet along with her shield and big Smokey hat. She snapped her holster onto her wide black belt, taking note of the fact that her uniform trousers, which had been snug a few weeks back, were now almost falling off of her hips. She wasn't eating. It was that knot in her stomach. The one she always used to have before she'd met Mitch. The only time in her whole life it had ever gone away was when the two of them had been together.

Odd that she'd been dreaming about him just now when the phone rang. It had been three whole months since she'd given him back his grandmother Sadie's engagement ring. Had to after Brandon had shown up on her doorstep and begged her to forgive him. He'd split up with Anita. Got himself transferred from D.C. back to Connecticut. And he wanted her back.

"Brandon, you don't even know me anymore," she had said.

To which he had said: "Yes, I do. You're still the woman I fell in love with. We weren't ready for each other, Desi. And we both got a little lost. But now we've found each other again."

When he'd taken her in his arms and kissed her it was as if he'd never left. And she had never even known that overweight Jewish film critic from New York City named Mitch Berger. There was Brandon and there was no one else. He was everything she'd ever wanted. Everything. They belonged together. So she had forgiven him. That's what you did when you loved someone. Okay, sure, their marriage had failed. But Des believed in their marriage.

Believed in commitment. That was who she was. Life with Brandon was who she was. He had a new high-powered federal prosecutor's gig in New Haven. Exciting plans to run for the U.S. Congress as the Democratic Party's great black hope. They were getting along great. Life was good. It was all good.

Mitch hadn't been a mistake. He was simply what she'd needed at the time. Just as her art had been what she'd needed. Her walk on the wild side. The one she'd never had when she was such a straight arrow at West Point. She would always look back on Mitch fondly. Dream about him, too, apparently. But that time in her life was over now. She was back to real.

When the coffee was ready she filled her travel mug and went out the side door to her Crown Vic, sipping the strong brew as she eased her way down the hill to the Boston Post Road, then south toward Old Shore Road. Soon it would be Des's busy season here on the Gold Coast. After the Fourth of July Dorset's sedate year-round population of 7,000 would swell to a boisterous 14,000. Right now, the historic shoreline village at the mouth of the Connecticut River, halfway between New York and Boston, was fast asleep in the hazy dark of night. Des drove with her high beams on, the eyes of night creatures shining at her from the brush alongside the deserted road.

She got off Old Shore Road at Turkey Neck Lane, which wended its way through meadows and marshland before it arrived at Sour Cherry Lane, onetime home of the landing for the ferry that in days of yore was the only way across the river to Old Saybrook. These days, Sour Cherry was a remote little enclave tucked away among the wild orchards that gave the lane its name. There were three weathered farmhouses, rentals, all of them. And perched high on a rocky ledge above them, a white-shingled mansion that commanded a view of the farmhouses, the river, Big Sister Island and Long Island Sound. There were lights on in the mansion.

And lights blazing inside and outside the first farmhouse on the left, where Dorset's volunteer ambulance van was wedged in the driveway between a red Saab convertible and a portable basketball hoop. The name on the mailbox said Beckwith. Des knew the Beckwith name. Patricia Beckwith, who lived in that mansion up there, was the village's richest, most fearsome old widow. Des also knew Sour Cherry. Keith Sullivan, the young electrician who'd rewired her house, lived in a little place next door to this one with his new bride, Amber, who was a grad student at Yale. Des had been to a cookout at the Sullivans' house back when she and Mitch were still together. She did not know who lived in the house directly across the lane from the Beckwith farmhouse. The van parked in the driveway there, which belonged to Nutmegger Professional Seamless Gutters, reminded Des she needed to call someone to come clean out her own downspouts. Because when it came to such dirty household chores Brandon qualified as a never.

Marge and Mary Jewett, two no-nonsense sisters in their fifties, ran Dorset's volunteer ambulance service. Marge was loading their gear back into the van when Des got out of her cruiser. Mary was still inside the house.

"Hey, Marge, what have we got?"

"A slightly freaked out sixteen-year-old named Jen Beckwith," Marge responded with cool professional detachment.

No familiarity. No warmth. Just that same cold shoulder so many of the locals had been giving Des since the breakup. Her romance with Mitch had been a feel-good story in Dorset. The single black female trooper and the Jewish widower from New York were beloved prime-time entertainment. But now that Mitch was out and Brandon was in, Des was simply one half of That Black Couple who lived on Uncas Lake Road. She hadn't known how good she'd had it before. She'd enjoyed Dorset at its most welcoming. Now she was experiencing its other side. In a small town, other people felt they owned your life.

"It seems Jen was hosting a party," Marge continued crisply. "There were boys. There was alcohol. And she's on Zoloft, a prescription antidepressant that does not interact well with alcohol. She claims she downed a couple of Mike's Hard Lemonades. Then her heart started racing so fast she thought she was having a heart attack and she called us. But her heart rate was totally normal when we got here. Blood pressure, too. She's alert, responsive and seems completely sober. Frankly, if she had more than two sips of anything I'd be surprised."

"Were they doing drugs?"

"She says no."

"And do we believe her?"

"*I* do," Marge said defensively. "With all due respect, I know Jen. She's as straight as they come. A National Merit Scholar. First team All-Shoreline at basketball and soccer. My guess? Reaching out to us was her way of hitting the panic button. Something was going on here tonight that upset her."

"Something sexual?"

"Doesn't look like she was fighting anybody off. But she won't tell us a thing."

"Any of the other kids still around?"

Marge shook her head. "They were hightailing it up Turkey Neck just as we were getting here."

"Recognize any of them?"

"I was just trying to keep my bus on the road. But I do know who some of her friends are, if it comes to that. They're athletes, most of them. Good families."

"And where are her parents?"

"Single parent, Kimberly. Jen says she's out of town for a couple of nights." Marge gestured with her chin over in the direction of the mansion. "Jen's dad was Johnny Junior, old lady Beckwith's son. He died three, four years ago."

Now Mary Jewett came out the front door of the house and joined them. Marge was three years older but the sisters looked enough alike to be twins.

"The latest I heard," Mary put in, "is Kimberly's been having her spine readjusted by Steve Gardiner, that chiropractor over in Old Saybrook. He's her boss. He's also married, which is nothing new for Kimberly."

"She left Jen here alone?"

"Her grandmother's supposed to be looking out for her," Marge answered.

"You're not expecting *us* to call her, are you?" Mary's voice grew heavy with dread.

"No, I'll take over from here. You girls can go back to bed."

The small living room was strewn with beer cans and hard lemonade bottles. Since Des hadn't personally witnessed any illegal drinking she had wiggle room, which was a good thing. Under a new Connecticut state law, adults were being busted for allowing underage drinking in their homes—even if they hadn't known it was going on. The law complicated her life as a resident trooper. She preferred to work with parents and their teenaged kids, not treat them like felons.

Cushions were heaped here and there on the floor. A lot of candles lit, the lights turned low. The air reeked of heavy perfume and cologne. She did not smell any pot smoke. Saw no roaches in the ashtray on the coffee table. What she did see on the table were five, six, seven different lipsticks in colors ranging from tangerine to bronze to grape.

Right away, Des had a pretty good idea what had been going on. She just hadn't known it was going on in Dorset.

The lipstick Jen Beckwith had on was hot pink. She wore no other makeup. Jen was a slim girl with blue eyes and long, shiny blond hair. She was almost but not quite pretty. Her forehead was a bit high, chin too pointy. And her mouth was drawn terribly tight. Hers was not the face of a girl who smiled easily. Jen wore a cropped, sleeveless belly shirt, a pair of thigh-high shorts and flip-flops. She took care of her body. There wasn't an ounce of extra flab on her toned, muscular arms or shapely golden legs. Her right knee jiggled nervously as she sat there on the sofa. Her hair and clothing appeared totally neat. No scratches. No signs of a struggle.

Des took off her big hat and sat in the armchair across the coffee table from Jen. Outside, the Jewett girls backed out of the driveway and steamed up the lane for home. "Hey, Jen, I'm Resident Trooper Mitry."

"I know who you are." Her voice was small.

"I won't ask you who else was here tonight because I know you won't tell me and it would just be embarrassing for both of us. But do you want to tell me what happened?"

"I had some friends over," Jen replied, her eyes fastened on the carpet. "We had some beers and stuff. Nothing major. But then my heart started beating *really* fast and I remembered I'm not supposed to drink because of these pills I'm taking so I—"

"Going to stick with that story, are you?"

"It's not a story," Jen insisted, raising her sharp chin at her.

"Okay, fine. But tell me something—was this your first?"

"My first what?"

"Rainbow Party."

Jen reddened. "I don't know what you mean."

"Girl, do you honestly think I don't know what was going on here? These things started in the inner city at least eighteen months ago."

"Look, I *don't* want to talk to about it, okay?"

19

"Then do you want to wipe that dumb-ass lipstick off your mouth? You look like you just chugalugged a whole bottle of Pepto-Bismol."

Jen heaved a suffering sigh, then reluctantly got up and fetched a tissue from the kitchen.

"Okay, here's what I'm guessing happened," Des said as the girl sat back down, wiping her mouth clean. "Tonight was your very first one. Maybe you weren't even totally up for it. It was more like something of a dare. And when things started moving right along, well, you realized you *really* weren't happy."

"I didn't punk out," Jen objected heatedly.

"Didn't say you did. I'm saying you showed a healthy dose of respect for yourself. Trouble was, you couldn't exactly take off because this is your own house—so you dialed nine-one-one and pulled the plug. Smart move, Jen. Give yourself a high five. Only, now here comes the bad news: I have to contact your mother. *And* take you to Shoreline Clinic for a blood sample to determine your drug and alcohol level."

"But I didn't do anything!"

"Your call was logged, Jen. I have to follow the rules. If I don't, I lose my job."

"My mom's on Block Island. I'm not even sure of the phone number."

"Then I have to call your grandmother."

The girl's eyes widened. "You mean right now?"

"Uh-huh."

"Have you ever *met* my grandmother?"

"No, I've never had that pleasure."

"Oh, this is going to be just great. . . ."

"Do you have to tell her everything?"

"She already knows about the drinking," Des pointed out as

she steered her cruiser back toward Dorset. It had been quiet at the clinic tonight. They'd whisked Jen in and out. Now the two of them were headed for her grandmother's house.

Patricia Beckwith was waiting up for them. When Des had phoned her the old lady hadn't tried to talk her out of the blood test. Or demanded to accompany them, as was her legal right. She'd simply intoned: "Our society's laws apply to everyone. Do what you must. My porch light will be on."

"And I'm afraid I do have to tell her what else you were up to," Des added.

"But that *is* everything," Jen pointed out.

"Then I guess I have to tell her everything," acknowledged Des, who was not entirely happy about it. Because if she landed too hard on a kid like Jen then Jen would never reach out to her if something truly awful was going down. Kids got high. Kids got busy. It wasn't Des's business to tell their parents how to raise them. But it *was* her business to make sure nobody got stupid. Some of those kids who Marge Jewett had seen hightailing it from Jen's may have been over the legal limit. And that was the very definition of stupid. She glanced over at Jen, who'd thrown on a Dorset High hoody and was hugging a book bag in her lap, looking all of thirteen. "How about you? Do you have someone who you can talk to about this?"

Jen let out a hollow laugh. "I have my shrink. She's the one who put me on Zoloft."

"What happens when you're not on it?"

"Why do you care?"

"Just asking."

"I obsess, okay?"

"About . . . ?"

"My flaws. Like if I screw up a single answer on a test. Or miss one free throw in a game. Trust me, I can turn myself into a real nut job."

"Not everyone gets sixteen hundred on their SATs and scores a hundred points a game. It's okay to fail."

"Now you sound just like my shrink."

"Do you have a boyfriend?"

"No way. I mean, there's a guy I used to like but they're all such immature assholes."

"Most of them." Des turned in at Patricia Beckwith's mailbox now. As she started up the steep, twisting driveway she could feel the girl shrink into the seat, both knees jiggling. "Was he one of the boys at your party tonight?"

Jen nodded her head, swallowing.

The driveway crested at the top of the hill and circled around in front of the big house, which was one of the oldest center chimney colonials in Dorset, dating back to the early 1700s. The porch light was on, as promised. Des pulled up out front and parked. From where they sat she could see the lights of Old Saybrook across the river.

"Jen, I wear a lot of other hats besides this big one. If you ever want to sit down over a cup of coffee, call me, okay?"

Jen didn't respond. Just took the card Des offered her and stuffed it into her book bag.

Patricia Beckwith stood out on the front porch waiting for them in a blue silk robe and red and white striped pajamas, her feet in a pair of sheepskin slippers. She was a tall, straight, silver-haired woman of rigid dignity. About seventy-five, with a long, seamed face and wide-set blue eyes. It was a face unaccustomed to spontaneous laughter and smiles. It was the face that Jen had inherited.

"Real sorry about this, Nana," the girl murmured as she slipped past her into the house.

"As well you should be, young lady." Patricia didn't sound angry. Her voice was surprisingly gentle.

The entry hall had an umbrella stand with a mirror. A

grandfather clock that wasn't running. A steep, L-shaped staircase that led up to the second floor.

"I've made up the room next to mine," she called to Jen, who was already halfway up the stairs. "We shall have a proper talk in the morning."

"Whatever you say." Jen paused on the stairs and added, "Nice meeting you, trooper."

"Make it Des. And I meant that about the coffee, you hear?"

Jen nodded her blond head. "I hear you. Thanks." Then she went up to her room and shut the door.

"Why was she thanking you?" Patricia demanded to know.

"For listening, I suppose."

"To what, her feverish adolescent rants? Did you know that a psychiatrist has put that girl on happy-happy pills? What rubbish. Jen's a bright, healthy young woman who excels at anything she sets her mind to. She's a born achiever. Has a wonderful life ahead of her. And instead of enjoying it she pops pills and sits in a room three times a week whining to a total stranger. We all have problems in this life. When you have a problem, you solve it. And if you're unhappy, well, get used to it. Life isn't for sissies."

"Mrs. Beckwith, you and I need to have a talk."

"Certainly."

She led Des into a small, paneled parlor that was stuffy and smelled of old books and mold. The ceiling was very low in there, the beams exposed. There was a walk-in stone fireplace. One entire wall of built-in bookcases crammed with hardcover books. There was a chintz loveseat and matching wingback chair. Next to the chair was an end table that had a collection of Edith Wharton stories on it along with an open box of chocolate-covered cherries, a bottle of Harvey's Bristol Cream sherry and a half-empty wine goblet.

A gray-muzzled dachshund was dozing in the chair. Patricia

picked it up and sat with it in her lap, the dog not so much as stirring. Des sat on the love seat, twirling her hat in her hands.

"Now what is this all about, trooper?" There was a fixed brightness to the old lady's gaze that was meant to intimidate, and did. "And kindly do not pander to me. I cannot abide people who treat me like a doddering old fool. Speak plainly and accurately and we shall get along fine."

"Jen was throwing a party at her house. There was alcohol. And no adult supervision on the premises."

"An obvious failure on my part," Patricia conceded readily. "Jen is studious and sensible—nothing at all like her mother. I had no idea she was planning any such party." She took a small sip of her sherry. "Tell me, was there sexual activity?"

"Of a sort, yes."

Patricia's gaze turned icy. "Just exactly what sort?"

"That's something I'd prefer to discuss with her mother."

"And you shall. I have the phone number of the inn where Kimberly is presently shacked up with her married chiropractor. She will return to Dorset on the very first ferry tomorrow morning if I have anything to say about it. And believe me, I do. I allow her to live in their cottage rent-free. I provide health insurance for her and Jen both. I paid for Jen's car. I intend to pay for her college education. Furthermore, it is *I* who you've phoned at two A.M. So you will kindly provide me with the details."

Des shoved her heavy horn-rimmed glasses up her nose and said, "There's a game the kids play. They call it a Rainbow Party. It's, well, think of it as an X-rated version of Spin the Bottle."

Patricia reached for a chocolate-covered cherry and popped it in her mouth, chewing on it slowly before she said, "Please elaborate."

"Each of the girls wears a different color of lipstick. Whichever girl leaves her mark on the most boys wins."

"They perform fellatio on them, is that it?"

"Yes, ma'am."

"Well, I can certainly understand what the boys get out of it, but what would possess a group of bright, self-respecting young women to debase themselves in such a fashion?"

"A combination of alcohol and peer pressure. For what it's worth, Jen told me it was her first such party. And it appears she got cold feet."

"You're saying that's why she called the Jewett sisters?"

"It would appear so."

"Please thank them for me if you happen to speak to them before I do. And thank you for attending to Jen." The old lady shook her head. "It's as if the women's movement never even happened. If only these girls knew how hard it was for those of us who came before them to get up off of our knees. But for them it's ancient history. The sad truth is that they don't even care." She studied Des carefully for a moment, as if she were trying to decide something about her. "I worked my entire adult life, you know. I was *not* about to be one of those ladies who play bridge and conduct meaningless affairs out of utter boredom. My late husband was involved in international banking in Brazil, Portugal, Singapore. Wherever we went, I taught English at a school for the underprivileged. After John left the bank and we returned here, I taught at the women's prison in Niantic." She reached for another of her chocolates. "Jen's father was raised here. Johnny was never a strong boy, physically or emotionally. He lacked decisiveness and drive. Had a difficult time finding a career. Intelligent young women saw him as a poor choice for a husband, despite his wealth and good name. All of which made him easy prey for a conniving little gold digger like Kimberly. I insisted that he find work. I cannot abide slackers. So my boy was selling suits in the Business Casuals section of the Mens Wearhouse in Waterford when he dropped dead of a brain aneurysm three years ago last month. He was thirty-eight years old. I also insisted that Kimberly sign a prenuptial agreement when they married. Consequently, she got very little after Johnny passed. The bulk of his assets are in a trust fund that Jen can't touch until she graduates from college. Although she's already displaying a good deal more emotional maturity at age sixteen than her mother has ever possessed. Running off to Block Island with a married man, the little fool. And he's an even bigger fool." Patricia stroked the sleeping dog in her lap, gazing down at it fondly. "Has it ever occurred to you that the reason we can't live forever is that we know too much?"

"About what, ma'am?"

"What pathetic frauds we all are. Only the young can be taken in by the false promises of others. When you get to be my age you can see right through everyone. And believe me, that is one hopeless way to exist. I sleep very little now." The old lady had become so chatty it occurred to Des that she might be lonely. "Mostly, I read. Are you a reader?"

"When I have time."

"And how up are you on the village gossip?"

"I hear what people tell me."

"I'm wondering about one of my other tenants. Perhaps you know them."

"I know the Sullivans."

Patricia nodded her head. "Very nice young couple. Keith is so amiable and helpful. He's done any number of electrical repairs for me. Plows my driveway, installs my air conditioners. The man won't ever take a nickel. And Amber is a terribly gifted scholar, I'm told. You wouldn't think they would be happy together, being so different. But there's just no telling with love, is there?"

"So they tell me."

"Actually, I was wondering about Richard and Carolyn Procter. They rent the house directly across the lane from Kimberly and

Jen. They've been hoping to purchase it should I ever decide to sell—which I haven't. Their little girl is named Molly."

"Don't know them, I'm afraid."

"Richard is a very distinguished historian at Wesleyan," Patricia went on, practically glowing at the mention of him. "There is no one alive who knows more about the early economic and social structure of the Connecticut shoreline than Richard Procter. He's written numerous volumes. And Carolyn is a noted author of children's literature herself, as well as a tremendous beauty. Comes from a fine old Massachusetts family, the Chichesters." Now Patricia's face dropped. "But it seems they have split up. Richard has moved out and Carolyn has taken up with some sort of a tradesman."

"And are you having trouble collecting the rent?"

"No, it's nothing like that. I simply wondered if you'd heard where Richard has ended up. He used to stop by regularly to drop off books that he thought I might like. I'd read them and then we'd discuss them over tea. I haven't many friends left, to be frank. Stimulating ones, anyhow. The village hens mostly wish to talk about their aches and pains. Richard shares my passionate love for the novels of Henry James. He's also keenly interested in the Beckwith family history. The Beckwiths were this area's earliest industrial settlers, you know. Operated the very first sawmill right up the road on Turkey Neck. Old Cyrus himself built this very house back in 1725." Her sherry goblet was empty. She poured herself some more and took a sip, staring into the big stone fireplace. "The last time Richard came by he promised he'd drop off a novel called *Time and Again* by someone named Jack Finney. It's about a modern day fellow who travels back in time to old New York. Richard was positive I'd adore it." She glanced at Des challengingly. "I don't suppose you've ever . . ."

"Know it and love it." The book had been a favorite of Mitch's. She still had his dog-eared old paperback around somewhere.

"My point is that Richard hasn't brought it by or so much as called. He's always been so thoughtful that I suppose I'm worried about him."

"Have you asked Carolyn where he's living?"

The old lady's eyes widened. "Oh, no, that would be inappropriate. I did try the phone company, but they've no new listing for him in Dorset or in any of our neighboring towns. Yesterday I placed a call to Professor Robert Sorin in Moodus. He's Richard's closest friend in the history department. But the lady with whom I spoke, his dog sitter, said Professor Sorin's away at a seminar in Ohio and won't be back for a couple of days." Patricia hesitated, her thin lips pursing. "You no doubt think I'm being clingy."

"Not at all. He's a friend and you're concerned. Perfectly understandable. I'll ask around," Des said, climbing to her feet. "If I hear anything, I'll let you know."

"Thank you." Patricia relinquished her chair to the dog and led Des back to the front door. "Trooper, there's one thing you haven't told me that has left me exceedingly puzzled. The girl who 'wins' one of these lipstick contests of theirs . . . What does she get?"

"Do you mean beyond unlimited social cachet? She gets payback."

"Payback?"

"The boy of her choice has to return the favor—in front of everyone."

"Why, that's d-disgusting," the old lady sputtered.

"It's the world we're living in."

"Well, I don't care for this world."

"Sometimes I don't either, ma'am. But it's the only one we've got."

CHAPTER 2

"AND *FOUR AND FIVE*. Do not wimp out on me now, Berger! And *six*. Come on, *feel* that weight lifting off of the earth!"

As Mitch lay there on the pressing bench, straining to push the barbell toward the ceiling, he could *feel* his shoulder sockets about to explode. His arms shook; sweat poured off of him.

"And *seven*. Give me one more, Berger!"

Somehow, he did—spurred on by the high-octane encouragement of the bodacious Liza Birnbaum, who happened to be a New York State kickboxing champion when she wasn't working as a personal trainer here at the Equinox Fitness Center in Columbus Circle.

"You are kicking ass!" she whooped as she helped him cradle the barbell, which he was about to drop on his windpipe. "Now go hit the cycle for a twelve-minute cardio cooldown and you're done. Come on, shake your booty! Shake it!"

Gasping, Mitch staggered over toward a Lifecycle.

"Damn, you are one stone fox," Liza exclaimed, heaping the flirty on him now. "I'd do you myself if you weren't a client." She never got busy with her clients, which meant she hadn't done the likes of Harry Connick Jr., Matt Lauer or Sarah Jessica Parker.

Mitch pedaled, amazed by his reflection in the mirror. He still couldn't believe how much progress he'd made in three months. A whopping thirty-six pounds of blubber *gone*. His man-boobs replaced by a high, solid ridge of pectoral muscles. He had a flat stomach, bulging biceps and a ton of pep. All thanks to working out five times a week with Liza and following a supervised diet.

Believe it or not, Mitch Berger, roly-poly lead film critic for New York City's most prestigious daily newspaper, was now a fitness freak. Partly this was out of professional necessity. The camera made everyone look ten pounds heavier. First time he'd seen himself on TV he thought he bore way too close a resemblance to the young Zero Mostel. Partly this was how he was getting over the green-eyed monster named Desiree Mitry. Mitch was not the man he'd been when Des had accepted his proposal of marriage and then dumped him all in the same week. He was a stronger man. She'd blown him away, no question. But he'd already withstood the death of his beloved wife, Maisie, and he would survive this. Des had made a choice. You accept the choices that people make and you move on. And so he had.

He relaxed in the sauna for a few minutes, then showered and toweled off. Ran his fingers through his newly styled short hair, which was camera ready without combing.... *"All right, Mr. De Mille, I'm ready for my close up...."* He also had camera ready teeth (whitened), eyebrows (waxed, which hurt like hell) and an engaging new on-camera delivery, thanks to Sylvia One, the media coach who had de-ummed his delivery and taught him to *embrace* the camera like a good friend. And he *embraced* it in an entirely new Ralph Lauren wardrobe courtesy of Sylvia Two, his personal stylist (for some unknown reason, all of the people in New York who did this kind of thing were women named Sylvia). Today Mitch was dressed in a dazzling white oxford cloth button-down, cashmere single-breasted navy blazer, Polo jeans that were four sizes smaller in the waist than he used to wear and black penny loafers. Basically, it was the same outfit he used to schlump around in except much nicer. Plus he was no longer shaped like an avocado. Actually, here was how Sylvia Two had put it: Mitch now *owned* his look.

Energized by his workout, he bounded out the front door of the club into the bright sun beating down on Columbus Circle, a buoyant spring in his step that was like Astaire walking on air. Equinox had two other branches downtown but Mitch no longer lived downtown. His old apartment on Gansvoort in the now impossibly chic meat-packing district was being converted into an impossibly chic French bath and bedding emporium. He'd just moved into a ground floor apartment on West 105th Street with a wood-burning fireplace and a deep, narrow garden where he could continue to grow herbs and Sungold tomatoes like he had out on Big Sister. Clemmie, his snuggly Dorset house cat, had happily gone Manhattan with him. But Quirt, his lean outdoor hunter, had run and hid in the woods. So Bella Tillis, who'd rented his carriage house, had inherited Quirt when she took over the place. Quirt was really more Des's cat anyway.

It was 11:30, but by no means the start of Mitch's day. He'd been up since dawn writing his review of the new Nick Cage film and generating fresh content for his Web sites *and* polishing up his proposal for *Ants in Her Plants,* the new film reference guide that he hoped would do for screwball comedies what his first three bestselling guides—*It Came from Beneath the Sink, Take My Wife, Please* and *They Went That-a-Way*—had already done for sci-fi, crime and the western.

Mitch's feet still wanted to take him to Times Square, but the newspaper had relocated to a new complex on West 57th Street and Ninth Avenue when a giant media empire gobbled it up earlier that year. Lacy Nickerson, the distinguished, old-school arts editor who'd lured Mitch to the paper from a scholarly journal, had been ousted in favor of Shauna Wolnikow, age twenty-eight, who went by the title of intergroup manager, not editor. Shauna's mandate was to *platform* Mitch's career, which meant turning him into a multimedia content provider for all of the empire's outlets.

He was now a highly visible on-camera personality for its twenty-four-hour cable news network. Contributed film reviews and on-air chat time to its talk radio network. Hosted a weekly online interactive chat group. Maintained a daily blog. And ran an advertiser-supported Web site tied in with his reference guides, where he provided capsule reviews, DVD picks, movie trivia and all sorts of amusing video downloads. Thanks to Mitch, cineastes across the globe could now, with a mere click, catch Troy Donahue singing the theme song to *Palm Springs Weekend*. Shauna had also taken to flying him around the country for speaking engagements before college film societies in places like Houston and Columbus—where the empire happened to own television stations that were just dying to have Mitch appear on their local morning news shows.

Even though Mitch had always been much more at home in a darkened screening room than in the limelight, he was throwing himself into his new career with enthusiasm. But it was a bit of whirlwind. He was so busy he barely had time to watch the movies he was reviewing. He definitely had no time to play the blues on his beloved sky blue Stratocaster anymore.

Yet here's something he noticed as he made his way through the crowd of humanity on West 57th Street: He was a Somebody now. People recognized him. Good-looking young women checked him out with frank interest.

And here's a thought he couldn't chase from his head: *When Des sees me on TV she'll be sorry she picked the other guy.*

The first thing he did was head straight for the fourth floor radio booth to tape his Nick Cage review. Then he dashed into the TV studio to be fitted with a lapel mike and earpiece for his five-minute spot on *Midday Live*. The studio looked every bit like a newsroom, complete with desks and computers. Beyond an artfully placed glass partition, people with rolled up sleeves were rushing around doing important, newsy things. But the studio was actually a made-for-TV newsroom that had been erected inside of the real one. Those people with rolled up sleeves worked next door in the sports department. At first, this bit of on-camera fakery had unsettled Mitch. He'd felt like an actor playing a role. But he'd done it so many times that he was used to it.

And now the Los Angeles–based host of *Midday Live,* a yummy young hairdo whose most recent gig had been Miss Hawaii, was doing Mitch's lead-in on the monitor before him. Then the green light came on and, *bam,* Mitch and she were on the air live, bantering like two best friends about the upcoming summer blockbuster season. She wondered him if there was a theme to this season's crop. "I'm calling it the summer of the sequel," Mitch replied. "Which, ironically, makes it a sequel to last summer's blockbuster season." Any predictions? "No must-sees until the new Brad Pitt in August." Any recommendations? "Yes, stay home and rent a DVD of *Breathless* with Jean Paul Belmondo and Jean Seberg," Mitch advised. "Then fly to Paris for a long weekend." She asked if she could come with him. He said absolutely—*if* she promised to buy the escargots. She told him she wasn't sure she was ready for that kind of commitment. He called her a chicken, flashed her his new smile and they were over and out.

Then Mitch was on his way downstairs to meet with Shauna, who'd left word that she wished to see him. Mitch's new editor— make that intergroup manager—was a cross between Tina Brown, Parker Posey and Satan. Previously, she'd been the brains behind a snarky entertainment webzine that had made the empire a fortune. Shauna was pale, hyper and freakishly thin. She wore a nose stud as well as a collection of heavy, clangy silver bracelets on both wrists. Purple highlights in her lank blank hair. She was dressed in a cropped pink T-shirt, skinny black jeans and Converse Chuck Taylor high-tops. On her cooked spaghetti of a left bicep was a tattoo that read: *Me*. Some kind of postmodern wink-wink that Mitch didn't entirely get. For him this was not unusual with Shauna. She often gave him the impression that the two of them were in on a joke that he didn't understand.

Her office TV was tuned to *Midday Live*.

"You, sir, are starting to pop," she exclaimed, flicking it off as he came in her door.

"Thank you," Mitch responded. "I think."

"No, no. Popping is good. Popping is exciting." Shauna spoke in clipped bursts. Everything with her was an exclamation. "I have awesome news. They're giving you a half-hour show. Every Saturday morning. You'll review the new movies, show clips, interview the stars. The suits in L.A. want you out there this week to meet. Your assistant has your itinerary. Your agent has their offer. It's a go, Mitch. They've already assigned you a producer. You're not saying anything. Why aren't you saying anything?"

Mitch sank into the chair opposite her, wondering how he'd find the time. He was already stretched thin. He'd have to hire another full-time assistant for sure. Maybe a Web intern to take over his online load. . . .

Shauna studied him across the desk, her eyes narrowing. "What do you think of L.A.?"

To Mitch Los Angeles was the very definition of hell on earth—Levittown meets *The Day of the Locust*. "Why?"

"They want you to tape out there. From now on, you'll be L.A. based for one, possibly two weeks a month."

"Not a chance. I'm a New York critic."

"We don't think of you as region-specific, Mitch," Shauna countered. "You're national. And we want you embedded within the Hollywood community. Here's what I'd love to see you doing: Asking ten Hollywood heavy hitters to name what movie they'd choose if they could only watch one movie before they died. Can't do that from here. Don't have the access. Out there, you go to a red carpet premiere with a camera crew and nail all ten in nothing flat."

"Hold on, I don't do the red carpet. I'm not an entertainment reporter."

"Which brings me to another thing—is it just me or is there natural chemistry between you and Mary?"

"That all depends. Who's Mary?"

"The newswoman you were just on air with."

"Miss Hawaii is a journalist?"

"They want to pair you two up. You'll do the reviews and serious interviews. She'll do the red carpet. She'll look fabulous. And she's a big, big movie fan. I hear she's seen *Groundhog Day* over twenty times."

"Okay, I think there's some irony buried in there if you wait for it."

"What do you say, Mitch?" Shauna pressed him.

"She seems nice and I'd be delighted to work with her—*provided* we tape the show here in New York."

"She can't. She broadcasts five days a week from Los Angeles. Plus she just got engaged to a pitcher for the Dodgers. Look, do me a favor, will you? Don't decide anything now. Call your agent. Because this is *huge*."

"Absolutely," he assured her. "Listen, I have the germ of an idea for my Sunday piece. Have you got time to spitball?"

She gave him an impatient shake of her head. "I've told you before, you don't have to run your pieces by me."

"I know, I just . . ." He just missed the stimulating rapport he'd enjoyed with Lacy. But Shauna wasn't Lacy, and never would be. He had to learn to live with that. "Thank you. I appreciate your confidence."

"Hey, are you pumped?" she called to him as he headed out the door.

"Totally."

Which he was, except for the part about spending one, possibly two weeks a month in L.A. But his concerns disappeared as soon as he went in his office and phoned his agent, who'd already been told by Business Affairs just how many thousands Mitch would be getting paid for that one, possibly two weeks a month in L.A. Not counting profit participation.

After Mitch had hoisted his jaw up off of the floor there was nothing left for him to say except, "I hear the weather's always spectacular in L.A. this time of year."

Then he had to dash to a screening of Will Farrell's big new summer comedy, which was a genuine laugh riot provided you were eleven years old and had never seen the Marx Brothers, Abbott and Costello, the Three Stooges or Wile E. Coyote. By the time the closing credits rolled it was after six o'clock and, apart from his gym break, Mitch had been working for twelve hours straight. And his day still wasn't done. Although he did get to go home to Clemmie. Not that she was there to greet him when he came through the door and called out, "Honey, I'm home!" Not Clemmie's style, being a cat.

Mitch's new place was a brownstone floor-through. The bedroom was in front, off the entry hall, which led into the kitchen and living area in back. Someone had smacked his kitchen with an ugly stick in the '70s, but it was functional. And the living room had exposed brick walls, parquet flooring and French doors out to the garden. His framed poster made from a rare Sid Avery black-and-white group photograph of the cast members of the original *Ocean's Eleven* seemed right at home over the fireplace. So did the leather settee and club chairs set before it.

Clemmie had been out cold in one of the chairs. She raised her head to acknowledge his arrival, yawning hugely. Mitch went over to her and fussed over her. She got lonesome when he was gone. And definitely missed Quirt.

He dumped the contents of his day pack on the Stickley library table that he used as his desk and opened the French doors to let in some fresh air. On went some music—Bob Dylan's legendary plugged-in performance at Royal Albert Hall in 1966. He changed into a sleeveless T-shirt and gym shorts. Popped open the one Bass Ale per day that he allowed himself and sat down at his computer to write his Will Farrell review, most of which he'd already composed in his head on the 1 train riding home. As he tapped away, Clemmie climbed into his lap and padded at his no-longer soft tummy, purring. Mitch polished his review carefully, trimming any and all excess. Then he filed it.

Starved, he fired up the gas grill out on his bluestone patio. The old Mitch subsisted mainly on hot dogs, American chop suey and Entenmann's doughnuts. But those days were as gone as his blubber. He put on brown rice to cook. Made himself a big green salad. Cut up an organic chicken and marinated it in olive oil, lemon juice, Dijon mustard and some fresh rosemary from his garden. He grilled the chicken on low heat so it wouldn't dry out. By the time it was done the rice was ready.

He'd bought a teak dining table and set of chairs for the patio. He lit a couple of candles and ate his dinner out there, enjoying the warm night air and the sounds of life coming from the brownstones around him. The giddy laughter of a dinner party. The Scott Joplin rag someone was banging out on a piano. The televisions and ringing phones and raised voices. The way the city positively pulsed with life. He'd missed this out on his remote little island in the Sound.

He checked his e-mail before he did the dishes. Discovered one from his tenant, Bella, the prickly Jewish grandmother who'd been Des's roommate until the return of Brandon:

To: Mitch Berger
From: Bella Tillis
Subject: Annoying Cottage Query

Dear Mr. Hotshot New York Film Critic—Pardon me for being blunt, but is this little house of yours haunted? I have two very good reasons for asking such a question. One is that I keep hearing very strange tap, tap, tapping noises in the walls late at night. Am I living with dozens of teeny-tiny ghosts? This is Dorset, after all. Weird, unexplained things have been known to happen here. That brings me to my second question: Do strangers typically hang around on the island after dark? Please don't think I'm being a nutty old broad, but I keep getting the feeling that someone has been spending the night on that ratty old sofa out in the barn. And I'd swear he or she is stealing food from me. I asked Bitsy Peck next door if she'd noticed anyone hanging around, but Bitsy looked at me like I was crazy. So did little Molly Procter, who has been helping me with the cats. You remember Molly, don't you? Her parents split up, and she is one sad, lonely little girl.

Anyhow, does any or all of this sound like your idea of normal island life? Answers, mister. I need answers.

I've had no luck corralling Quirt, though I'm certain I will soon prevail. When I do I'll be happy to bring him to you in the city. It'll give me an excuse to visit you. I'm sorry to say our resident trooper is unwilling to take him. Her current roommate is not a cat lover, which should tell you everything you need to know about that arrogant, manipulative bum.

I know, I know. I promised you I wouldn't talk about Him anymore. I'm just so accustomed to saying whatever pops into my head that I can't help it. You're like a son to me. And Desiree is my best friend. The fact that you two aren't together anymore, aren't even speaking, makes me mad enough to spit. I still can't believe you let that man take the love of your life away from you. But I suppose I just have to deal. You've certainly moved on. I saw you on TV today flirting with that Polynesian high school girl. You probably don't even think about Desiree anymore. Or Dorset. That's what the old hens at Town and Country beauty salon are saying.

I choose to disagree with them in my own quiet way.

Much love, Aunt Bella

p.s. Between you, me and the lamp post: What in the hell did they do to your eyebrows???

To: Bella Tillis
From: Mitch Berger
Subject: Re: Annoying Cottage Query

Dear Aunt Bella—You'll be happy to know that the house is not, repeat not, haunted. That tap-tapping you hear in the walls at night is nothing more than the mating call of your friendly native powder post beetles. They are small, pill-shaped bugs that live in the chestnut beams. Every year when the weather turns warm they come out and bang their little heads (or whatever it is they have) against the wood to announce to their opposite numbers that it's time to get busy.

I am not making this up.

They're totally harmless. Well, not totally. They will, in fact, eat the house eventually. But it will take at least another 200 years, and I don't want to fumigate. So you have housemates. Sorry I forgot to warn you. I promise you they'll disappear back into the cracks in another few days and blessed silence will return. It's all just part of the rich cavalcade of life on Big Sister.

As to your question about strangers hanging around in the night: Sometimes high school kids sneak out there to get high and engage in recreational boinkage, particularly when it gets warm (see above re: powder post beetles). This is why the lighthouse is always kept locked. But they don't usually stay over. And they for sure aren't welcome to come in our houses and help themselves to food. If you think someone is doing this then you should definitely contact our resident trooper. Her name and number are listed in the phone book.

For the record, Brandon didn't "take" Des from me. She made the decision that was right for her and I have to respect it. It's nobody's fault. In the immortal words of that great philosopher Donald Rumsfeld, "Stuff happens."

I'd love to see you any time you can make it into the city. But I must warn you that I can't take Quirt. He is a roamer, not an apartment cat. He belongs out there. I don't mean to sound cold and heartless, but he would not be happy here.

Molly's a terrific kid. One hell of a first step to the hoop, too. I e-mailed her recently but never heard back. Tell her I said hey. And I'm sorry to hear about her folks.

Best regards, Mitch

p.s. Honestly, I have no idea what you mean about my eyebrows.

It was past midnight when he finished his dishes, by which time Clemmie decided she was in the mood to frolic. Mitch tossed her mousy toy up and down the hall and she chased after it with murderous intent until she'd tired herself out. Then she padded into the bedroom, jumped up on the big brass bed and waited there for him. She liked to sleep on his chest.

He smiled at her and said, "Clemmie, old girl, we are doing pretty damned good, know that?" Because it was true. Hell, if he'd had a sword, Mitch would have launched it triumphantly into the ceiling just like Tyrone Power had in *The Mark of Zorro*. But Mitch had no sword. So instead he wept.

CHAPTER 3

IT FELT VERY STRANGE to be easing her cruiser *thumpety-bumpety* over the narrow wooden causeway out to Big Sister again. Des couldn't help recalling the very first time she'd set eyes on this private Yankee eden with its choice handful of Peck family mansions scattered across forty acres of meadows and woods. That snug little carriage house where she'd first met a certain pudgy, sad-eyed widower named Mitch Berger. She'd driven down from Central District headquarters in Meriden that day to investigate the body he'd found. She was still a homicide investigator on the Major Crime Squad then. A lieutenant. One of only three such women in the state. And the only one who was black. She'd been hot stuff all right—until she stepped on the wrong toes.

Seeing the place once again, Des realized that Big Sister felt a lot like home. There was that strip of private beach where she and Mitch had walked together for the very first time. And the sandy, twisting path they took home the night they went skinny dipping in the moonlight. And the lighthouse where he'd proposed marriage to her.

It all seemed so long ago now. And yet it was still right there inside of her heart. She could feel her chest tighten as she pulled into the driveway next to Mitch's plum-colored 1956 Studebaker pickup. He'd left it behind for Bella. Had no use for it in the city.

Quirt came running across the garden toward her when she got out, rubbing up against her leg and yowling in outrage over her prolonged absence. She bent down and picked him up. He wouldn't let her hold him. Just squirmed in her arms until she released him. When Bella came out the front door to greet Des he darted inside the house.

"Oh, thank god!" Bella said excitedly. "I've been trying to get him inside for weeks. Quick, quick, close the door. . . ."

Des shut the door behind them. "What are you going to do with him?"

"Find a good home for him—unless you want him."

"Bella, you know I can't take him."

"I don't know *anything* anymore," Bella blustered, standing there in her ratty, ancient black ERA–YES sweatshirt and black stretch pants. She looked like an angry Jewish bowling ball. "I used to, but those days are over."

Des let her rebuke slide on by. "I like what you've done with the place," she said, glancing around.

Bella had opened up Mitch's drop-leaf dining table and moved it in front of the bay windows, which gave the room a much homier air. There was a bowl of fruit on it. Also her laptop computer. Mitch's sky blue Fender Stratocaster and stack of amps were stashed in a corner by the door. Des was surprised he hadn't taken it all with him to New York.

"He said he hasn't felt like playing his music lately," Bella explained, following her gaze.

"He called that music?"

"To him it was. Which, being an artist, you ought to be able to understand. How is your drawing coming?"

"I've been a bit short on time lately."

"Uh-huh."

"What does that mean?"

"It means uh-huh."

"Sounded like something more."

"Then you're having a conversation with yourself, not me."

Bella looked her up and down, brow furrowing. "Tell me, just exactly how many pounds have you lost?"

"Who says I've lost any?"

"I do. You're nothing but skin and bone. As for your color . . ."

"My *color?*"

"It's distinctly sallow. You used to glow. You don't glow anymore."

"Bella, is this a for-real prowler call or did you just lure me out here to tell me how lousy I look?"

"You don't look lousy. You look unhappy."

"Just step off, okay? Brandon and I are getting along great. Why can't you accept that?"

"Because I lived through this before, that's why. I remember how close he came to destroying you."

"Bella . . ."

"And don't you tell me he's changed because he hasn't. People never do."

"Bella, if we're going to stay friends then the subject of Brandon will have to remain off-limits. Deal?"

"Fine," she snapped. "But only if you eat a little something. How about a nice, thick brisket sandwich? I've got fresh challah."

"Why don't you just tell me about this prowler?"

"I'm not sure it's a *prowler*. But I do keep finding signs that someone has taken up residence out here."

"You mean like a homeless person?"

"Come, I'll show you."

She led Des outside to the barn. The stray cats that they'd rescued together were parked inside in their cages, waiting not-so-patiently for homes. A lanky, bespectacled girl of about ten was feeding them.

"Hey, Bella," the girl said, studying Des guardedly.

"Molly, this is Trooper Mitry."

45

Molly had curly blond hair and freckles and a pink, busy little nose. "Hullo . . ."

Des smiled at the girl. "Hello, yourself."

"Now, do you see the way these tarps and dropcloths are all laid out?" Bella was motioning to the sprung, moth-eaten old sofa. "Every morning, I find them rearranged. One morning, there was a pea coat here. A man's coat. Next morning, it was gone. Also, someone has been taking food from me. When I came home from the dentist the other day my fruit bowl on the table was empty."

"Have any of the other residents seen him?"

Bella shook her head. "Bitsy Peck thinks I'm seeing ghosts."

Which was only natural, Des reflected. The whole damned island felt haunted. "How about you, Molly? Have you seen anyone out here who doesn't belong?"

"Absolutely not," the girl answered vehemently, her cheeks mottling.

Des studied her curiously. "You sound pretty sure about that."

"Because I am."

Des gestured for Bella to follow her back out into the sunlight. "Talk to me about this Molly," she said to her softly.

"She helps me with the cats. Lives on Sour Cherry Lane. She's a bright little thing, but a bit lost. Her parents have split up."

"Last name Procter?"

"That's right."

Des stood there thinking about her conversation of last night with the regal Patricia Beckwith. Putting two and two together. Wondering what it added up to. "If you don't mind," she said, her voice raised, "I think I will have that brisket sandwich."

They went back inside, Bella charging straight into the kitchen. "Do you want mustard or mayo on that?" she called to Des.

"Neither," Des replied, watching the barn through the bay window in the living room. "And you can hold the sandwich."

"I don't get it, *tattela*. What are you doing?"

"Playing a hunch."

Sure enough, little Molly soon came scurrying out of the barn. She shot a wide-eyed glance over her shoulder at Mitch's cottage, then skedaddled down the path to the lighthouse. Des went out the door after her, following from a careful distance as the path wound its way through the wild beach plum and beach roses. Molly dashed past the lighthouse toward the island's narrow stretch of beach. Her destination was a little sand knoll about thirty feet back from the high tide line. A valiant cluster of little cedars grew there. Molly squeezed in between them and then vanished.

Des followed, her footsteps silent on the soft, dry sand.

There was a protected little burrow there amid the trees where the man was seated on his pea coat. He was thin and unshaven, with receding sandy-colored hair and a long, sharp nose. He wore a torn, bloodstained blue button-down shirt and khaki trousers that were filthy. He'd been in a fight. His eggplant-colored left eye was swollen shut. His lower lip all fat and raw, as was his left ear. In his hand was a plastic bottle of Poland Spring water.

The girl was trying to get him to drink some of it. He wasn't showing any interest.

"Your dad may need professional help, Molly," Des spoke up, startling the hell out of her.

Richard Procter didn't react at all.

"Just leave us alone, will you?" Molly cried out angrily. "He's *okay!*"

Des knelt before the professor. He didn't seem okay. Dazed was more like it, his gaze unfocused and blank. "Richard, do you know where you are?"

"They both threw me out." His voice was a hollow murmur.

"Can you tell me what day this is, Richard?"

"They both threw me out," he repeated.

"Richard . . . ?"

"Leave him *alone!* "

Gently, Des pushed the man over onto his side so she could snatch his wallet from his back pocket. He offered no resistance. His Connecticut driver's license did indeed identify him as Richard Hearn Procter. As did his credit cards. There was no money in the wallet.

"Molly, how long has he been this way?"

"Why?"

"Honey, I know you're trying to help him but he needs medical attention. Trust me, it's for his own good."

"Oh, what would *you* know about it?" Molly demanded. "You're going to wreck everything. *Everything!*" Then the little girl gave her an angry shove and went sprinting back across the beach in the direction of Mitch's cottage.

Her father didn't seem to notice. Just stared out at the water, unblinking, and said it one more time: "They both threw me out."

Shaking her head, Des reached for her cell and called the Jewett sisters.

CHAPTER 4

"HONESTLY, I CAN'T REMEMBER the last time I was this happy," Mitch exclaimed as he wolfed down some more of his chef salad. "The job is fun. Being on TV is fun. And I feel incredible."

Lacy Nickerson took a bite of her ten-ounce bacon cheeseburger, gazing admiringly at Mitch's biceps inside his fitted polo shirt. "Well, you certainly look incredible. But just between us, kiddo, what happened to your eyebrows?"

"Why, what's wrong with them?"

"Not a thing. I simply never realized before that you bear such an eerie resemblance to Joan Crawford."

Mitch's former editor speared some fries with her fork and washed them down with a swig of New Amsterdam ale. Lacy ate and drank like a longshoreman, yet remained needle thin. She was a tall, impeccably groomed tuning fork of a woman who, at age fifty-seven, had been the most influential cultural arbiter in New York until the empire pushed her out in favor of the younger Shauna. Not that Lacy seemed at all bitter. She was her same upbeat, A-list self. It was she who had called Mitch to meet her for lunch at Pete's Tavern, the historic landmark on East 18th and Irving Place that opened its doors when Lincoln was in the White House and had never closed them. She lived right around the corner in a three-bedroom apartment overlooking Gramercy Park with husband number five, a Wall Street titan.

And she still had pull—they were sharing one of Pete's prized sidewalk tables. Lacy dabbed at her mouth with her napkin and studied him there in the afternoon sunlight. "If you're doing what you want to be doing then I couldn't be more pleased for you. Although that does mean I'm wasting my time."

"Wasting your time how?"

"I'm here to proposition you."

"Lacy, I'm flattered but I've never thought of you as more than a friend."

"Stop! This is me being serious. Mitch, I've been reading your pieces very closely of late and I don't feel you're doing your best work. Your insights lack their usual depth and passion. You seem hurried."

Mitch sipped his iced tea with lemon, no sugar. "Only because I am. I'm still learning how to manage my time better. I've decided to take on a Web intern for all of the Peg Entwistles."

"All of the what?"

"The movie trivia for my Web site. We get a ton of hits. Shauna says people are totally hooked."

"And Peg Entwistle is . . . ?"

"*Was* the struggling young actress who jumped to her death from the letter H of the HOLLYWOOD sign on September 18, 1932. Caused quite a stir at the time, believe me."

"Oh, I do." Lacy cocked her head at him slightly. "And I think I get it now. This new editor . . ."

"Intergroup manager."

"She's trying to dumb you down."

"She is not. I'm free to write what I want, how I want. She's just not much for spitballing is all. Maybe that's what you're noticing—how much I miss *us*."

"Stop it, you're going to make me weep."

"Sorry."

"Don't tell me you're sorry," she huffed. "Tell me what you're working on for Sunday."

He grinned at her. "I thought you'd never ask. Okay, here it is: I keep noticing how there are two distinct species of leading men— those who ripen and mature before our eyes and those who simply become aging boys. Take Tom Cruise . . ."

"You take him," she sniffed.

"For me, he's still a boy up there on that screen even though he's, what, forty-six? Same goes for Hugh Grant. Sean Penn, on the other hand, has become a man."

"Just like Harrison Ford," Lacy said, nodding her head. "He gets better the older he grows. Meanwhile, Sly Stallone has become a total joke."

"Hold on, Sly Stallone was always a total joke."

"I am absolutely loving your premise, Mitch. Trust me, I have dated a lot of successful men in my time. . . ." In her wild youth Lacy claimed to have bedded the likes of Irwin Shaw, Mickey Mantle and Nelson Rockefeller. "It doesn't matter whether they're forty or fifty or even sixty—some grow up, others never do."

"And the screen merely reflects it," Mitch said, nodding. "Like a great big wide-screen mirror—complete with Dolby sound."

"God, a million names are suddenly racing through my head," Lacy said excitedly. "Like Newman . . ."

"A grown man."

"And Redford?"

"Still a boy, definitely."

Their waiter came by and cleared their table. They ordered espressos.

"I've missed this, too," Lacy sighed. "Mitch, we owe it to ourselves to be together again."

"How?"

"Funny you should ask," she said, wagging a long, manicured finger at him. "I've spent these past months figuring out what I would do if I could do anything. And I'm doing it. Kiddo, I'm starting up a new arts magazine. Or I should say Webzine, since my money genius has convinced me it's the only way to go. I'm bringing all of the finest young critics and essayists I know together on one site. Our primary focus will be on New York at first, but I believe we'll build a national following very quickly because I'm convinced that fresh, passionate writing is still what people want—no matter whether they live in Tribeca or Billings, Montana. I want the best, Mitch. And when it comes to movies that means you. It'll mean less money, of course. I can't compete with the empire. I'm not even sure I can offer you a health plan. But it's a chance for us to be together again. And to hell with Peg Entwistle."

The waiter returned with their coffees.

Mitch took a slow sip of his before he said, "They're giving me my own weekly half-hour show, Lacy. I'll be spending a lot of my time in L.A. from now on."

She looked at him in surprise. "You never wanted that sort of thing before."

"You're right, I didn't. But the world is changing, and I have to embrace change."

She nodded her head at him sagely. "This is all about Des, isn't it?"

"It has nothing to do with Des. Why would you even think that?"

"Because I've been dumped by the best—and *embraced change* like you wouldn't believe. God, I even moved to Tibet for six months after my Harry Reasoner thing. Honestly, kiddo, you're doing great. You're positive. You're productive. I just want to make sure you're not turning yourself into a sculpted Roger Ebert wannabe because you think it will impress her."

"Lacy, I'm completely over Des."

"If that's the case then I have a terrific woman for you."

"Not interested. I'm really not looking to get involved again.

Not for a long, long time." Mitch drained his espresso. "Why, who is she?"

"My new dance critic. She just moved here from London. In fact, she's living in my spare room until she finds a place. Her grand-daddy was the Earl of somewhere. She's a graduate of Oxford. A gourmet chef. Tall, slim *and* a dead ringer for Diana Rigg."

"Diana Rigg then or now?"

"She's twenty-eight. And don't be mean. Her name is Cecily Naughton. She goes by C.C. in her byline."

"Sure, I've read her pieces in *Vanity Fair*. She's wicked funny. And so insightful."

"She used to be a dancer herself."

Mitch's eyes widened. "Really?"

Lacy let out a hoot. "What is it with men? I can talk until I'm blue in the face about a terrific woman and get nowhere with you. But if I so much as mention the word 'dancer' or 'model' you start drooling like horny teenaged boys."

"That's totally your imagination."

"Do you want to call her?"

"Lacy, I'm afraid I just don't have the time right now."

"I'm sorry to hear that, Mitch. And very sorry that you and I won't be working together again." Her eyes searched his for a mo-ment before they let go. "My door is always open in case you change your mind."

"That's incredibly nice of you, but I won't be." Mitch beamed at her. "Honestly, I can't remember the last time I was this happy."

CHAPTER 5

"You've got a nice soft touch, girl," Des observed as Molly Procter sank jumper after jumper in the driveway of the farmhouse that Jen Beckwith shared with her mother, Kimberly. There were no cars in the driveway. Neither Jen nor Kimberly was around. Nor was anyone home at the Sullivans', whose cottage was a hundred feet farther down Sour Cherry in the direction of the river. The only thing sitting in their driveway was a huge pile of cedar mulch that had been heaped onto a blue tarp. Across the narrow lane, that same Nutmegger Professional Seamless Gutters van was parked at the Procter place. Two men sat out on the front porch drinking beer and trying to pretend they weren't watching Des's every move.

Molly didn't want to look at Des. Or say one word to her. Just play ball. She was all gamed out in a UConn Lady Huskies T-shirt, gym shorts, sneakers and floppy socks that harked back to the heyday of Pistol Pete Maravich.

Des went over to the basket and retrieved the ball after Molly drained it. Bounce-passed it crisply to her, leading her to her left. Molly caught it in stride, stutter stepped right and parked a twelve-footer. Now Des led her to her right. Again, nothing but net.

"Did you used to play?" she asked Des finally, her voice cool.

"Rode the bench in high school. I've got no skills, but if you're tall they point you toward the hoop." Des flashed her a smile but got nothing but a glower in return. "Your dad's going to be okay, Molly. No concussion or other serious physical injuries. He's suffering from what they call situational depression, which is a fancy way of saying he's been kind of thrown for a loop."

"Okay," Molly responded quietly as she put up another jumper.

According to Marge Jewett, Richard Procter would be kept overnight at Connecticut Valley Hospital in Middletown for observation. Since he did not appear to be an imminent threat to himself or others, chances were they'd prescribe an antidepressant and counseling—and release him in the morning. It seemed cold but that was the sad reality of medical life today. Unless someone was running down the street waving a gun or threatening to jump off a roof then they were likely to be medicated and kicked.

The only question with the professor was kicked to whom.

"I had to do what I did, Molly. Really, I had no choice in the matter. I'm heading over to talk to your mom about it now."

"Good luck," Molly said scornfully.

Des raised an eyebrow at her but Molly had nothing more to say. Just more baskets to shoot.

The two men on the porch were drinking Coors. One of them sat in an old wooden rocker, the other on the front steps. The one on the steps, a husky young Hispanic in a tank top and baggy jeans, was very anxious to let Des know that he was not someone to be messed with. His chin was stuck out, his gaze hard and cold.

"Good afternoon, gentlemen," she said pleasantly, tipping her big hat at them.

"Right back at you, trooper," the man in the rocker said with an easy smile. He was older, about forty. Wiry and weathered, with slicked back dark blond hair and a lot of squint lines around his eyes. He wore a T-shirt, low-slung jeans and beat up Top-Siders.

"I'm Resident Trooper Mitry. Is Carolyn home?"

"She sure is, ma'am," he replied, just a real pleasant and accommodating fellow. Unlike his mute, glowering young friend on the steps. "May I ask what this is about?"

"A situation has arisen concerning her husband Richard."

"Is the prof okay?"

"I'll talk to her about it, if you don't mind."

"You can talk to me if you want. What I mean is, I'm the man of the house now. The name's Clay Mundy." Clay lit a Marlboro with a disposable lighter, cupping it in his large, knuckly hands. "This here's Hector Villanueva. Hector works for me."

"Glad to know you, Hector."

Hector muttered, "And to know you, too." He had no trouble with English. It was her uniform that was his problem.

"You fellows clean roof gutters, am I right?"

"That's what the van says," Clay replied, grinning at her.

"I could use some help with mine. They haven't been cleaned in at least three years. Can you swing by and give me an estimate?"

Clay shook his head. "Sorry, ma'am, but we wouldn't be able to get to you for at least six weeks. This is our busy season."

Des stood there thinking they sure didn't seem real busy. It was, what, three in the afternoon and they were sitting around drinking beer? "I'm in no rush. If you'll give me your business card I'll call you."

Clay patted his chest pocket absently. "There's a batch in the van somewhere, isn't there, Hector?"

Hector grunted in vague response. Neither of them got up to fetch her one. Just sat there nursing their beers.

Des studied them, feeling a prickly sensation on the back of her neck. She didn't necessarily smell yard on them, but she did smell something. "Have you been in Dorset long, Mr. Mundy?"

"Why are you asking?"

"It's a small town. I like to get to know the people who I serve."

"Rolled in a couple of months back from Atlanta," he replied, pulling on his cigarette. "Me and Hector both."

"And how did you pick our fair town?"

"I've just always loved this area. Done a lot of different things in my time. Worked construction in West Texas. Oil rigs in Louisiana. Long-haul trucking out of Atlanta these past few years. That's how I came to know this this area. Soon as I saw it I made a promise to myself I'd settle down here and do my thing. It's a slice of heaven, really. You've got the water right outside your door. The fishing's good. Casinos are a half-hour away. That's where I met Carolyn— playing the slots at Foxwoods. I really hit the jackpot, too. She's a doll. Only, she's not feeling too well right now. Lying down last time I looked."

"I really do need to talk to her. Or both of you, if you prefer."

"Whatever you say, ma'am." Clay flicked his cigarette butt out across the front lawn. "Come on in."

She went on in with him. Hector stayed behind on the porch.

The parlor was cozy. There were a couple of overstuffed chairs and a love seat to curl up in. The framed covers of Carolyn's animal books for kids, which had titles such as *Molly Lays An Egg* and *Molly Finds a Fox,* were displayed on one wall. The artwork was colorful and cheerful. Her photo on the back cover was that of a beautiful and confident looking blonde with high cheekbones, bright eyes and a terrific smile.

"Let me see if I can rouse her," Clay said, crossing to a short hallway off of the parlor.

There was a sunny eat-in kitchen with French doors leading out to a deck. It would have been a nice kitchen if it weren't such a mess. The sink and counter were heaped with dirty dishes. The stove covered with greasy pots and pans. The trash container by the back door was overflowing with empty pizza cartons and beer cans. There were more empty beer cans on the long oak kitchen table, as well as assorted liquor bottles, ashtrays and magazines devoted to the joys of stock car racing and naked women with giant boobs. At one end of the table, someone had been playing a game of solitaire.

Des heard a murmur of voices coming from the bedroom. Carolyn's a plaintive whine of protest. Clay's low and insistent.

Then he joined Des in the kitchen with that same crinkly-eyed grin on his face. "Poor girl's been knocked low by some darned virus. All she seems to do is sleep. But she'll be right out."

"Fine. Thank you."

"Kind of repulsive in here, isn't it?" he acknowledged, glancing around. "You'll have to forgive me. I'm no good around the house, and I can't seem to get Molly to help out one bit. She's resents me being here. You know how that goes."

"Sure do," Des said, turning at the sound of Carolyn Procter's footsteps.

They were not steady footsteps. In fact, Richard Procter's estranged wife could barely put one foot in front of the other as she staggered her way weakly through the doorway in a soiled white T-shirt and nothing else, a wavering hand groping at the door frame for support. Carolyn barely resembled the cheery, beautiful woman pictured on the cover of her books. She was deathly pale, with dark blue circles under her bleary eyes. The skin on her bare arms was all scratched and blotchy. And it seemed to hang loose from her, as if she'd lost a great deal of muscle tone very quickly. Her long blond hair was stringy and filthy. She gave off a sour odor, as if she hadn't bathed in a week.

One look was all it took. Des knew instantly it was no virus that had hold of Carolyn Procter.

"How are you feeling, Carolyn?" Des asked, feeling Clay's eyes on her. "I understand you haven't been well."

"I am . . . so sick," she moaned, slumping into a chair at the kitchen table.

"But she's getting better every day," Clay said encouragingly. "You just need you a nice hot bath, hon. Freshen you right up."

"I'm Trooper Mitry, Carolyn. I've come to see you about Richard."

At the mention of her husband's name Carolyn reached for a cigarette and lit it, her hands shaking badly. Then she sat back in her chair, one slender, dirty foot propped up on the table. She wore no panties under her T-shirt yet didn't seem to care that she was flashing her goodies. Her long leg started twitching as she sat there pulling anxiously on her cigarette. She was sweating. And grinding her teeth. And picking at the skin on her face with her fingers.

Carolyn Procter: Portrait of a tweaker.

There was no doubt in Des's mind that Carolyn Procter had gotten herself hooked on crystal meth, which kept you up, up, up for twelve or more hours straight, then sent you crashing into the shaky, agitated state Des found her in now. True, a woman who was as accomplished and classy as Carolyn hardly seemed the type. But Des had learned long ago that when it came to dope there was no type. And crystal meth was very popular around the casinos. Gamblers got off on its all-night rush.

She was shaking her head at Des in confusion. "You said . . ." Her voice seemed disconnected, as if the words had to travel several time zones from her brain. "Something about . . . Richard?"

"Yes, ma'am. I found him today out on Big Sister Island. I'm afraid he's been in a fight of some kind."

"He swung at me first." Clay spoke up defensively. "And if he says otherwise he's—"

"Professor Procter's not saying much of anything right now, actually. He's quite dazed and despondent."

"I was just standing up for myself," he went on. "And, speaking candidly, I don't see any place for the law in this."

"Mr. Mundy, no one is swearing out a complaint. I'm simply trying to help. So why don't you just tell me what happened, okay?"

Clay shrugged his shoulders. "Not much to tell. He stopped by a few nights back and we had us a little scuffle out in the driveway."

"Over . . . ?"

"Him refusing to accept the new reality of his situation."

"When I encountered him today he kept mumbling, 'They both threw me out.' By 'they' he was referring to Carolyn and you?"

"That's right," Clay confirmed. "I was trying to set the man straight, you know? And maybe things got a bit rough. But he started it. And he seemed okay when he took off. I wouldn't have let him go if I thought he was in bad shape. That's not my style at all. I try to get along with people. Right, hon?"

Carolyn didn't answer him. Didn't seem to hear him. Just sat there, bare leg twitching, cigarette burning down in her fingers.

"He's been admitted to Connecticut Valley Hospital for observation," Des informed her. "When he's released he'll need to be in a supervised home setting. Any idea who he can stay with?"

Slowly, Carolyn stubbed out her cigarette in a ceramic ashtray full of butts. Then she hurled the ashtray against the kitchen wall, shattering it and sending butts and ashes flying everywhere. "*Not* here!" she screamed, her eyes blazing with rage. "He *can't* stay here!"

"That's fine," Des said to her gently. "I understand perfectly. Does he have any other family in the area?"

"Not . . . here," she repeated, quieter this time. Slowly, she got back on her feet and weaved her way back toward the bedroom.

"That's right, you get yourself back into bed," Clay called after her. To Des he said, "Poor girl. Those viruses sure can hang on sometimes."

"Yes, they certainly can," Des said, starting for the front door.

Clay stayed right with her. "Real sorry about this business with the professor, ma'am. It was just one of those things. I had no idea he'd take it so hard, being he's such an educated guy and all."

Hector was still sitting on the front steps, burly shoulders hunched over a stock car magazine.

"Maybe you're better off being a dumb ass like me," Clay added with a not so easy laugh. "Know what I'm saying?"

"I absolutely do. Don't sweat it, Mr. Mundy. And thanks for your time." Des tipped her big hat at him and headed back across the lane, thinking about how she was going to run a criminal background check on these two just as soon as she had a chance.

Molly was still over there shooting baskets. A silver VW Passat was now parked behind her in the driveway.

"It's happened to her, too, hasn't it?" Molly said glumly.

"What has, Molly?"

"My mom's body is still there but *she* isn't. She's been taken away same as my dad. It's just like *I Married a Monster from Outer Space* with Mr. Tom Tryon."

Des snagged the ball and bounce-passed it to her, feeling sorrier for this bespectacled little waif than she had for anyone in a long while. "How do you know about such a black-and-white oldie?"

"Mitch was always uber-cool about loaning me DVDs. I'm really into old-school sci-fi. Also anything that has haunted houses with secret passageways and dungeons."

"You and Mitch really spoke the same language, didn't you?"

"Totally. I really miss Mitch. He's like my dad—real smart but he doesn't try to make you feel stupid." Molly drove to the hoop and laid it in off of the glass. "Why'd you break his heart?"

"Is that what you think happened?"

"Duh. It's why he left town. Everybody knows that."

"Sometimes two people just don't belong together anymore."

"Will you guys ever get back together?"

"No, Molly, we won't."

"But you're supposed to be together," Molly said insistently. "You *belong* together."

"You've been talking to Mrs. Tillis about us, haven't you?"

"Have not. I just know it, that's all. I know about a lot of things."

Des glanced back across the lane. Clay and Hector had gone inside the house. "Do you know if your mom has been to see a doctor lately?"

Molly shook her head. "She hasn't been anywhere in weeks. Just sleeps all day. Clay does all of the grocery shopping and stuff."

"Do you like Clay?"

"I hate him," she said flatly. "He's bossy and he's mean. Always acting like he can tell me what to do."

"Has he ever put his hands on you?"

"You mean like hit me? No way." Molly lowered her eyes evasively before she added, "Hector's okay. He shoots hoops with me sometimes."

"And where does he live?"

"With us. Except sometimes he goes away for a few days. So does Clay."

"They go away together?"

"No, when one of them leaves the other one stays behind. Hector crashes on the sofa usually. Except if Clay's out of town. Then he gets to . . ." Molly trailed off, her pink nose twitching. "One morning I saw Hector coming out of my mom's room without any clothes on. He sleeps in her bed just like Clay does. And sometimes they're *both* in there with her at the same time." Molly gazed up at her now, wide-eyed and earnest. "Trooper Des, what's wrong with my mom?"

"Nothing we can't set right," Des answered confidently, even though she sure wasn't feeling that way. The girl's father was out to lunch and her drugged-out mother was getting it on with the entire staff of Nutmegger Professional Seamless Gutters. The truth was that this situation was edging dangerously close to actionable—if Des had reason to suspect that Molly was being abused, neglected or exposed to criminal behavior then she was supposed to toss it to the Department of Children and Families.

A driveway side door to the Beckwith farmhouse opened now. A fortyish, frizzy-haired redhead in a short-sleeved pink blouse and white slacks came bustling out with a basket of laundry and started around back with it.

"Don't you worry, Molly," Des said with a reassuring smile. "And hey, my folks split up, too. So if you ever want to talk I'm around, okay?" She offered the girl her card. Molly just stared at it. "Look, I know you were mad at me this morning, but I need for you to come up big for me now, okay?"

Molly frowned at her. "Big *how?*"

"By being my eyes and ears. If anything goes down over there that scares you, pick up the phone and call me, deal?"

Grudgingly, Molly tucked the card inside of her sneaker. Then she went back to draining jump shots.

Kimberly Beckwith's small backyard was weedy and untamed. She was hanging sheets and towels on the clothesline when Des made her way back there, the wet sheets billowing and flapping in the breeze off of the river.

"Good afternoon, Mrs. Beckwith."

"Hiya, Trooper Mitry. Call me Kimberly, okay? When I hear Mrs. Beckwith I think of that bitter old broad sitting up there in her parlor chugalugging that god-awful sherry." Jen's mother spoke with the folksy nasal bray that was characteristic to working class Hartford. She was a small woman, five-feet-four, tops. Riding a tiny bit low in the caboose but still plenty curvy—particularly in the boobage department. Kimberly had the look of someone who'd been tons of cute, cuddly fun when she was younger. A real cupcake. But the years and the extra pounds were starting to show in her face. Her cheeks had plumped up. Her chin was disappearing into a soft puddle of jowls. And her blue eyes looked out at Des with weariness and disappointment. "You have *no* idea how humiliating it was to get a call from that old hag at four in the morning ordering me home because my daughter's been throwing a drunken sex orgy. Patricia already thinks I'm a terrible mother. Not to mention the slutsky of the century. She'd be thrilled if I just went *poof* so she could raise Jen herself. Well, screw her. I'm not going anywhere."

Des nodded politely. Nothing but happy families here on Sour Cherry Lane.

"That woman gives me nonstop grief," Kimberly rattled on. "I was never, ever good enough for her precious Johnny. Just a conniving piece of Polish ass after his money. So what if I graduated from Bod College? So what if my dad worked the line at Stanley in New Britain for thirty-two years? I married Johnny because I loved him." She let out a bitter laugh as she reached for another handful of clothespins. "Some gold digger, hunh? Here I am in the lap of luxury trying to save twenty bucks a month on my electric bill by hanging this crap out to dry. I'm a single mother doing the best I can to scrape by. I spend fifty, sixty hours a week in the therapy room at Dr. Gardiner's listening to those goddamned old ladies bitch, bitch, bitch about their sciatica and lumbago. I get *one* chance to go away for a couple of nights and have a teensy bit of fun with a nice guy and that old hag treats me like I'm out on the street selling my . . ." She halted, glancing at Des uneasily. "Sorry, I talk a blue streak when I'm nervous."

"I don't mean to make you nervous."

"It's the uniform, honey. Every time I see one I feel like I'm sixteen again myself—by which I mean sprawled in the backseat of Pauly Mondello's Trans Am with my panties down around one ankle and a half-smoked joint in the ashtray." She squinted at Des, her nose wrinkling. "Just so we're clear here, did you take Jen into custody last night? Cite her for a violation or anything?"

Des shook her head. "Nothing will go on her record."

Kimberly let out a sigh of relief. "Good, because my Jen has a chance to go to some very, very good colleges. The sky's the limit for her. I stopped off at The Works on my way home and she told me everything about their . . . what do they call it, Rainbow Party? Believe me, that'll never happen again. Well, it will. But not in my house it won't. No more parties. Listen, when will you have the results from her blood test?"

"Not for at least a couple of weeks."

"That long?"

"I'm afraid so. This is real life, not *CSI: Dorset*."

"Well, I guarantee you it'll turn up clean. Jen doesn't drink or smoke dope. If she did she'd tell me. We're best friends, and she's never lied to me. I asked her straight up just now if she needs to go on birth control. She said no. Even sounded offended that I asked. But I had to, right? Honestly, she has very nice friends. The girls are jocks just like her. And the boys aren't druggies."

"I didn't find any drugs," Des confirmed. "But there was alcohol. And I need for you to know that you're legally responsible for what goes on in your home—even if you're not around. If one of those kids, say, got loaded here last night and then smashed into somebody on Old Shore Road, guess whose fault that would have been? Understand what I'm saying?"

Kimberly nodded her head, gulping.

"Fortunately, nobody got hurt. And we all learned a lesson. Believe me, I'm on your side. Just trying to make sure that good kids like Jen and her friends stay in one piece. Because at that age there is such a fine line between good and idiot."

"No need to remind me. God, when I think back to some of the stuff I put my own folks through . . ." Kimberly smiled at Des faintly. "With Jen I count my blessings every day. She *is* a good kid. And it's just us two. Well, two and half if you count Diana Taurasi Junior out there," she added, cocking an ear to the steady thud of the basketball in the driveway out front.

"So you see a lot of Molly?"

"Are you kidding? She must have dinner with us four, five nights a week. Sleeps over in Jen's room a lot, too. Especially when it rains. Poor thing's really bothered by storms for some reason. Not that Jen minds. Molly's like a kid sister to her."

"Are you tight with the Procters?"

"We don't exactly move in the same crowd, if you know what I mean. *Not* because of Richard." Kimberly blushed instantly at the mention of his name. Had herself a small crush on the professor, it seemed. "He is such a sweet guy. Nice manners. Never puts on any airs. But that Carolyn is a whole other story. The great big fancy author with her Miss Porter's this and her Radcliffe that. They split up, you know. Some other guy moved right in. A real roughneck, too, if you ask me. Does gutters for some big outfit. Has himself a Mexican helper who's always hanging around, and I don't like the way *he* stares at Jen. They're hard workers though, I'll give them that."

"Is that right?"

"Absolutely. I've seen two, three of those white Nutmegger vans parked over there at a time. Sometimes I even hear them out there in the middle of the night."

"Doing what?"

"Unloading their gear. They try to be quiet about it but I'm a real light sleeper. Didn't use to be when I had a man in bed next to me. Now the slightest breeze wakes me." She hung the last of the towels, grabbed the empty basket and started back toward the house. "It's funny, isn't it?"

"What is?" asked Des, walking with her.

"How you can live fifty feet away from someone, wave to them every day in the driveway, take in each other's mail, exchange cookies at Christmas—and really not know them at all. If you'd asked me six months ago I'd have told you that the Procters were the ideal family. Now look at them."

Des climbed into her cruiser, waved good-bye to Molly and started her way back toward Turkey Neck, not liking what she was hearing about the Procters one bit. Clearly, the little girl was being neglected. Clearly, Des ought to be reaching out to the Department of Children and Families. Starting the bureaucratic process rolling. DCF would send an investigator down to interview the family members. Possibly place Molly in a foster home until her parents could sort out their lives. That was the required procedure. It was also the easy thing to do. But shoving Molly into the system wasn't necessarily the right thing to do.

So what was?

As Des eased her way around a bend, mulling her options, she rolled up on a young couple walking slowly along, hand in hand.

She pulled up next to them, lowered her window and barked, "Folks, I'll need to see your driver's licenses *and* passports if you intend to proceed any further down this lane."

In response, Keith and Amber Sullivan both broke into big smiles.

Keith was thickly built and sunburned, with wiry sun-bleached hairs on his tree-trunk forearms. No more than twenty-five but already losing his wavy blond hair. So Keith looked much younger when he had his Sullivan Electric Co. baseball cap on. He wore it with a weathered T-shirt, cargo shorts and work boots. When Des got acquainted with him she'd discovered that Keith was one of those rare individuals who knew who he was, where he belonged and who with. Which put him way ahead of most people. Keith was by no means a slacker. He and his older brother Kevin worked plenty hard at their business. But it was Kevin who was the real go-getter of the two. Keith was more easygoing. A man who made time for a leisurely walk down a country lane with his bride on a beautiful June afternoon.

Amber was a slender, lovely little thing in a sleeveless summer dress and rubber flip-flops. She was Portuguese on her mother's side. It showed in her olive complexion and thick, shiny black hair, which she wore cropped short like a boy. Amber's big, brown eyes were shiny and searching. She and Keith had been married for four months now, but it could just as easily have been four days the way he kept gazing at her. "And what brings you out this way?" she demanded in that spunky, forthright manner of hers.

Des filled them in on Richard Procter's situation.

"This is *so* upsetting," Amber lamented, her brow furrowing. "Richard was my mentor at Wesleyan. I wrote my senior thesis for him." She was keenly interested in the social history of the Portuguese mill workers who'd settled in Southern Connecticut and Rhode Island a hundred years back. "It's thanks to his recommendation that I was accepted into the master's program at Yale. He also found us our cottage. I can't believe he . . . It's just *awful* him going to pieces this way. And it's been real hard on Molly since he left."

"We try to keep tabs on her," said Keith, whose love-struck eyes never left Amber. Des tried to remember if Brandon had ever looked at her that way. The short answer was no. "I can't tell you how many times we've asked that girl over for dinner. Or to watch a movie with us on TV. She always says 'Gotta go' and splits."

"And do you know where that child sleeps at night?" demanded

Amber, hands parked on her slim hips. "In her tree house. I can see her up there reading by flashlight."

Which explained why Molly bunked with Jen whenever it rained, Des reflected as she continued to idle there in the road. You could sit in the middle of Sour Cherry for ten minutes and not encounter another vehicle. "Would you happen to know if either Richard or Carolyn have any family nearby?"

"None," Amber replied with a shake of her head. "Both sets of parents are dead and Richard's an only child. Carolyn's sister, Megan, lives on an organic farm up in Blue Hill, Maine, with her life partner, Sue. The Procters go there every summer for their vacation. Or at least they used to."

"Carolyn's maiden name is Chichester?"

"Yes, that's right."

Des jotted down that information before she said, "Did Richard and Carolyn used to fight a lot?"

"No, but . . ." Amber glanced up and down the lane just to make absolutely certain no one was within earshot. "Apparently, Richard got himself involved with another woman. And when Carolyn got wind of it she threw him out."

"He brought this on himself," Keith said soberly. "Not that we're taking sides or anything. These things happen, right?"

"Any idea who the other woman is?"

Amber studied Des intently. "Why do you ask?"

"Because Richard's a man who needs all of the help he can get right now."

"We haven't the slightest idea who she is."

Meaning the odds were she wasn't someone local. In Dorset it was practically impossible to play in the dirt without people finding out.

"And if Richard hasn't sought her help," Amber added, "then she must not be in a position to help."

"You mean because she's married herself?"

"That would be my guess."

"This whole business came as a total shock to us," Keith said. "Richard used to stop over for a beer all of the time. Him and me would talk carpentry projects. He'd ask Amber about her studies. He was always upbeat. We had no inkling that he was unhappy at home."

"Carolyn we've never been quite as close to," Amber said. "She's so devoted to her responsibilities. Running Molly to and from school, working on one of her books. And ever since Richard has moved out she's, well, how should I put this. . . ."

"Gone skanky," Keith put it bluntly. "Drinking morning, noon and night. Bringing strange guys home at all hours. One of them was this Clay who, near as I can tell, never does a day's work. Not one guy I know has ever seen him on a job anywhere in town. You ask me, he's just a drifter who's found someone he can sponge off. Him and his buddy Hector both."

Amber said, "I caught a glimpse of Carolyn on her porch the other day and I almost didn't recognize her. The poor woman looks like she just walked away from a train wreck."

"Only because she has." Des wished the two lovebirds well, then eased her cruiser down the lane and up Patricia Beckwith's steep, twisting driveway.

Dorset's meanest, richest widow wasn't sitting in her stuffy parlor sipping sweet sherry. She was perched regally on a kneeling stool, weeding one of the flower beds in front of her house. She wore green garden gloves for the job, with a fraying old seersucker shirt and raspberry-colored slacks. Her little dachshund was stretched out in the grass near her. It didn't bark when Des climbed out of her cruiser, delivery in hand. Just watched her, black nose quivering.

"Good afternoon, Mrs. Beckwith," Des called out, pausing to savor the old lady's panoramic view of Long Island Sound.

"And to you as well, trooper," Patricia responded cordially. "What's that you've got in your hand?"

"I bumped into it this morning," Des said, holding Mitch's worn paperback copy of *Time and Again* out to her.

Patricia took it from her gratefully. "How very thoughtful. I'll look forward to reading and discussing it with you. And I promise to take good care of it. Would you like to come in for some lemonade?"

"Thank you, no. I can only stay a second. I just wanted you to know that I've located Professor Procter. It seems he's been sleeping in somebody's barn out on Big Sister."

The old woman's eyes widened in shock. "Why, the poor man must be out of his mind."

"Situational depression is what they call it."

"To do with his problems at home?"

Des nodded. "Apparently, he even got into a scuffle with the new man in Carolyn's life. He's presently up at Connecticut Valley Hospital in Middletown. Likely to be released tomorrow."

"I see. Well, I thank you for the update. And for your thorough professionalism of last night. I apologize for the manner in which Jen inconvenienced you."

"It was no inconvenience. That's why I'm here."

"Nonetheless, I've spoken with First Selectman Paffin and told him what an outstanding asset you are to our community."

"That really wasn't necessary, ma'am."

"I assure you it was. And if I can ever repay you . . ."

"You can, as a matter of fact."

The old woman stiffened ever so slightly. "Yes, what is it?"

"Richard is going to need supervision for a while. Someone making sure he takes his medication and shows up at his counseling appointments and so forth. He doesn't seem to have anyone to turn to. Or a place to stay."

"Then he shall stay here with me," Patricia said without hesitation.

"Are you sure that's okay?"

"Absolutely. I have plenty of room."

Des had obtained the name and phone number of Richard's doctor from Marge Jewett. She jotted the information down and handed it to Patricia. "Will you be able to pick him up tomorrow in Middletown?"

"I choose not to drive long distances anymore," she replied. "But I can certainly arrange to retrieve him. Don't you worry about Richard. He will be fine here. I'll make sure he follows his doctor's orders. Eats three square meals, gets his proper rest. And he and I shall sit down together and talk things over. He's a highly intelligent man. He just needs a little time. And someone to listen to him."

"You're very kind, Mrs. Beckwith."

"I assure you I am not. I'm the nastiest old bitch in town. Ask anyone."

Des got back in her ride and started down the driveway, thinking about how all of this spoke to the single most important lesson she'd learned about Dorset: No one was who they appeared to be. Those frosty, scary patrician dowagers weren't necessarily so frosty or scary. And those blond, perfect families like the Procters turned out to be just as screwed up as everyone else. More so, maybe, since they were such strangers to trouble in this orderly, privileged, unreal place. When they fell they fell hard. Which explained how a respected historian ended up out on Big Sister, mumbling to himself and subsisting on whatever food his daughter could steal for him, while his wife got strung out on crystal meth and allowed a pair of relative strangers to climb into her bed and do God knows what to her.

It was all just another nice, neat Dorset family snapshot, suitable for framing.

Des headed back up Turkey Neck to the stop sign at Old Shore Road. Made a left onto Old Shore Road and started home to change clothes for tonight's big event. She hadn't gone more than a half-mile when she noticed the big black Chevy Suburban in her rearview mirror coming up fast on her. Its driver, a jarhead in aviator shades, was way over the speed limit. And now the bastard was actually riding right up on her tail. Anybody dumb enough to climb up on a Crown Vic either had to be several drinks over the line or a complete chowderhead. She was wondering which this one was when he flashed his brights at her several times and gestured at her to pull over. As she slowed down he rocketed past her and made a hard, screeching right onto Mile Creek Road. She pursued him. Found him pulling onto the shoulder there and coming to a stop. Des pulled in behind him.

Before she could get out he'd leapt out of the Suburban and come charging at her with his his chest all puffed out. He was young, muscle-bound and terribly full of himself. A real testosterone cowboy in a red Izod shirt, jeans and running shoes. "Master Sergeant *Mitry*," he blustered at her, his voice positively dripping with contempt. "Whatever are we going to do with you, Master Sergeant *Mitry*?"

"That all depends on who you are and why you pulled me over."

He whipped off his shades, his eyes icy blue slits as he peered at her through her open window. "Are you trying to tell me you don't know?"

"I am."

"You must think I'm a total cretin."

"Too soon to say, wow man. But give me time."

He made an elaborate show of reaching into his back pocket for the FBI shield that identified him as Agent Grisky. "Now, I don't know whether you've got a lost puppy or stolen tricycle or whatever it is you resident troopers do, but we can't have you and your big hat tromping around in our pea patch, understand?"

"Not even a little, agent."

Grisky sighed impatiently. "Back the hell off, will you? Because I will *not* let you take a crap all over six months of hard work."

"Um, okay, are you trying to say I've walked into something?"

"As you know perfectly well."

Des shoved her heavy horn-rimmed glasses up her nose. "And how would I know that?"

"So, what, you're really going to keep playing dumb?"

"I really am. Because I really don't know what you're talking about."

"Fine," he snapped. "You want to play games, we'll play games. For starters, stay put." And with that he strutted his mad skills back toward his Suburban.

Watching him, Des felt absolutely certain he was a consummate quick draw artist between the sheets. A red hot thirty seconds from launch pad until blastoff, max. Following by ten good minutes of self-congratulation.

He reached inside the Suburban for his cell, flipped it open and speed-dialed someone. Talked into the phone. Listened. Then flipped it shut with a flourish and came back to her. "Tomorrow morning at ten in your barracks commander's office," he said. "And, lady, be prepared to get your ears chewed off."

"I'll be there. But I sure would appreciate it, one law enforcement professional to another, if you'd tell me what's going on."

"Not authorized to. But here's an extreme idea—why don't you give U.S. Attorney Stokes a nudge tonight and ask him?"

"Why, what's Brandon got to do with this?"

Agent Grisky wouldn't go there. Just smirked at her and said, "See you tomorrow, Master Sergent *Mitry*. Really dig the hat. Can I have one just like it when *I* grow up?"

The first time Des had seen Bitsy Peck's immense, natural-shingled Victorian mansion out on Big Sister she'd said to herself: People who aren't named Martha Stewart don't actually live this way. They don't own houses with this many turrets and sleeping porches. They don't enjoy such views of Long Island Sound in every direction. They aren't surrounded by such amazing gardens. But they did. They were. It was all for real. Same as Mitch's little carriage house nestled beyond those gardens was real.

The early evening sky over the Sound was a dusty pink when she arrived. Parked cars were jammed everywhere. And fifty or so very polite people were enjoying drinks out on Bitsy's deep wrap-around porch, where she was hosting the monthly get-together of the Dorset Town Committee, a nonpartisan group of highly in-fluential locals. Among other things, the Town Committee en-dorsed candidates for the State Senate, State Assembly and U.S. Congress. Tonight was a chance for its elite members to get to know Brandon. It was not a campaign fundraiser—although he'd warned Des there'd be people there from the party, not to mention photographers from the newspapers. It was simply a chance for Dorset's People Who Matter to hang with the man who wanted to be their next congressman. The district's current representative to D.C. had failed to carry Dorset, so for Brandon this was highly fertile ground.

And it certainly didn't hurt to have the town's resident trooper on hand to introduce him around and smile oh-so-adoringly at her brown-eyed handsome man.

The event was casual dress, which for the men meant madras blazers and for the women meant whatever was being featured in the current Talbot's catalogue that was neutral-colored and dowdy. Des wore an untucked orange linen shirt, trimly cut ivory slacks and gold sandals.

She met up with Brandon when he pulled into Bitsy's driveway accompanied by a pair of hyper, narrow-faced party operatives. He looked relaxed and ready. Also ultra-preppy in his new khaki-colored suit from Brooks Brothers. Used to be Brandon was more of an Armani man.

He smiled broadly at her as he got out of the car. "You're not wearing your uniform," he observed, giving her a big hug.

She batted her eyelashes at him. "You noticed."

"Desi, I thought we decided it wouldn't hurt to remind these good folks that I intend to be their law and order candidate."

"I never wear my uni when I'm off duty."

"Then why did you ask me if you should wear it?"

"Because I wanted to hear what your answer would be."

Brandon tilted his head at her slightly. "Well, you definitely made the right choice," he conceded, looking her up and down. "Although it's going to be difficult for me to keep my mind on politics."

"Brandon, we have to talk."

"Sounds serious."

"Only because it is."

"We'll find a quiet spot on the porch in a little while. Right now . . ." He took her hand as they climbed the porch steps, squeezing it. "Are you ready for this?"

"Ready as I'll ever be," she answered, taking a deep breath.

Together, they plunged in, Brandon towering over one and all at six-feet-six. Not that he was intimidating. The man could disarm anyone with his smile and rich, burgundy voice. Des introduced him straight away to Dorset's snowy-haired first selectman, Bob Paffin, who still wasn't totally comfortable having a resident trooper who was so young, female and black. And to Glynis Fairchild-Forniaux, the blond, blue-blooded attorney who felt just fine about Des—and soon hoped to unseat Bob Paffin. To Arthur Lewis, president of the local chapter of the Nature Conservancy, and Emma Knight, who ran Dorset's No. 1 real estate agency. To the Inlands Wetlands commissioner and the commissioner of the Historic District. To the head of the school board, a mother of three whose oldest girl, Shannon, played on the Dorset High basketball team with Jen Beckwith. Des found herself wondering if Shannon had been at Jen's Rainbow Party, and if so which color lip-gloss she'd worn.

There were platters of sweaty cocktail wienies and ice cold shrimp. Potluck dishes of ham and scalloped potatoes, tuna casserole and Mitch's perennial favorite, American chop suey. All of which looked heavy and gloppy and way too much like warm vomit.

And there was talk, talk and more talk—most of it coming from Brandon's mouth. He told the soccer moms how much he believed in public education. The chesty Lions Clubbers how antiterror he was. The environmentalists how he intended to protect the Sound from natural gas pipelines. The realtors that he was for "quality" development. The man never came up for air. Never stopped smiling. Never stopped working, working, working the crowd. As Des watched him it dawned upon her for the very first time that Brandon Stokes wasn't an attorney at all. He was a natural born performer. Someone who could be hip or square, funny or serious, compassionate or outraged. Whatever the person who he was belly up to needed from him at a particular moment. Then he could move right along and do it all over again with someone else—and make the transition seem utterly effortless. Truly, this porch was Brandon's stage. And he was totally at ease on it.

Which made exactly one of them.

Des was watching her man do his thing, utter fascinated, when without warning she felt another of her damned blackouts coming on. The porch swaying under her feet. The voices and laughter growing fainter. Horrified, she groped her way out to the farthest end of the porch and slumped into a wicker chair with her head down. Breathed slowly in and out, waiting for it to pass. Which, thank God, it did. But she did not want to risk hitting the deck in front of all of these people. So she stayed put for a while, directing her mind elsewhere.

To the phone call she'd just made to Megan Chichester, Carolyn Procter's very capable sounding sister up in Blue Hill, Maine. Megan was aware that Richard had moved out, but knew nothing of Clay Mundy. She'd been shocked by Des's description of her sister's physical state and by her concerns over Molly's welfare. Promised Des she'd drive down to Dorset as soon as possible—if not tomorrow then the day after—to get Carolyn whatever help she needed. And, if necessary, bring Molly home with her for an early summer holiday. "I'll take charge of the situation," she assured Des. Which made it a good day's work all in all. This was the job, Des reflected. Giving a family a chance to heal itself. Piecing together a way to keep the law out of it. She'd tried, anyhow. The rest was up to them.

As she sat there, Des found herself gazing across the gardens at Bella's lights in Mitch's windows. Wondering how many more months it would take before the doughboy was no longer inside of her. When he would finally, mercifully, fade away.

She heard footsteps clacking toward her now. It was her hostess, Bitsy, bringing her a goblet of white wine.

"I thought you could use this," she exclaimed brightly.

Des took it from her gratefully. "You thought right."

"Your Brandon is certainly one handsome man. Do you know who he reminds me of?"

Des nodded. "Denzel Washington."

"I was going to say Harry Belafonte."

"Really? My bad."

Bitsy Peck was a round, snub-nosed woman in her fifties with light brown hair that she wore in a pageboy. She had always been very warm and friendly toward Des, and got on extremely well with Mitch. It was Bitsy who'd taught Mitch the joy of gardening. "I did invite Bella," she said, her gaze following Des's. "But she told me she couldn't make it."

Des drank down some of the wine. "I know," she responded quietly.

Bitsy studied her shrewdly. She was one of those Dorset housewives who gave the impression of being unfailingly merry and dim, and was neither. She was smart and tough. Had lost her husband right after Des came to town. And seen her daughter, Becca, battle heroin addiction. "Are you okay, Des?"

"Never better."

"We're going to lose you, aren't we?"

"Excuse me?"

"I can see it in your eyes as you look around. It's as if you're trying to memorize everything. My kids looked at this place that way when they were getting ready to leave me."

"Bitsy, I don't know what you mean."

"Yes, you do."

Some of the Town Committee members were starting to trickle back to their cars. Bitsy scurried off to say her good-byes. Des stayed put, sipping her wine.

Brandon found her there a few minutes later. He was all pumped up, his eyes gleaming. "Man, this is some way to live," he exclaimed, taking in the remains of the sunset over Long Island Sound. A few sailboats were still out on the water, taking advantage of the breeze. "It's almost enough to make you want to be white."

She smiled faintly. "But not quite."

He turned and looked at her. "This is going to take you some getting used to, isn't it?"

"I'm afraid so."

"Same here. I still have to get over my long held personal belief that all politicians are assholes." He let out a big laugh. "But we did good tonight. Huge thanks, Desi. These people carry a lot of weight."

"Brandon, there's something serious I need to talk to you about."

"So talk to me. But smile or it'll look like we're having a fight."

"I got pulled over by a fed named Grisky just before I came here. He told me to keep away from Sour Cherry Lane. I phoned my C.O. right away and got another earful from him—mostly about Grisky and his strong-arm tactics. But he confirmed that the guy's legit. It seems there's been an independent operation going on here in Dorset."

"And you're telling me this because . . . ?"

"When I asked Grisky what it was he told me to ask you."

Brandon's face dropped. He said nothing.

"I ran criminal background checks on Clay Mundy and Hector Villanueva. Both out of Atlanta, supposedly. I came up empty. Brandon, what's going on?"

"I can't discuss it with you," he responded quietly. "All I can say is they wanted you kept clear of it."

"Kept clear of *what?* This is my town. If something's going on here, I have a right to know."

"Don't get all huffy."

"Trust me, *this* is not huffy. But if you want huffy I'll be more than happy to—"

"Keep your voice down, Desi. And please listen to me, will you? We are talking about a highly classified investigation involving multiple federal and state agencies. They've had trouble with leaks in the past, so a high-level policy decision was made to keep local uniformed personnel out of the loop. They want you going about your normal business."

"That's them. What about you and me?"

"What about us?"

"If you'd given me any kind of a heads-up I'd have watched my step. Instead, you let me blunder my way right into the middle of *whatever*. And so tomorrow I'm getting called on the carpet. Do you realize how humiliating this is?"

"I had no idea you were working anywhere near Sour Cherry. You didn't tell me."

"I shouldn't have to. You're my man. I expect you to be watching my back."

"I'm watching out for *us*. Desi, this is the biggest case of my career. It just may put me over in this district." His eyes found and held hers. "What's good for me is good for you. You know that."

"I know that you're good at keeping secrets. I know I don't like secrets. And I don't like being with anyone who does."

"I am not about secrets."

"Brandon, your whole damned life is divided into secret compartments." Like the one that had contained his law school classmate, Anita, and the affair that they never broke off the whole time he and Des were married. "For me, it's real simple. Either we're honest with each or we're not. Either we're together as a couple or we're not."

"Now you're not being fair," he objected.

"I think I'm being more than fair. Are you going to tell me what the feds are doing in my town?"

"You know I can't."

"Okay, fine. Then I'll listen to what they have to say tomorrow. And until then you're sleeping in the guest room."

"I'm *what?*"

"My house, my rules. If you don't like it you can take up residence at the Frederick House. The innkeepers are standing right over there by that pillar." She drank down the last of her wine before she added, "And hey, not to worry. When I said it I had a real sweet smile on my face."

CHAPTER 6

To: Mitch Berger
From: Bella Tillis
Subject: Eureka

Dear Mr. Hotshot New York Movie Critic—I'm pleased to re-port that I've finally managed to corral your roaming friend Quirt. He's here in the house with me, though I'm not sure how much longer I can keep him here. The little fiend keeps pacing around like a caged lion. Yowling at me in angry protest. Sharpening his claws on the beetle-infested chestnut posts that barely hold this place up. He's one giant pain in the tuchus, frankly.

At your suggestion, I phoned our resident trooper about my phantom nighttime visitor out here. I hadn't seen Des for a while. Not that you asked me but she looks awful. Scrawny as a half-starved Chihuahua. She says she's fine. She's not fine. And it pains me to report that she has abandoned her art. Do you remember how she always used to have that charcoal residue under the nail of her index finger? She doesn't have it anymore. Not so much as a trace. This is not a happy woman, Mitch. I thought you should know since you were once so fond of her.

Anyhow, it turns out I *have* been sheltering a homeless man in the barn—Molly Procter's father, who seems to have suffered a breakdown since he and Carolyn split up. Molly has been hiding Richard out here and stealing food for him. The Jewett sisters have carted him off and now Des will no doubt try to patch the family back together again. It never ceases to amaze me how a woman whose own life is broken keeps trying to repair everyone else's.

Actually, Des is out here on Big Sister at this very moment. Or *they* are. Bitsy Peck got talked into hosting a bash for the Town Committee to get acquainted with our next congressman—assuming, I should say, that Brandon can carry this district without my vote. I was invited to the event but am staging a one-woman boycott. And voting Green Party all of the way should he receive the party's . . . Oops, hang on, somebody's at my door . . .

Hi, I'm back. That was just Bitsy dropping off some of the leftover food. And to tell me something very interesting. She suspects Des will soon be leaving Dorset. This certainly wouldn't surprise me. Now that you're gone Des no longer has any reason to stick around here. Bitsy also told me she thought Brandon didn't go over particularly well with Dorset's old guard. People thought he was a bit too slick and/or insincere. This was definitely Bitsy's own reaction. And perhaps her loyalty to you shining through.

Oy, Quirt has just started yowling at me again. Such a set of lungs he's got on him! Mitch, I'm not sure how long this little arrangement will last, since I do enjoy a night's sleep now and then. Do you think you can come fetch him some time soon? If not, I'll shove him into a carrier and bring him to the city on the train. Mind you, I'll have to provide earplugs for my fellow passengers. But I'm game. Please advise.

Love, Aunt Bella.

p.s. I don't mean to be such a yenta regarding you and Des, but it so happens that I am a pure-blooded Jewish mother. And let us never forget that the word *smother* is just *mother* with an extra S in front of it.

To: Bella Tilllis
From: Mitch Berger
Subject: Re: Eureka

Dear Aunt Bella—I'm happy that you've managed to corral Quirt. But I could have sworn I already told you that Quirt will never be happy living with me here in the city. I can't take him, Bella. Quirt's a roamer.

And so am I, it turns out.

I wasn't going to say anything until the deal is officially inked but the empire's cable news network is giving me my own weekly half-hour show, complete with Miss Hawaii as my comely sidekick. I made it, ma! Top of the world! On the downside, it means I'll be out in Los Angeles for a while, setting up a staff and so on. Actually, the newspaper would love it if I relocated out there permanently. But that's not going to happen. I intend to stay in New York. Once the show's up and running, I'll be able to spend more time here. But, short term, I'm simply not going to be around. That means I'll have to beg my assistant to cat-sit Clemmie. Throwing Quirt into the mix is out of the question.

I'm very sorry to hear about what's happened to Richard Procter. Molly is so devoted to him. I did try e-mailing Molly again but I never heard back from her.

It's funny about being away from Dorset. When I was living there full-time the lives of the people there seemed incredibly important to me. That's what it means to be a Dorseteer. But now that I've left I don't feel connected to them at all. I really enjoyed my time there, Bella. I'll never forget the exquisite pleasure of sitting in a lawn chair with a cold Bass Ale watching the migratory shore birds fly by. But now that I'm back here living my normal life it's almost as if none of that was truly real—especially Des and me. We never really made a whole lot of sense, if you stop and think about it. A black state trooper and a Jewish movie critic? How farfetched is that? If you put it in a movie nobody would buy it. And how in the hell would you cast it? Well, okay, you'd go with Halle Berry for Des. That's a no brainer. But who on earth would play me? And don't say Ben Stiller or we will never speak again.

Bella, I guess what I'm trying to say is that my Dorset interlude is over. I've moved on. You're welcome to visit me in NYC any time. I'd love to see you—provided we talk about something, anything other than the resident trooper of Dorset, Connecticut, USA, a place that is now so far removed from my thoughts that I honestly can't imagine what it would take to drag me back there again.

Much love,
Mitch

CHAPTER 7

HER TROOP COMMANDER WAS a sagging accordion of a man named Rundle. Rundle was less than a year away from retirement. All he cared about was making sure Troop F ran friction-free. No emotional or jurisdictional conflicts of any kind. So it was not exactly a happy man who sat there behind his steel desk from them. Grumpy was more like it.

His office was small and plainly furnished. Some photos on his desk of his beloved grandkids and even more beloved fishing boat. The standard issue photo of the governor on the wall. Not much else. The Troop F Barracks practically kissed the southbound right-hand lane of I-95 in Westbrook. You never stopped hearing the interstate traffic whizzing by. If you stood over by Rundle's window you could even watch it.

There were three others there besides Des. The supervising agent, who was a bland, buttoned-down DEA man named Cavanaugh. Capt. Joey Amalfitano, the point man for Connecticut's Narcotics Task Force, who Des had worked a drive-by shooting with back when she was still on the Major Crime Squad. Everyone called him the Aardvark due to his huge, down-turned snout of a nose. And Agent Grisky of the FBI, who was dead wrong about the purpose of this meeting. It was not a tongue-lashing. Everyone was real polite and professional. Everyone, that is, except for Grisky himself. He was still acting all chippy when he wasn't busy styling in his tight T-shirt and chewing gum with his mouth open.

It was Cavanaugh of the DEA who did most of the talking. "Master Sergeant Mitry, I'm afraid you've stumbled your way right smack dab into the middle of Operation Burrito King."

Des sat there with her hands folded in her lap, wondering how it was the feds always came up with such cute names.

"This operation originated with some wire surveillance we had going on in Tucson," he informed her in a clipped, quiet voice. "An informant of ours happened to be meeting a dealer at a fast food restaurant of that name."

Okay, that answered that question.

"We've gotten our hooks into a major drug ring with ties to the Vargas family, Mexico's largest cocaine trafficker in this country. Lately, they've started moving into crystal methamphetamine in a huge way. The why is pretty simple. We cracked down on the sale of over-the-counter cold medicines and other household ingredients that were being used to produce the ice domestically. Felt darned proud of ourselves, too. Trouble is, the Mexican traffickers immediately saw an opening and jumped right in."

"Nobody ever said they weren't smart businessmen," Des said.

Cavanaugh nodded his head. "They mass produce it south of the border, then ship it into the U.S. I am talking about hundreds and hundreds of pounds of methamphetamine crystals that are crossing into this country every day. As to what happens to it once it gets north of the border, well, our investigation has led us to Atlanta."

Right away, Des felt an uptick of her pulse.

"Atlanta's their distribution center, okay?" Grisky put in now, chomping away at his gum. "All of the ice shipments headed for the midwest and northeast pass through there, okay?"

Des said, "Okay." He wasn't going to be happy until she did.

"Over the past six months," Cavanaugh continued, "we've assembled a joint task force made up of the DEA, the FBI, the Connecticut Organized Crime Task Force and, most recently,

Captain Amalfitano and his Narcotics Task Force. U.S. Attorney Stokes has also been involved in an advisory capacity for quite some time."

"And why did you end up in Dorset?" Des wanted to know.

"Because they did," the Aardvark told her, slurping from a Styrofoam cup of coffee. "Like you said, they aren't dumb. If they stash a huge quantity of product somewhere like the South Bronx then it's always at risk. You're talking about a high-crime area crawling with dealers, users and various and sundry lowlifes. Maybe a rival dealer rips them off. Maybe a strung-out snitch whispers in some beat cop's ear. Bottom line, their product is never secure and they know it. So they've started using stash houses in nice, quiet little towns like yours where there isn't a whole lot of crime or drug traffic or scrutiny. It's under the radar there. Who would think to look for three hundred pounds of crystal meth in Dorset, am I right?"

"You're not wrong," Rundle wheezed, putting the lie to Des's theory that he'd fallen asleep behind his desk with his eyes open.

"Just last year," Cavanaugh revealed, "one of the other Mexican cartels was using a lovely little village in the Pennsylvania Amish country."

"Yeah, right up until we nailed their sorry asses." Grisky let out a cocky bray of a laugh.

"And Dorset is ideally situated," the Aardvark went on. "It's halfway between New York City and Boston. It's close to I-95. Perfect locale for a wholesale supply house."

"Clay Mundy is their point man here," Cavanaugh said. "He and his sidekick Hector set up the stash house on Sour Cherry Lane, and they're operating it quietly and efficiently right there under everybody's noses. That so-called seamless gutter business of theirs is strictly a shell. The only thing Nutmegger uses its vans for is transporting product in and out."

"I knew they smelled wrong," Des said. "Neither man has a sheet, though."

"Because they're cautious and they're smart," he said. "Mundy also appears to be a world-class player when it comes to the ladies. He moved right in on the Procter woman after her husband left. We gather she was already drinking heavily. He turned her on to crystal meth and ever since then she's been floating in the clouds while he and Hector go about their business. We've been running a tap on their calls, intercepting their mail. The full monty. But these boys are incredibly careful. They conduct no business over the phone. Not a single incriminating call. Not a coded message. Nothing. Either their delivery schedule is prearranged or it's communicated to them strictly face-to-face."

"Meanwhile," said Grisky, "we're staked out in the woods twenty-four seven. Three of us on eight-hour shifts. Near as we can tell, they've got the ice stashed somewhere inside of the house. Neither man ever goes near the barn or wanders into the woods. Once a week, one of them will take off in their van to make drops. He'll be gone for a day, sometimes two. The other one stays behind to guard the stash. They get resupplied every couple of weeks by another Nutmegger van—usually late at night. They keep an ultra-low profile. No parties. No hangers on. No fooling around. These are total pros. The neighbors don't suspect a thing."

"Have any of them made you guys?" Des asked him.

"Only Molly, the little girl. I told her I was with the DEP. She bought it."

"Don't bet on it," Des said. "Molly is way savvy. She will also, I hope, be far, far away from this mess very soon."

Cavanaugh stared at her for a moment before he said, "Master Sergeant, I think you'd better explain that remark."

"When I stopped by Carolyn Procter's yesterday I found Carolyn to be in a highly drugged-out state. Molly is currently living in the presence of illegal behavior. She is also unsupervised."

"We share your concerns," Cavanaugh said. "And we intend to remove the girl to a safe location when the time is right."

"That's fine for you," said Des. "But I'm blessed with no such wiggle room. As my commander can tell you, I'm required to report my observations to the Department of Children and Families."

Grisky immediately let out a groan of protest.

"Molly also happens to be one of my people," Des added, raising her voice over him. "I don't want to see anything happen to her."

"And you think we do?" Grisky demanded.

"I think you gentlemen have your priorities and they don't include the welfare of the Procter family. Which is why I resent you keeping me in the dark all of these weeks. You had to have witnessed the altercation between Richard Procter and Clay Mundy. Yet you did nothing to intercede. Nor did you alert me. Hell, for all I know you were aware that Molly had hidden him out on Big Sister Island."

Grisky didn't dispute this. No one did.

"I understand where you're coming from," Cavanaugh said to her quietly. "But we've had some huge cases go into the crapper lately because too many people knew about them. We desperately want this one. Secrecy is vital. Which is why I must point out that bringing in the Department of Children and Families would not be a very good idea right now."

"Really, really bad idea, girlfriend," echoed Grisky. "Last thing in the world we need is a bunch of social workers hanging around."

"Okay, two quick things," Des responded. "I am not your girlfriend. And DCF caseworkers do not travel by the bunch. And, okay, *three* things—I'm no fan of the DCF bureaucracy myself.

I reached out to Carolyn's sister. My hope is she'll take the girl home to Maine with her. Maybe get Carolyn into some kind of rehab."

Cavanaugh considered this carefully for a moment, his eyes narrowing. "We'll be happy to see the girl relocated. Even happier if it's expedited outside of official channels. As far as Carolyn is concerned, no one here wants to see the woman destroy her life. My only worry is if the sister topples the apple cart. Leans on Clay and Hector to move out, for instance. We're at a very sensitive juncture right now. I'm talking days, *hours* away from landing on them. Our informant down in Atlanta has tipped us off to a big shipment of ice that'll be making its way north to the Sour Cherry house within the next seventy-two hours. We intend to dog the delivery van from the moment it leaves there until the moment it arrives here—witnessing every drop it makes along the way. This is our chance to roll up the entire operation, master sergeant. It's the culmination of a lot of hard work. And we do not want Clay suddenly getting spooked."

"Understood," Des said. "And, again, if you gentlemen had included me before now I would have made every effort to accommodate you."

"Perhaps we should have," Cavanaugh conceded. "If we've created an awkward situation for you, I apologize. We know you have a job to do. We're just under a lot of pressure to deliver this one. Also, speaking candidly . . ." He cleared his throat, coloring slightly. "What I mean is, we were assuming that U.S. Attorney Stokes was keeping you up to speed. Strictly off the record, of course."

"Well, you assumed wrong. Brandon hasn't said one word to me about it."

"The man is a pro's pro," Grisky said admiringly.

Indeed. A pro's pro who'd spent last night bedded down in Bella's old room. When Des woke up he'd already taken off for work. Left her a note on the fridge that read: *I love you. Let's sit down and talk tonight, okay?*

"Now that I'm up to speed," Des said to Cavanaugh, "exactly what is it that you want me to do?"

"Go about your normal business," he replied. "Just don't do it anywhere near Sour Cherry Lane. Stay away from there."

"Not a problem. But what if the unforeseen happens?"

"Such as?"

"Such as I get another routine call to go out there."

Cavanaugh opened his mouth but nothing came out.

Which left it up to Rundle to tell her, "Pray that you don't."

"You're not pregnant, if that's what you were wondering."

"This much I already know. I took a home test."

"Have you taken any allergy or cold medication? Used a nasal spray?"

"No, why?"

They were all done with the physical part of her examination. Des had been poked inside and out. Blood and urine samples taken. Now she had her uniform and dignity back on as she and Dr. Lisa Densmore sat there in the tiny examining room on Park Street in New Haven. Lisa was a generously sized slab of a sister out of Newark, by way of Yale Medical School. Also a friend dating back to when Des and Brandon were living in Woodbridge. Lisa's husband Ron, a research chemist, used to play basketball with Brandon Saturday mornings.

"How about diet pills?" she asked as she pored over Des's medical file.

"Why on earth would I take diet pills?"

Lisa smiled at her. She had a space between her two front teeth that gave her the look of a mischievous little girl, which she was not. She was a serious, tough-minded doctor. "Desiree, you are one of the most superbly conditioned patients I've ever treated. When a fine, healthy specimen such as yourself tells me she's been blacking out I start with the basics, okay?"

"Such as . . . ?"

"Your blood pressure, which today registers one-forty-three over eighty-eight. Would you like to know what it was when you were here for your regular physical back in February?" She glanced down at Des's file. "One-twenty-five over seventy-two. It's *been* one-twenty-five over seventy-two for as long as I've been treating you, give or take a few points. Not only is your pressure significantly higher, it's *high*. You and I will need to have a serious conversation if we establish this as your new baseline. Which it may not be. Could just be a one-time deal. *Except* there's more. Such as your resting pulse rate. This afternoon it's ninety-seven beats per minute. In February, it was seventy-four. Somehow, my dear, you have also managed to lose nine pounds."

"I haven't been very hungry lately."

"Why not?"

"I'm a bit wound up. When I get tense, I lose my appetite."

"We should all be so lucky," Lisa sighed, patting her soft tummy. "How much coffee do you drink?"

"One cup in the morning."

"Alcohol?"

"A glass of wine now and then."

"How about drugs? Please be honest or I can't help you."

"I don't do drugs, Lisa."

Lisa set the file aside and crossed her arms before her chest. "Talk to me about these blackouts. How many have you had?"

"A few over the past couple of weeks."

"Are you on duty when they occur?"

"No, I'm usually at home. Or out socializing."

"Do they happen after you've just stood up?"

"No, I'm already standing up. I'll just suddenly feel very light-headed and dizzy. And my heart will speed up. Next thing I know, I'm either out cold on the floor or sitting there with my head between my knees, praying."

"I know this is embarrassing, but when you black out do you lose control over your bladder or bowels?"

"No."

"Have you been experiencing any blurring or loss of vision lately? Hearing loss? Impairment of memory or motor skills? Do you notice yourself slurring your words?"

"Nothing like that. Lisa, what's happening to me?"

"Darned good question. You have no buildup of fluid in your ears or sinuses. Your cardiogram is normal. I *could* order up a whole bunch of really elaborate brain scans, but I'm not sure that's called for at this point. Obviously, I'll want to look at your blood work. But most likely what we're dealing with here is something lifestyle related."

"Lifestyle related," Des repeated doubtfully.

"You say you don't eat when you're stressed out. Start eating—three square meals a day, doctor's orders. And let's talk about your stress load. Lord knows there's plenty of it in your job. How is that going?"

"I enjoy what I'm doing. Sure, it can be frustrating sometimes. But I'm happy being a resident trooper. I feel like I'm helping people. Although I'd be lying if I didn't admit that I'm thinking about transferring to a different community. Some place where they don't know every single damned thing about my private life."

Lisa raised her chin at her slightly. "Does this have to do with you and that nice Jewish boy you were seeing?"

Des lowered her eyes, nodding.

"Then you've answered my next question."

"Which is . . . ?"

97

"Have there been any major changes in your life? The answer is Hell, yes. You've ended a serious relationship and taken up again with your ex-husband."

"Are you suggesting that Brandon is hazardous to my health?"

"Not at all. But there's no way you aren't feeling conflicted, possibly even a bit freaked out about your decision. I know I'd be."

"And that's why I've been blacking out?"

"You want my best guess? Yes, it is. And if you were someone else I'd write you a prescription for a mild antianxiety medication."

"No way, Lisa. I'm a first responder. I carry a loaded semiautomatic weapon that I'm expected to be—"

"Down, girl! I know this. So I am not even going to bother. But I am not happy about your blood pressure. If you're anywhere near a clinic in the next few days I want you to stop in and have it checked again. Keep track of your numbers. If your systolic continues to average around one-forty with a diastolic of over ninety then we will have to consider putting you on medication. Let's talk again when you call me to discuss your blood samples, okay?"

Des nodded unhappily. She was not used to warnings. Or anything short of perfect health.

"This other man you were seeing . . ."

"His name was Mitch. Still is."

"Are you still in contact with him?"

"No, not at all."

"Would you like to be?"

"It's over with Mitch, Lisa. Brandon and I are getting along great. I'm very happy."

Lisa flashed Des her gap-toothed smile. "Then go home and *be* happy."

So Des followed doctor's orders. Stopped off at The Works on her way home and picked up the fixings for a major romantic supper.

A thick porterhouse steak for two from Paul the butcher. A wedge of Cato Corner Farms Hooligan from Christine the cheese lady. Baby greens and fingerling potatoes from Ben the produce man. And a sinful strawberry cheesecake from the bakery, where Jen Beckwith was working the counter. Little Molly was parked on a stool at the adjacent coffee bar, basketball on the floor at her feet, her nose buried in a library book.

"How goes it?" Des asked as Jen boxed up her cheesecake, face set tight with determination.

"Molly's all excited that her dad's coming home today. Well, not *home*, but you know what I mean. Nana's hired Fred to drive her to the hospital to get him." Dorset was too small a place have a commercial taxi or car service. What it had was Fred Griswold, a retired chimney sweep who chauffeured Dorseteers to and from the airport or wherever in his Buick Regal. "Nana wanted *me* to drive her," Jen went on, "since she paid for my car and is, like, incredibly cheap. But I have to be here all afternoon. It'll be really great for Molly, her dad being walking distance away. And I know my mom will be thrilled."

"Your mom? Why is that?"

"She has a major, major thing for Professor Procter. Goes into her whole cocker spaniel deal every time she sees him."

"Her cocker spaniel deal is . . . ?"

"Mom's way of gazing oh-so-adoringly up at a man. She cocks her head to one side and her eyes get all huge and swoony. . . ." Jen treated Des to a demonstration, complete with slackened jaw and shallow panting. "It's totally embarrassing, believe me."

"Does Professor Procter have similar feelings for her?"

"I really wouldn't know."

Another customer joined at the bakery counter now—old Rut Peck, Dorset's apple-cheeked retired postmaster, who was a loyal chum of Mitch's. Des smiled at him. Rut wouldn't smile back.

Des sighed inwardly before she said, "Jen, why don't you take care of Mr. Peck first? I'm in no rush."

Jen thanked her. Rut didn't. Just pointed a stubby, wavering finger at what he wanted.

Molly was totally absorbed in her book, which was Harper Lee's *To Kill a Mockingbird*. Her half-eaten doughnut lay forgotten at her elbow. "This is due back at the library *tomorrow*," she explained urgently, barely looking up from it. "I absolutely have to finish it. My dad doesn't believe in overdue fines. He calls them the hallmark of a sloppy mind."

Des slid onto the stool next to hers and said, "Molly, you mentioned to me yesterday that you don't much care for Clay."

"No, I didn't." Molly's eyes remained glued to the page. "I said that I hate him."

"He isn't real fond of you either, is he?"

"Which is fine by me."

"Has Clay ever ordered you to stay out of a certain part of the house? Told you not to go in a particular room or anything like that?"

The child looked up from her book, studying Des curiously through those bent wire-framed glasses of hers. "Why are you asking me that?"

"Just curious."

"Are you investigating a *crime*? Because I've got awesome skills, you know. I always help my mom figure out what happens next in her books. Tell me, what did Clay steal?"

"Who says he stole anything?"

"I do. He's bad news. I just know he is. What are looking for, Trooper Des? Come on, you can tell me."

A dozen or so rambunctious, sun-browned high school boys and girls joined them at the coffee bar now, full of banter and laughter. They were lively, good-looking kids. Although one of the boys, a tall, blue-eyed blond, did wear his hair braided in exceptionally silly-looking cornrows. Glancing over at the bakery counter, Des noticed Jen coolly watching the kids as she rang up Rut Peck. This was her crowd, Des figured. The ones who'd been at her Rainbow Party. Des wondered which one of the boys she liked. Fearing it was Mr. Blond Boy from the 'Hood.

Molly was tugging impatiently at her sleeve. "If I tell you what I know will you promise to let me help you?"

"I promise."

"Okay," she agreed. "He ordered me to stay out of the root cellar under the kitchen. Told me there are snakes down there. Which is, duh, total bull. I've been down there a million times."

"Have you gone down there since he told you not to?"

Molly shook her head, eyes widening with fright.

Des looked at her in concern. She didn't doubt that Clay would threaten this girl to keep her out of there. What else was he capable of doing? "Molly, I know things seem pretty messed up right now but it'll all be better soon, I swear. Just promise me one thing, will you?"

"What is it?"

"Don't get too curious."

"About what?"

"Stay out of that root cellar."

"*Why?*"

"Because it's important, that's why. And I am not fooling around, hear? Promise me."

"Okay, okay. I promise you," Molly said sullenly.

Des patted her on the shoulder, then went back to the bakery counter. "Feel like taking a break?" she asked as Jen rang her up. "I'll buy you a smoothie."

"Can't," Jen answered. "I'm all alone here until five. Responsible for everything."

While her friends goofed around over coffee, not a care in the world. Jen was still watching them, her jaw clenched, eyes wary. Such a bright and promising girl if only she'd learn to lighten up a little. But Dorset's teenagers came in only two flavors, Des was learning. Either they cared too much or they didn't care a goddamn about anything or anyone.

"How are you doing, Jen? Going any easier on yourself?"

"Why, is that what *you* do?" she demanded. "Go easy? Just smile and, *ta-daaa,* everything is all right in the world?"

"No, that only works in old Frank Capra movies." Damn, there was Mitch again, right inside of her head. "Besides, you wouldn't want to go by me. I'm strictly a work in progress."

Jen didn't respond. Just put Des's boxed cheesecake in a shopping bag and handed it across the counter, her tight, narrow face a blank.

Des tried a different approach. "I'm kind of worried about Molly."

"Don't be. I totally look out for the little squirt. She's perfectly . . ." Jen halted, frowning at her. "You don't think her dad might hurt her or something, do you?"

"No, no. It's nothing like that."

"Then it's Clay, isn't it? You think *he* might do something."

"She just needs a friend is all I meant. The Sullivans told me she's been sleeping in a damned tree."

"I *thought* we were going to be honest with each other," Jen shot back, her cheeks flushing with anger.

"Well, we are, aren't we?"

"Not one bit. You're not telling me something. I can see it in your eyes."

"Jen, I'm merely trying to—"

"Damn, it is *always* that way with you people!"

"By 'you people' you mean . . . ?"

"Adults." Jen made it sound like the dirtiest word in the English language. "You are *all* such hypocrites. You came at me the other night like you wanted to be my friend. Gave me all of this blah-blah about how I can confide in you and trust you. But it's nothing but a one-way street. You are *so* holding out on me. And I know why, too. Because *you* don't trust *me*. So why don't you just do me a humongous favor and take your cheesecake and go, okay? Because I am *never* going to be your friend. Not now. Not ever. I don't make friends with anyone who is so totally and completely full of shit."

CHAPTER 8

IN HIS WILDEST FILM fantasies, Mitch could not have concocted a better blind date than Cecily Naughton.

She told him over the phone that she was tired of eating out and wanted to cook him a proper meal at his place. She insisted on bringing all the groceries. Even the wine. All Mitch had to do was be home on time to let her in. And it was a good thing he was because Lacy's new dance critic was exceedingly punctual. Showed up at seven o'clock sharp clutching shopping bags that were filled with loin lamb chops, eggplant, onions, tomatoes, salad greens, organic whole wheat couscous, fragrant strawberries, fudge sauce and two bottles of Chianti Classico.

Oh, and Cecily also turned out to be slender, leggy and startlingly beautiful, with long russet hair that was parted down the middle, big brown eyes, flawless milk-white skin and a devilish grin. She wore a snug-fitting sleeveless T-shirt with no bra, tight hip-hugger jeans, leather flip-flops and an interesting assortment of toe rings. And she was no bashful English rose. Charged right on in. Dumped the groceries on his counter. Pronounced his new place "utterly fabulous." Accepted a cold Bass Ale. Declined a glass. Kicked off her flip-flops and sat on his leather love seat with her legs crossed before her, raptly attentive.

Somehow, this gorgeous woman managed to give Mitch the impression that there was absolutely nowhere else in the world she'd rather be than right here with him.

Clemmie immediately crept into her lap and curled up there, purring.

Mitch sat in a leather chair facing her. For the occasion, he had chosen a powder blue single-ply cashmere crewneck over a white T-shirt, plain front khakis and suede Pumas. The sort of effortlessly casual look that had only taken him seven wardrobe changes and three calls to Sylvia Two. He'd spent another twenty minutes choosing the evening's musical selections. He'd opened with Stevie Ray Vaughan.

"It is *such* a thrill to meet you," Cecily exclaimed, taking a thirsty swig of her ale. "You used to be my favorite of the American film critics."

"I'm flattered. Only why 'used to be'? Don't you read me anymore?"

"I never miss one of your articles," she responded brightly.

Which threw Mitch decidedly off balance. "So . . . what brings you to New York?"

"London was beginning to feel stale. I've been wanting to try America for a while. Particularly New York. I've always loved its energy. The streets here are like pure adrenaline. I decided if I don't do it now I never will."

"Lacy told me used to be a dancer."

"Until I couldn't any longer," she confirmed, nodding. "Recurring stress fractures in my left foot. So I decided to write about it instead. I know the dance world inside and out, after all. And writing is something I've always had a facility for. I was very fortunate, actually. Began placing commentaries and things right away. It all just fell right into place. And then I heard from Lacy. She is such a dear. Is it true that she once slept with Lord Snowdon?"

"I wouldn't be the least bit surprised. If that woman ever decides to write a kiss-and-tell memoir she'll smash a lot of china."

Cecily tilted her head at him fetchingly, studying him now.

"I don't wish to be rudely personal, but she warned me that you'd had a bad breakup a while back."

"Is there such a thing as a good one?"

"Excellent point."

"It's true, I did. And I should warn you that I'm not looking to get seriously involved with anyone. Not for a good long while anyway."

"Excellent." Cecily gazed at him over her Bass bottle. "Neither am I."

Definitely on the prowl, if Mitch Berger knew anything about women. Which, let's face it, he did not.

"Good God, what am I thinking?" she declared suddenly. "I must start dinner." Moved Clemmie onto the loveseat, leapt to her feet and started for the kitchen. "I'm doing grilled chops with couscous, a salad and a quick skillet ratatouille of my own devising. I already roasted the eggplant this afternoon at Lacy's. Honestly, I don't believe she's ever used that oven. Would you like to know what she keeps inside of it?"

"No, I really wouldn't."

"I'll need a large skillet, Mitch. Cast iron if you have one."

He fetched her the biggest of his Lodge pans. "There's rosemary, mint and thyme growing out in my garden, if that's of any interest."

"My god, the perfect man!"

He went out onto the patio to cut some for her and fire up the grill. When he returned, the onion and garlic were sizzling in the pan and Stevie Ray had slammed his way into "The House is Rockin'," a rollicking Texas toe-tapper that had Cecily Naughton shaking her hips, her butt, her everything as she sautéed away. She was no Des Mitry. Hadn't the green-eyed monster's moves. Or booty. But she could get down pretty well for the daughter of English royalty.

Watching her at that moment, Mitch was very happy to be alive.

"Dance with me," she commanded him, grabbing him by the hand and swinging him around.

"No, wait, I don't dance."

"Nonsense," she scoffed, bumping hips with him. "*Move* to the music. Come on, show me what you got! Give it to me, boy! Get down and let your . . ." Abruptly, she released his hand. "You really *don't* dance, do you? Not a problem, the only good male dancers I've ever known were gay. You I have other plans for."

"Such as . . . ?"

"You can set the table, for starters," she replied, her eyes twinkling at him.

They ate out on the patio by candlelight. The night air was soft and warm, the food delicious, wine perfect.

"What did you mean about my work?" he asked her as he cut into his lamb chop.

Cecily tilted her head at him fetchingly. "Sorry?"

"You said I 'used to be' one of your favorite critics."

She took a sip of wine before she said, "I'm not entirely certain you wish to have this conversation with me, Mitch. I'm known to be rudely caustic."

"I'm plenty thick-skinned. And I want to hear what you have to say."

Cecily dabbed at her mouth with her napkin and sat back in her chair. "As you wish. At the risk of sounding like an overt bum licker, you were one of my heroes when I first set out to write about dance. I idolized you, actually. Chiefly because of the way you absolutely refused to accept what the film community was doing. You established high standards of your own and you stuck to them. Wrote about the movies not as they are but as they should be. Demanded more. Held the bastards to account. You stood for something, Mitch. Go back and look at some of your Sunday pieces from two or three years ago. Then look at last week's quote-unquote reappraisal of Brian De Palma."

"I simply said that not all of his films are outright terrible," Mitch responded easily. "The guy's career goes way, way back to *Carrie* in '76. He's been making movies for over thirty years. A lot of them bad movies, yes, but you have to admire his perseverance. Besides, I've actually enjoyed a couple of them. *Scarface* is wonderfully kitschy. And Sean Penn slays in *Carlito's Way,* which is actually a terrific movie if you can get past Penelope Ann Miller."

"Why, what's wrong with Penelope Ann Miller?"

"Aside from the fact that she can't act? Not a thing."

Cecily held her ground. "You've given in, Mitch. You used to rage against the machine. Now you're merely another cog in it. Someone who spends his time operating a Web site devoted to cute, diverting trivia. Lacy told me you're even launching your own television program out in Los Angeles."

"They've given me a twelve-week commitment."

She shook her head at him gravely. "That's not you."

"Sure it is. I'm just using a new delivery system, that's all. I'm still the same me."

"So you've always waxed your brows, have you?"

Mitch opened his mouth but no words came out. Glanced down at his hands and discovered that his fists were clenched. "You think I'm becoming a total media whore, is that it?"

"I do, Mitch. And it upsets me terribly to see you doing this to yourself. I admire you more than you can imagine." She reached for her wine glass and took a sip. "I warned you that I can be rude."

"Quite all right. That's your opinion and I respect it. But this is simply a new career challenge, that's all. I'll rise to it."

"How, by striding the red carpet with Miss Hawaii?"

"Wait one second. . . ." Mitch said, shaking his finger at her. "*Now* I get it."

"Get what? And don't do that with your finger. It's very rude."

"Lacy put you up to this, didn't she? She sent you here to coax me into leaving the evil empire for her new e-zine. That's what this whole evening has been about, hasn't it? The gourmet meal and wine. The tight jeans. Your nipples. You've come here to twist my arm."

"Mitch, I haven't the slightest idea what Lacy's designs were. As for my own . . ." Cecily gazed at him through her eyelashes. "I assure you that they involve twisting an entirely different part of your anatomy."

Mitch swallowed hard. "Are you always this shy?"

"Actually, I've demonstrated admirable restraint considering that I've wanted to jump you since the moment I walked in that door. The only thing that's held me back has been my acute sense of propriety." She studied him seriously. "One thing does concern me, however."

"And that is . . . ?"

"Do you have something against my nipples?"

"Not a thing. They seem very nice. I'd like to get to know them better."

Cecily yanked her T-shirt off over her head and flung it in the general direction of Mitch's Sungold tomato plants. "So what the devil are you waiting for?"

CHAPTER 9

"I DON'T MAKE FRIENDS with anyone who is so totally and completely full of shit."

The bubble bath felt heavenly after the punishing hour in her weight room capped off by a five-mile run through the hills around Uncas Lake. Des's body was good and relaxed now. All muscle tension gone.

If only her mind would ease off, too.

She could not stop obsessing about her encounter with Jen Beckwith at The Works. Replaying their conversation. Wondering how she might have handled it differently. Teenagers were just so damned hard. Trust was hard. Hell, *Dorset* was hard. It always got tricky when she waded into the lives of these people. Sometimes, as much as Des hated to admit it, she missed the moral clarity of a nice, clean gunshot wound to the head.

She shaved her long fine legs. Rubbed them with baby oil after she'd rinsed off. Dabbed some perfume behind her ears and between her breasts. Put on her tiny, low-cut red mini with not a stitch underneath. Barefoot, she set the table with her good china and silver and wine goblets. Lit the candles. Got the Reverend Al Green going on the stereo, feeling tingly and girlie-girl all over.

Brandon arrived home at six on the dot bearing a dozen long-stemmed red roses and two chilled bottles of Dom Perignon. "My god, Desi!" he gasped, gaping at her from the front hallway. "You look so foxy you're going to throw me completely off my game."

She sashayed over to him, worked his tie off and draped it around her own neck. "Which game is that?"

"I . . . had this speech all worked out."

"This isn't a courtroom, baby," she said, gazing up at him. "It's just us. Talk to me."

"Fair enough," he began, his Adam's apple bobbing up and down. "I understand why you were upset last night. It was wrong of me to shut you out of Operation Burrito King. I should have told you what was going on. You had every right to know. I simply let work get the best of me. I have to do a better job from now on, and I promise you I will. I've already lost you once, Desi. Lord knows I don't want to lose you again. I'm nowhere without you. I really mean that. And I-I . . . Damn, this was all going to sound fine until I saw you in that little dress."

"It sounded plenty fine," Des assured him. "Besides, it's not all on you. They told you to keep it quiet. You were being a professional. It was wrong of me to judge you. Sometimes I get a little turfy about this place and these people. I feel responsible for them."

"I know that." Brandon's eyes gleamed at her. "And it makes me so proud."

She glanced over at the champagne he'd brought. "Are you planning to open one of those or are they just for show?"

He went to work easing a cork out while she fetched their goblets from the tablet. He poured. They clinked glasses. They drank, gazing at each other as Reverend Al crooned smooth and silky on the stereo.

"So how awful was your meeting at the barracks?" he asked her.

"Let's just drop that, okay? I've punched out. Don't want to talk about work anymore."

"Well, what do you want to talk about?"

She put her arms around his neck. "Who wants to talk?"

They kissed, her heart pounding so hard she felt weak in the knees.

"All day long I've been wanting to hold you in my arms," he purred at her.

She melted into him, her head nestled on his shoulder as they slow-danced right there in the kitchen, pausing now and again to sip their champagne and get lost in each other's eyes. Just like it was when they first met. When she couldn't believe this one in a million man noticed her, liked her, wanted her. Couldn't believe how gentle he could be. How lucky she was.

"God, you smell good." He ran his big hands up and down her bare back. "And you are *smooth* all over."

"Thank you, sir," she said, raising her mouth to his. "Just so you know, there's steak."

"How can you think about food at a time like this?"

"Why, are you thinking about something else?"

"Girl, you are naughty. Know what happens to naughty girls, don't you?"

"Haven't the slightest idea." She put a finger to his lips before he could say another word. "Don't tell me. Show me."

For starters, that dress came right off over her head. And now Brandon's tongue was on her breasts. And now, oh, God, it was slip-sliding its way downtown. He fell to his knees, the better to devour her. She threw one leg over his shoulder and let out a groan, her breathing growing deeper and deeper . . . until he picked her up and carried her off to their bedroom.

It was long past dark out, nearly ten, by the time she stirred and got up, searching for something to throw on.

"Where are you going?" he asked her sleepily, sprawled there in bed.

"To start dinner."

"Now that you mention it, I'm starved," he admitted. "Only, wait, there's something else I wanted to say to you. Let's disappear from this place for a couple of days. Jump in the car tomorrow morning and head for the Cape. Find ourselves a little inn near a beach somewhere. What do you say?"

She flashed her wraparound smile at him. "I say, what time do we leave?"

That was when her phone rang. It was the 911 dispatcher. A call had come in from the Sullivan residence on Sour Cherry Lane. Amber Sullivan phoning to report she'd just heard some sort of a fight out in the lane. Followed by the sound of a man screaming.

There were plenty of lights on at Kimberly and Jen's, as well as across the lane at the Procters. But the lane appeared to be deserted as Des eased past their cottages. Until little Molly suddenly loomed before her there in the road—standing out in front of the Sullivan cottage with her eyeglasses shining in the headlights.

Des rolled down her window and called out, "Girl, what are you doing out here at this time of night?"

"I heard something," Molly answered in a quavering voice. "Somebody's hurt."

Des nosed her cruiser up to the pile of cedar mulch in Amber and Keith's driveway and got out, flashlight in hand. The night air was very heavy and still. It smelled of a skunk that had been marking its territory. With her light, Des looked the girl over carefully as Molly stood there in her UConn jersey, baggy shorts and floppy socks. She seemed frightened but unharmed. "Were you up in your tree house for the night?"

Molly nodded her head, swallowing.

"Did you see anything?"

She shook her head gravely.

"Well, what did you hear?"

"Voices. Men's voices. They came from out *there* somewhere." Molly pointed past the Sullivan place toward the utter darkness at the end of the lane.

Des shined her light out there. Saw nothing other than wild, overgrown brush crowding both sides of the pavement. The road dead-ended at Jersey safety barriers after a hundred feet or so. Beyond the barriers was the bank of the Connecticut River.

"How many men did you hear?"

"Two, I think."

"And you're sure they were both men?"

"W-What do you mean?"

"Could one of them have been a woman?'

"I don't know. Maybe. One of them . . . he *screamed*."

"Then what happened?"

"I don't *know*. I listened real hard, but I didn't hear anything else."

"And you're sure you didn't see anyone?"

Molly gazed up at her, mystified. "Like who?"

"Someone running away from here. Or driving away. Did anyone pass by your place after you heard the scream?"

"I didn't see anybody. But I-I was . . ." She faltered, lowering her gaze.

"You were what?" Des asked, hearing footsteps now. Amber and Keith were approaching them.

"Scared to come down." Molly let out a sob. "I *hid* in my tree house until I saw you coming."

Meaning she may not have seen someone fleeing in her direction. Des knelt and hugged the frightened girl, her thoughts on Grisky's team in the woods. What had they seen and heard? And where in the hell *were* they? "You did the right thing, Molly. You were smart to be afraid. But you don't have to be afraid now, okay?"

Actually, Amber looked plenty scared herself. Those big brown eyes of hers were huge and shining. "Des, I really, really hope I didn't get you out here on a wild goose chase," she said in a frantic voice.

Beefy, blond Keith trailed along a few steps behind her clutching a bottle of Sam Adams. He wore a T-shirt, shorts and a pissed off expression. A vibe of tension was coming off of the two lovebirds.

The source of which tumbled straight out of Keith's mouth: "I am totally sorry about this, Des," he growled. "I told her not to waste your time."

"Stop being such a know-it-all," fired back Amber, all ninety pounds of her in a halter top and linen drawstring trousers. "I am a sentient adult being. I know what I heard."

"What you 'heard' was a couple of raccoons," Keith argued. "I've heard 'em fighting in the night a million times—and you'd *swear* it was a person being gutted with a grapefruit knife."

"It wasn't raccoons," Molly said in a low, insistent voice.

"You see?" Amber huffed at him. "Molly heard them, too."

Keith shook his head disgustedly. "Fine, whatever."

"I heard them when I was taking out the trash." Amber gazed toward the end of the lane same as Molly had. "They were down there somewhere."

"And how about you?" Des asked Keith.

"I was watching the Red Sox game in the living room," he replied, swigging from his beer. "Didn't hear a thing."

"How are our boys doing tonight?"

He made a face. "Toronto's killing us."

"That figures." Des looked over in the direction of the Procter and Beckwith houses, guessing that no one in either place had heard anything. If they had, they'd be out here in the street telling her about it by now. "I'm going to ask you folks to please follow me, okay?"

She strode back to her ride with the three of them and left them standing there in the driveway. Backed out into the road and pointed the cruiser so that its high beams lit up the end of the lane right down to the Jersey barriers. Then she got out and slowly checked out the wild brush growing alongside of the pavement, left hand gripping her flashlight, right hand resting lightly on the holster of her Sig. She trained the light on the tangled profusion of sour cherry trees, blackberry bushes, forsythia and lilac. She saw no broken branches. No signs of trampling. The brush did not appear to be disturbed on either side of the lane.

Until, that is, she got to within twenty feet of the barriers. Here, the lane began to dip downward as it neared the shallows of the river, the wild brush giving way to boggy salt marsh where Spartina grass and phragmites grew.

Here, the marsh grasses were newly trampled. There were mucky shoe prints on the pavement. And there was more.

There was blood. There was a lot of blood. And droplets leading down toward the water.

Stepping carefully around them, Des approached the riverbank and waved her light out into the water. She wondered if someone had pitched a body out there—figuring it would float out to sea on the current.

She did not have to wonder for long. She spotted the floater maybe fifty feet downriver where a dead tree had washed up in the mud. One of its branches had snagged him as he'd drifted past. Or at least it looked like a *he* from where she stood. The body lay facedown in the water, bobbing up and down in the gentle current of the river. Des didn't want to disturb the crime scene. But she also didn't want the body to break free and drift out into Long Island Sound. So she went down there and fetched it, keeping a watchful eye out for shoeprints or any other disturbances in the mud as she tiptoed her way along the water's edge.

It was a man, all right. Dressed in a light blue shirt, khaki trousers and hiking shoes. Gently, she untangled him from the branches that held him there. Then she pulled him ashore and flopped him over, her abdominal muscles clenching as the pang of recognition hit.

It was Richard Procter. Someone had cut his throat from ear to ear.

It took the uniformed troopers less than ten minutes to get there from the Troop F barracks. They immediately set up a vehicular cordon all of the way back up Turkey Neck at Old Shore Road. And another cordon around the perimeter of the crime scene itself, which included all of Sour Cherry Lane, the riverfront and, at Des's suggestion, the woods between Sour Cherry and the Peck's Point Nature Preserve.

Soon after that, the Major Crime Squad crime scene technicians rolled up in their blue and white cube vans along with a death investigator from the Medical Examiner's office.

By now it was nearly midnight. The residents of Sour Cherry were huddled together out in the lane like the survivors of an apartment house fire. By now Des had expected to see or hear from Grisky. But she'd had no contact from him or Cavanaugh or anyone else associated with Operaton Burrito King. She didn't know what to make of that beyond the fact that they seemed content to let the normal investigative process unfold. So she went ahead and did her normal thing, which was to conduct preliminary interviews of the neighbors.

Kimberly and Jen Beckwith were standing out there with Molly. Kimberly was sobbing and moaning, utterly blown away. Her frizzy red hair was wet and uncombed—she'd been in the shower when Jen answered Des's knock on their door. When Kimberly heard what had happened to Richard she threw on a purple caftan and came running, a damp towel still wrapped around her neck. Neither she nor Jen had heard the screams. Nor had they seen anyone fleeing the scene.

Jen seemed quite shaken herself, but unlike her mother was trying to keep her emotions in check for Molly, whose own mother was nowhere to be seen.

Molly had a surprisingly serene look on her freckled face as she stood there holding Jen's hand. It was almost freakish how composed the girl was.

She was certainly holding up better than Amber and Keith, both of whom had turned goggle-eyed with shock and disbelief when Des told them what she'd discovered.

Patricia Beckwith stood slightly apart from the others, her posture erect, facial expression stony. Whatever emotions she was experiencing were private. Not to be displayed in front of others. "Richard and I ate a good dinner together," she told Des in a firm, measured voice. "Scallops, rice and string beans. He had a fine appetite. He seemed very positive and upbeat. After we'd had our coffee he said he felt like taking a walk. I asked him if he would like some company. He said he'd be fine on his own, and went striding out the door shortly after nine."

"Mrs. Beckwith, did he happen to speak to anyone on the phone before he left?"

"Not that I am aware of," Patricia responded, pursing her thin, dry lips. "I shouldn't have let him go by himself, I suppose."

"He wasn't your prisoner," Des told her. "He was free to come and go as he pleased. So don't blame yourself for this, ma'am. Whatever *this* is."

Actually, Des thought she had a pretty fair idea what it was as she gazed over at Clay and Hector. The two of them were seated on the front porch of the Procter house drinking Coors and acting completely innocent. They'd been playing Texas Hold 'Em at the kitchen table all evening, or so they claimed. Neither of them had heard a thing, or so they claimed. No screams in the night. No footsteps. No cars leaving the lane. Nothing but good ol' country quiet.

Neither man had a scratch on him. No indication that he'd been involved in anything remotely physical that evening.

As for Carolyn, she'd been sacked out in the bedroom since nine o'clock, according to Clay. "The poor woman still can't chase that virus," was how he put it to Des. "You want me to get her up?"

"No, let her sleep for now," Des replied, detesting the man. He and Richard had already fought once over Carolyn. Tonight, they'd fought again. There was no doubt in her mind about it.

What a mess. What a great big steaming turd of a mess this ruthless drug trafficker had made in her nice little New England town.

The homicide investigators from the Major Crime Squad were the last to get there from Central district headquarters in Meriden. They sent a two-person team that Des happened to know real well—Lt. Rico "Soave" Tedone and his half-Cuban, half-black sergeant, Yolie Snipes. Soave had been Des's stumpy, bulked-up young pup of sergeant back in her glory days when she was still the state police's great nonwhite hope. And Yolie, a brash hardcharger out of Hartford's burned out Frog Hollow section, was someone who Des had very high hopes for. Yolie had a Latina's liquid brown eyes. Lips, nose and an hour-and-a-half glass figure that said sister all of the way. The boys all called her Boom Boom because of what went on inside of her sweater. She wore a sleeveless one tonight, tattoos adorning both biceps. In her chunky boots she towered over Soave, who was still trying to win cool points with that goatee and shaved head look of his.

"Hey, Miss Thing," Yolie exclaimed, showing Des her smile.

"Back at you, girl."

"Haven't seen you since you and your ex got back together. How is that?"

"All good."

"And it shows. You look fantastic."

"Thanks. You're the first person who's told me that in . . . ever."

"Yo, dumping that fat doofus Berger was the smartest move you ever made," Soave declared with great assurance. "The two of you had zero future as a couple."

"Thank you, Rico," said Des, who was certainly ready to change the subject at any time.

"What have you got for us?" he asked.

"One dead Wesleyan history professor named Richard Procter. Our victim was the estranged husband of Carolyn Procter, who lives in that scenic farmhouse on your left. She recently took up with another man, Clay Mundy. He's the one sitting on the porch in the white T-shirt."

"Who's the other gee?"

"Hector Villanueva. Works for him. Are you ready to look at the victim?"

"On it," barked Yolie, who immediately went charging down toward the crime scene personnel gathered on the riverbank. She was more comfortable around techies than Soave, who tended to get edgy and snappish with them. Partly because he wanted quicker answers than they were able to give him. Mostly because he got insecure around people who he feared were smarter than he was. When it came to self-esteem Des's little man was still very much a work in progress.

She could see the flashbulbs go off down there as they photographed Richard's body. Not so long ago, she would have wanted a set of those photos. Wanted, needed to draw Richard. Richard with his carotid artery severed—the deep, puckering knife gash washed clean by the river. Richard with his eyes wide open and that look of complete surprise on his ghostly bluish face. Her fingers would have itched at the prospect. Tonight, she felt no such itch. Only the knots in her stomach.

She filled Soave in on how Richard and Clay had scuffled in the driveway a few nights back. How she'd found him in out on Big Sister in a despondent state. How he'd been hospitalized, then had moved in that very afternoon with Patricia Beckwith.

Which was when he stopped her. "Wait, who's Patricia Beckwith?"

"The elderly mother-in-law of Kimberly Beckwith."

"And she is . . . ?"

"That redhead over there in the caftan. Kimberly lives across the lane from the Procters with her daughter, Jen. Patricia was very fond of the victim. Happy to take him in for a few days until he got back his act together."

Soave mulled this over, nodding his gleaming dome. "Who called it in?"

"A neighbor named Amber Sullivan. She lives in the house that's nearest to the crime scene. Amber's a grad student at Yale. The victim happened to be her mentor, for whatever that's worth. She told me she heard a scream. Her husband Keith didn't. But Molly Procter did. She's the victim's nine-year-old daughter. Molly was up in her tree house at the time. Neither she nor Amber witnessed anyone fleeing the scene. Nor did anyone else I've spoken with. Translation: Whoever did this to Richard is still right here among us. Or took off through the woods. Or swam, though I highly doubt that. The current is treacherous down here at the mouth of the river."

"How about a little boat?"

"That's possible," Des allowed. "Though it suggests there was some degree of premeditation. To me this doesn't play out as any kind of planned thing."

"Fair enough. Anything else?"

Des shoved her heavy horn-rimmed glasses up her nose and said, "Couple of things. I still haven't spoken to Carolyn."

"She's next of kin. Why haven't you?" Soave started his way down toward the crime scene now.

Des walked with him. "Clay Mundy claims she's asleep in bed. He told me she has a quote-unquote virus. But when I visited yesterday I got the distinct impression she's way into crystal meth. Not to mention both Clay *and* Hector."

Soave let out a short laugh. "Nice, tight little bunch you got here."

"Welcome back to Dorset, Rico."

"I love this place, Des. Really, I do. Every time I think the real world's spinning out of control I come to this safe, sane little haven of yours and discover that things are even more whacked than I thought."

"Well, then you'd better prepare yourself, wow man. Because when it comes to whacked out I am just getting rolling."

"Why, what else have you got?" he asked, peering at her.

By now they'd arrived at the trampled marsh grass where Des had found the blood. Yolie was huddled with the medical examiner's man and several techies. Lots of ears. Too many. The rest of her story would have to wait.

"He's been in that water no more than two hours, boss," Yolie reported as they approached.

"Totally consistent with the time of the nine-one-one call," Des said, glancing at her watch.

"Mind you, that's strictly a preliminary estimate," cautioned the death investigator. "This is a tidal estuary. You've got your colder salt water from Long Island Sound ebbing and flowing with the warmer river currents. A formulation for determining the mean water temperature for any prolonged amount of time is highly complex. I'll have to reference the tidal charts for this evening as well as factor in the—"

"Yeah, yeah, yeah," blustered Soave, who had an extremely low geek speak threshold. "He put up any kind of a fight?"

"Doesn't appear so," Yolie answered. "No obvious defensive cuts or bruising. But we won't know for sure until they get him on the table. We're looking at a single cut, very deep. A smooth, sharp blade. Something along the lines of a carving knife. The cut was most likely made from behind, which means we're talking about a person who was strong enough to overpower him."

"Unless there were two of them," Des said.

"I'm down with that," Yolie agreed. "It would explain how the body was moved from here all of the way down to the water. We're talking, what, thirty feet? The victim was good-sized, yet there's no sign he was dragged."

"Meaning he was carried." Soave tugged at his goatee thoughtfully. "Got to figure his blood got all over the person or persons who did this. There ought to be bloody clothing and shoes around here somewhere. Not to mention the carving knife. Only, jeez, is it dark down here or what? Have they ever heard of a little thing called streetlights in this place?"

"You're in the country, Rico," Des reminded him.

"Whatever. Come daylight, I want our scuba divers down here searching the river for the knife and for weighted-down clothing. They can hook up with the DEP if they need a boat. And I want all available men combing this marsh, that brush back there, the woods, everywhere."

"Right, boss." Yolie flipped open her cell phone.

"Anything I can do to help, Rico?"

"Would you mind informing the victim's wife? We'll catch up with you in a minute."

Des strode back to the Procter house, her thoughts straying to

Carolyn's sister Megan. Wondering if she was en route here from Maine at this very moment. Wondering if her arrival just a few precious hours sooner would have saved Richard's life tonight.

Clay and Hector remained seated on the porch, eyeballing her calmly. They were cool customers. Des had to give them that much.

She tipped her hat and said, "Gentlemen, I need to give Carolyn the news about her husband now."

Slowly, Clay reached for a cigarette and lit it. "I'll be the one to tell her, if you don't mind."

"I appreciate you wanting to soften the blow, Mr. Mundy. But according to the laws of this state it's my official duty to notify the next of kin. You're not going to impede me, are you?"

"No, ma'am," he assured her. "Absolutely not. Do what you got to do."

A nightstand light was on in the bedroom, which was a soiled zoo cage reeking of sour sheets, overflowing ashtrays and its sweaty, unwashed occupant. Carolyn lay naked atop the wrought iron bed with an iPod plugged into her ears, head nodding lazily to the beat. Her eyes were open but she did not seem to notice Des standing there. Or Clay hovering behind Des in the doorway. She was in a stoned-out stupor. The lady was sporting a couple of fresh cigarette burns on her arms, Des noticed. But she did not spot a blow pipe or ice any other illegal drugs on the nightstand. Only beer cans.

"Carolyn . . . ?" she said, standing over her.

No response. Nothing.

She reached down and pulled the earphones off. "Carolyn . . . ?"

Slowly, Carolyn's eyes began to focus. Or almost. "You . . . still here?" Her voice faint and dreamy.

"That was yesterday, Carolyn. I'm back again now. I need to talk to you about Richard."

"He . . . left. I-I told you."

"I'm very sorry, but I'm here to inform you that he's dead."

Carolyn blinked at her. "Away. Richard went away."

"Carolyn, I just found him floating in the river. His throat has been cut. He's *dead*, do-you-understand?"

With tweakers there was no such thing as an emotional middle ground. One moment the lady was lying there in a persistent vegetative state. The next, as the reality of her husband's death hit home, Carolyn Procter turned into a wild woman.

"Where's Richard?" she screamed, vaulting from the bed with a surge of instant rage. "Richard, where are you . . . ? *Richaaard . . . ?*" She was still calling out his name as she went flying out of the room—past a stunned Clay—and right out the front door of her house, stark naked. Des in hot pursuit. The others, including Molly, standing out there in the lane gaping at her. "Where's Richard? I have to be with him! *Richaaaard . . . ?*"

Big Yolie, who happened to be there talking to Kimberly, grabbed Carolyn at once and frog-marched her back inside the house as Des phoned the Jewett sisters on her cell.

"Where's the bedroom, girl?" Yolie hollered, puffing as she wrestled the squirming madwoman across the living room.

Des led the way. When they got there Yolie threw Carolyn down on the bed and pinned her there. Although Carolyn wasn't done fighting her. She even tried to take a bite out of Yolie's forearm.

For which Yolie slapped her hard in the face. "Behave yourself! Your little girl is out there. Want her to see you this way?"

Des found a man's white button down-shirt hanging in the closet. Richard's most likely. It took both of them to muscle Carolyn into it.

"He needs me!" she groaned, thrashing around wildly, her head swiveling from side to side. "Richard needs me!"

"Richard is gone!" Des hollered at her. "It's Molly who needs you now!"

At the mention of Molly's name the fight seemed to melt right out of Carolyn. She lay there limply now, panting for breath, foul-smelling sweat pouring from her.

"Are you going to behave?" Yolie demanded.

Carolyn nodded her head up and down. Yolie released her. Slowly, she sat up and fumbled for a cigarette on the nightstand, her hands trembling so badly that Yolie had to light it for her.

"I need a drink," she gasped, drawing the tobacco deep into her lungs.

"You *need* to get clean," Yolie countered angrily. "What are you into? Crack? Smack? Ice? All of the above?"

Clay reappeared in the bedroom doorway. "Everything okay in here?" he inquired, the picture of tender concern.

"Fool, what do *you* think?" Yolie snarled at him.

Now Carolyn had the full-blown shakes. Des could hear her grinding her teeth. It was not a pretty sound.

"I think Carolyn got upset," Clay informed Yolie politely. "Which is perfectly understandable. Plus she's been under the weather lately."

"Oh, is that what you call it?" Yolie's eyes were daggers.

Outside, Des could hear the Jewett sisters rolling up to the state police cordon. She went out there to meet them. Hector watched her coolly from the porch, saying nothing.

"Where is she, Des?" asked Marge, her eyes taking in all of the residents and sworn personnel gathered there. Mary was getting their gear out of the back.

"In the bedroom," Des answered, lowering her voice as they hurried inside past Hector. "I want Carolyn Procter out of here, okay? Get her admitted to the hospital for acute psychological trauma. Or shock. Or a severe allergic reaction to prescription medication. I don't care what. Just take her where she can get help, understand?"

"Afraid not," Mary said briskly. "What kind of help?"

"Have either of seen her lately?"

They shook their heads.

"Then you had better prepare yourselves," she said as the sisters barged past Clay into the bedroom.

Mary let out a gasp as soon as she laid eyes on Carolyn.

"Can you do it?" Des asked Marge.

"Consider it done," she promised Des.

"Carolyn's doing okay, really," Clay tried to assure them. "Just needs a little shot of something to settle her nerves down."

Marge ignored him completely. "Honey, you are coming with us," she told Carolyn. "Can you walk?"

"She can walk," said Yolie, pulling Carolyn roughly to her feet.

"Where am I going?" Carolyn wondered, gazing at Mary in bewilderment.

"To get you a hot shower, for starters," Mary replied, wrinkling her nose. "You used to be the prettiest, most accomplished young mother in all of Dorset. I'd see you shopping for groceries in the A & P, always a smile on your face, always a polite word, and I'd say to myself *that* is one classy lady. Lord, honey, what on earth has happened to you?"

In response, Carolyn spat right in her face. Then began fighting with Yolie all over again. "Leave me the hell alone!" she cried out, struggling in Yolie's iron grip.

"Out of our way, mister!" Marge barked, elbowing Clay aside as they hustled Carolyn out of there.

Clay didn't try to stop them. He knew when to fold his cards. Just watched from the porch with Hector as the sisters loaded Carolyn into their ambulance, kicking and screaming.

Happily, Molly was no longer out there to see any of this. Jen had taken her inside her own house.

"Molly can stay with us for as long she needs to," Kimberly promised Des after the sisters had rolled out of there, lights flashing.

"We'll all look after her," Amber chimed in, clutching Keith's hand. "The important thing is that Carolyn get well."

"I'd like Molly to stay out of that house while her mother is away," Des said to them. "I don't want her in there. Kimberly, please make sure Jen understands that, okay?"

Kimberly glanced over at Clay and Hector on the porch, swallowing. "Yeah, sure. Whatever you say."

"It shouldn't be for very long. I've been in touch with Carolyn's sister Megan up in Maine. She's already on her way down to take charge of things."

"That'll be great," Amber said enthusiastically. "Megan's a really capable person."

"In fact, I'm expecting her to turn up pretty much any minute now." While she'd been waiting for the crime scene techies to arrive, Des had phoned Megan's farm in Blue Hill. Woke up her partner, Susan, who sleepily told her that Megan had left for Dorset that very day at around noon. It was generally an eight-hour drive if the traffic was light, Susan said. Ten if it wasn't. Which, according to Des's calculations, meant that Megan should have reached Dorset at about the same time Richard was murdered. Unfortunately, Susan had no idea where she presently was or how to reach her. Megan would not buy a cell phone. She was convinced they caused brain cancer. "Amber, would you mind keeping an eye out for her?"

"Be happy to, Des. I'll let you know just as soon as Megan gets here."

Now Soave waved to Des from his slicktop, where he and Yolie were hashing things over.

"Cut to the chase," he said to her when she joined them. "I know you schooled me to keep an open mind and all of that, but Clay Mundy's a slam dunk, right?"

"Why do you say that?"

"Oh, I dunno. Maybe because he stole the guy's wife. Got her strung out on dope. Moved into his house. Beat the crap out of him a few nights back. Plus he looks seven different kinds of skeegie around the edges *and* he has a running buddy. Two-man job, remember? Otherwise, I can't imagine why."

Des watched Clay and Hector there on the porch, smoking and talking. "It's whacked-out, Rico."

"Yeah, you said that before. Whacked-out how?"

Her cell phone rang. She took the call and listened. "Right, I understand," she said. Then she flicked it off and showed them her smile. "Prepare to get funky."

They were setting up a temporary command headquarters in the auxiliary conference room of Dorset's town hall, a stately, white-columned edifice that smelled all year around of mothballs, musty carpeting and Ben-Gay. Troopers in uniform were busy booting up computers and plugging in phones. Which was standard procedure for a murder investigation. But there was absolutely nothing standard about the collection of law enforcement professionals who had assembled by the time Des arrived with Soave and Yolie. Cavanaugh, the bland, cautious supervising agent from the DEA, was there. And Grisky, the testosterone cowboy from the FBI. And Captain Amalfitano from the state's Narcotics Task Force, alias the Aardvark. Also a very polished and polite U.S. Attorney out of New Haven by the name of Brandon Stokes.

Who Yolie absolutely could not stop staring at. She looked as if she were going to hyperventilate when Des introduced him to her. "Girl, have they got any more like him at home?" she whispered after Brandon had crossed the room to confer with Cavanaugh. "Has he got like a brother? A cousin? *Distant* cousin?"

"Sorry, Brandon's one of a kind."

"I'm down with that. Mitch was cute but this one is the bomb. Real, know who he reminds me of?"

"Let me guess—Harry Belafonte?"

"No, I was going to say Denzel."

"My bad."

"What's up with Maverick over there?" Now she was checking out Des's non-favorite G-man. "He ever stop flexing?"

"That's a no," Des replied, making a face.

The Aardvark asked the other uniformed troopers to let them have the room. Then he closed the door and they seated themselves around the conference table. Someone had picked up bags of burgers and spiral fries at McGee's diner before it closed for the night. Grisky attacked the food ravenously, biceps bulging in his tight T-shirt. So did Brandon, who had eaten no dinner. Neither had Des, but she wasn't hungry. Or happy. Her eyes found Brandon's across the table. He wasn't happy either. They were both thinking the same thing: So much for our wild and wet getaway to the Cape. So much for escaping from our responsibilities for a few days. That will have to wait. *We* will have to wait.

Soave listened to Cavanaugh's Operation Burrito King rap in respectful silence, nodding his shaved head as the soft-spoken DEA man detailed their six-month investigation into the Vargas drug cartel, the Atlanta connection, Clay and Hector, the stash house on Sour Cherry, it all.

When Cavanaugh was done talking Soave sat back in his chair, tugging at his goatee thoughtfully for a moment. "This is all awesome stuff, guys," he declared finally. "But I've got a homicide investigation to run. Homicide takes priority over whatever you've got going on. So I sure hope you aren't trying to strong-arm me."

Des had never been prouder of her little man.

Cavanaugh and Amalfitano exchanged an uneasy glance before the Aardvark said, "That's absolutely understood, lieutenant. Obviously, we've got a vested interest in keeping our own investigation under wraps. But we in no way wish to impede yours. We're just here to offer you whatever assistance and support we can."

"Glad to hear it," Soave said, turning his gaze on Grisky. "You can start by telling me what your men saw and heard from your setup in the woods."

"That would be me." Grisky dipped a spiral fry in a puddle of ketchup and chomped on it with his mouth open, splotches of blood-red ketchup flecking his lips. And Des couldn't imagine why she wasn't hungry. "I was up tonight. I was set up maybe a hundred feet behind the Beckwith house, angled slightly toward Turkey Neck so I'd have a direct sight line with the Procter place. That means the Sullivan cottage stood right smack dab between me and the crime scene. I was blocked out is what I'm saying. Didn't see a thing."

"Did you hear anything?" Yolie asked him.

"Maybe I did," he replied, taking a starved bite out of his burger. "Maybe I didn't. What I heard was a shriek of some kind. I thought maybe coming from the direction of the river. But I really wasn't sure. It's a warm night. People's windows were open. I thought maybe the Beckwith girls were watching a scary movie on TV. Or Amber and Keith Sullivan were getting it on yet again. They never quit, those two. And they are not quiet. Or maybe it was a couple of alley cats out there in the brush fighting over territory. I didn't know. I hear all kinds of noises in those woods at night."

"And so you did what exactly?" Soave asked him.

Grisky stuck out his jaw and said, "Stayed put. No way I'm

about to compromise my setup because of anything like that. Trust me, it wasn't that much out of the ordinary."

"I hear you," Soave said, nodding. "Subsequent to this, what did you call it, a shriek . . . ?"

"Shriek, scream, whatever," Grisky said with a shrug.

"Did you see or hear anyone leaving the scene—either through the woods or up Sour Cherry Lane? Did you observe a car going by? Any kind of activity whatsoever?"

"Not a damned thing, lieutenant. Not until *she* rolled in." Meaning Des. "At which point I checked in with Agent Cavanaugh by cell phone."

"After I spoke with Agent Grisky," Cavanaugh interjected, "Captain Amalfitano and I interfaced jointly with Captain Polito of the Major Crime Squad."

Polito was Rico's commanding officer, not to mention his brother-in-law.

"And we're all in agreement," the Aardvark declared. "Our best move right now is to stand back and give you folks a chance to do what you do."

Brandon didn't say a word. Just sat there and listened as he polished off his burger. The man was the tidiest burger eater Des had ever seen. Even his very last teensy-weensy bite was a perfectly arranged stack of patty, bun, lettuce, tomato and onion.

She cleared her throat now and said, "If I might . . . ?"

"Jump right in, Des," Soave urged her.

"What went on prior to this shriek, agent? The reason I'm asking is that the victim told Patricia Beckwith he felt like taking an after-dinner stroll. It's not unreasonable to assume he strolled in the direction of home. Possibly hoping to visit Molly or, worst case scenario, have more words with Carolyn and Clay. Did you see him come knocking on his own door?"

"Nope," Grisky answered flatly.

"Did you see anyone leaving the Procter house at any time?"

"I didn't see a soul walk up or down that lane. I never do. There are no streetlights."

"But you saw Richard and Clay going at it in the driveway the other night, didn't you?"

"Because the porch light was on," he confirmed, nodding. "Tonight, it wasn't. It was pitch black over there. The entire Fighting Illini marching band could have gone by and I wouldn't have seen them."

Des mulled this over before she said, "Sounds reasonable."

"Whoa, huge thank you," Grisky jeered at her. "I so totally live for your approval, master sergeant."

Des studied him curiously. "Something you feel like getting off of your chest?"

"Hell, yes, there is. It's because of *you* that this went down. You're the one who arranged for the victim to move in with the old lady when he got released."

"We don't really need to go here, do we?" Cavanaugh said to him.

"Why not?" Grisky shot back. "It's true, isn't it?"

"It absolutely is," Des acknowledged. "Because the poor man had nowhere else to go. And because when I made those arrangements I had no idea the Procter home was a stash house. That's on you, gentlemen. You're the ones who chose to keep me in the dark about your operation. So don't lay your stink on my doorstep, agent. I was just doing my job."

"And these jurisdictional battles are not helpful," Brandon asserted, speaking up for the first time. This was how he operated. He watched. He listened. Then he stepped in and took charge. "We are all fighting the same battle."

"Sure, take *her* side," muttered Grisky, just like a petulant little boy in need of a spanking. Trouble was, he'd probably enjoy it.

"I am not taking sides, Agent Grisky," Brandon said abruptly. "And I would urge you to get on board or first thing tomorrow morning I will recommend you be drop-kicked from this operation."

Grisky bristled but held his tongue, his chest rising and falling.

Des's cell phone rang now. She glanced down at the illuminated screen, then excused herself and stepped out in the hallway, closing the door behind her.

Amber Sullivan was calling to tell her that Carolyn's sister, Megan Chichester, had just arrived from Maine in her beat-up Chevy pickup. Upon being told the awful news about her brother-in-law, Megan had rushed over to Kimberly and Jen's to be with Molly. She wished to see her sister as soon as possible, reported Amber.

"Absolutely," Des said. "Carolyn is being treated at Middlesex Hospital. Can you tell Megan how to get there?"

Amber told Des that would be no problem. Des thanked her and returned to the conference room.

"Let's review where we're at, shall we?" Brandon said, glancing down at a lined yellow note pad as Des sat back down. "If no one was observed fleeing the crime scene then Professor Procter was most likely killed by a resident or residents of Sour Cherry Lane, correct?"

"Unless our search of the area tomorrow morning reveals evidence to the contrary," Soave said. "And our prime suspect appears to be your boy Clay Mundy, with an assist by Hector Villanueva. Unless I'm missing something. Did anybody else have a good reason to be pissed off at the guy?"

"How about his wife?" Yolie asked. "She's an all-out meth

rage monster. Also strong as a bull. I wouldn't cross her off of my list."

"Fair enough," Soave said, turning to Des. "Anyone else?"

Des thought it over carefully before she replied, "Not that I'm presently aware of."

"Then it seems we have ourselves a situation here," Cavanaugh said. "It so happens that your prime suspect is the very same individual who is the target of our own investigation. Now what are we going to do about that? Because we do not want to compromise Operation Burrito King if we can avoid it."

"I don't wish to belabor the obvious," Brandon said to him, "but this particular facet of our operation is already compromised. There is virtually no chance the crystal meth shipment from Atlanta will arrive here as planned. Not with the entire vicinity crawling with state police."

"No chance," the Aardvark concurred, thumbing his chin glumly. "You also got to figure that Mundy's plenty spooked right about now. He's pinned down there with a major stash *and* a murder rap hanging over him. I wonder why he and Hector didn't just try to run?"

"Admission of guilt," said Brandon.

"Plus they're responsible for that ice," Grisky added. "The Vargas family would not be happy about them ditching it. I've seen what they do to people who bail on them. Trust me, it ain't pretty."

"Those two can't run and they can't hide," Soave said. "They are totally screwed."

"And they're in it together," Yolie said. "Unless we can convince one to flip on the other."

"So what's our next move?" the Aardvark wondered. "Do we go ahead and show them our hand? Swoop down and nail them for possession with intent to distribute?"

"No way," Grisky argued. "If we do that then this ends right here. We can't connect it to the cartel."

"Then again, maybe we can," the Aardvark countered. "Clay and Hector are a pair of pros. Ordinarily, I wouldn't expect either of them to rat out the Vargas family. But Mundy is staring at a murder charge. That gives us big-time leverage."

"No question," Brandon agreed. "And my office would certainly consider a plea deal in exchange for detailed sworn testimony about the Vargas operation. Depending on how far he's willing to go, we might be able to reduce the whole package down to involuntary manslaughter."

"Sure, he thought the professor was a prowler," the Aardvark said, warming to it. "The man was defending his own home. He'd get, what, five years?"

"And shanked his first night in jail," Grisky said.

"So promise him witness protection," the Aardvark fired back. "I say we go right at him. And if he don't want the deal then maybe Hector will. We can play one of them against the other, like Sergeant Snipes said."

Cavanaugh stayed strangely silent throughout this back and forth exchange. Just sat there with his hands clasped before him, his eyes cast downward at the table. The supervising agent looked as if he were saying grace. Until he raised his eyes and said, "In principle, I agree with everything you're saying, Captain. And I appreciate your input. But I'm not ready to make such a move yet. Agent Grisky and I have been dogging these people for a whole lot longer than you folks from the state have. We've invested a lot in Operation Burrito King. I am talking months and months of man-hours, millions of taxpayer dollars. We are tasked to go after the really big game here. Not just a couple of petty hoods."

"You mean murderers, don't you?" Soave said.

"Nonetheless," he went on, undeterred, "I'd like to see how the next twenty-four to forty-eight hours play out before we show our hand. We still have our wiretaps and cell phone traces in place. Maybe Mundy will get shook enough to do something dumb—like break silence and reach out to Atlanta. Why not wait and see what he does before we roll up the whole damned operation?"

Des didn't like what she was hearing. If it were her call to make they'd land on Clay and Hector that very night. Swarm the house and sweat a murder confession out of them. Hell, they had the bastards right where they wanted them. So take them. Because if you didn't, if you got greedy and held out for more, then things had a not-so-funny way of slipping through your fingers. But it was Cavanaugh's case, not the Aardvark's and for sure not hers. And the Feds were always going to have it their way—because they could.

"Besides which," Cavanaugh added, "we don't even know where the damned dope is hidden."

"Actually, we do," Des said, all eyes turning her way.

"Don't play cute, master sergeant," he said, glaring at her. "What do you know that we don't?"

"That right after he moved in Clay Mundy ordered Molly Procter to stay out of the root cellar. It's directly under the kitchen, which is where the trapdoor is. It's a dirt floor crawl space, most likely. That's how they built the old farmhouses around here. Especially in low-lying areas like Sour Cherry. A full basement would just flood during the rainy season."

"Why didn't you tell us this yesterday?"

"Didn't know it then."

"It plays," Grisky said grudgingly. "We've never seen them go near the barn or anywhere else. And I've heard about dealers burying their crystal under dirt for safekeeping."

"Which leaves us where?" Soave demanded impatiently. "Last time I looked I still have a homicide investigation to run."

"So run it," Cavanaugh said easily. "We'll stay on the sidelines, watching and listening. Just do us a small favor and stay out of that root cellar for now. We can't have you stumbling over our evidence."

"But what if there's evidence down there that links Mundy to the murder?"

"Actually, you gentlemen are getting a bit ahead of yourselves," said Brandon. "I seriously doubt that a judge would even grant you a warrant to enter the house. Not based on what I've heard so far."

Soave shook his shiny dome at him. "Why the hell not? We're looking for the murder weapon and bloody clothing. The stuff's got to be somewhere."

"*Somewhere* doesn't constitute probable cause for entering a home."

"Mundy and the professor fought in that very driveway just a few nights ago," Soave argued, stabbing the table with his index finger.

"Not good enough," Brandon reasoned. "No one saw the victim entering the home tonight. No one saw Mundy or Villanueva leaving the murder scene and going in the home. The two men claim they were playing cards at the time of the murder. You have no evidence or testimony to the contrary. Neither man has so much as a single prior arrest. Consequently, you have no reason to believe the evidence is in that house. What you have barely even rises to the level of a suspicion." He paused to take a sip of his coffee. "Furthermore, Agent Cavanaugh makes an excellent point. You do not want to go anywhere near that meth while in the process of looking for something else. You'd be leaving the door wide open for defense counsel to claim an illegal search and possibly get it thrown out. You haven't even undertaken your search of the area yet, let alone exhausted it. If I were you, lieutenant, I'd stay out of that house altogether for now. If there's anything down there, it's not going anywhere. And neither are Clay Mundy or Hector Villanueva."

"I'll have to talk to my C.O. about this," Soave grumbled.

"Do what you have to do," Cavanaugh said with cool condescension. "Just touch base with us regularly so there are no communications lapses." To Des he said, "Yesterday, you had safety concerns regarding the family. The wife has now been hospitalized, correct?"

"Correct. And Molly's tucked in across the street with the Beckwiths. I've made it very clear to them that she's to stay out of her own house."

"Are they hip as to why?" Grisky wondered.

"No, they're simply of the belief that Clay and Hector are too unsavory for the girl to be around."

"Which, real, they are," Yolie said.

"Then I think we're all done here." A faint smile creased Cavanaugh's impassive face. "I'd like everyone to know that I'm extremely comfortable with our game plan." *His* game plan. "In fact, I have a remarkably good feeling about our chances." *His* chances. "Let's suit up, shall we?"

CHAPTER 10

To: Mitch Berger
From: Bella Tillis
Subject: Unhappy Turn of Events

Dear Mr. Hot Shot New York Movie Critic—I know you told me that you no longer feel "connected" to this place but I have some very sad news to send along concerning little Molly.

Her father, Richard, was murdered last night. Des found him floating in the river at the end of Sour Cherry Lane with his throat cut. Apparently his killer dumped him there thinking he'd drift out to sea. Although chances are he would have washed up right here on our little beach, as you know. Thank God he got snagged on a tree or I probably would have tripped over him on my walk this morning and suffered horrible nightmares for weeks.

They don't know who did it yet. Poor Molly was up in her tree house when it happened. She actually heard her father's screams. Such a thing for a child to cope with. Carolyn has been hospitalized, so for now Molly is bunking across the lane with Kimberly and Jen Beckwith. My impression is she'll soon be relocating to her aunt's farm in Maine for the summer, if not permanently. My point is, I'm not sure just how much longer Molly is going to be around Dorset. She is very, very fond of you, Mitch. I know you were once fond of her. And even though you no longer feel "connected" to this place if you could phone her or drop her a note at Kimberly's it would mean a lot to her.

Do you remember Des's friend Yolie? The one with the cazongas? And Soave, that strutting little weasel with no neck? They're both on the case, and currently of the opinion that Richard was done in by Carolyn's boyfriend, Clay Mundy. Possibly assisted by Hector, his hired man. But they haven't filed charges yet. About fifty men in uniform have spent all day today searching the countryside around Sour Cherry Lane for the murder weapon and other evidence. They've uncovered nothing so far, although the crime scene technicians did find some shoeprints near the murder scene that may have belonged to Richard's killer. They're from a man's shoe, a sneaker. The professor was wearing hiking shoes. Scuba divers are scouring the river bottom. Or trying. The bottom is so soft and muddy that anything like a knife would sink out of sight. They have to use a metal detector. The forensics people are searching Richard's body for any sort of hair or clothing fibers that may point them to whoever did this. All of which is slow, painstaking work that takes a great deal of patience. Certainly more than I possess.

You're probably asking yourself how I know so many details. The answer is that I just ran into our resident trooper at The Works and she filled me in over a cup of their fancy, shmancy hazelnut flavored coffee. Which, if you'll pardon me, still doesn't compare to Chock full O'Nuts back in its heyday. I used to get a cup of good, strong coffee *and* a slice of date nut bread with cream cheese for a nickel. That was my lunch when I was going to City College. Now it costs $3.95 for the coffee and you get no date nut bread, no nothing. But business is booming. The parking lot was loaded with state troopers standing around drinking their overpriced coffee and yukking it up. Not exactly how I choose to see my tax dollars being spent, but I'm just a fat old woman and no one ever asks me my opinion on this or any other matter.

Between you, me and the lamppost I think there's more going on here than Des is willing to let on. More than just the professor's murder, I mean. When I was on my way home I swung by Town Hall to pick up my new dump sticker and *someone* has taken over the auxiliary conference room. I spotted a few state troopers in uniform. But the rest of them had that smug, self-important look that is peculiar to federal agents and Republican members of Congress. Could it be that this Clay Mundy is involved in something even worse than cutting a man's throat? Des certainly wouldn't say, but I suspect that drugs are involved. The illegal kind. Because she did tell me that Carolyn Procter is all messed up thanks to him. Her exact words were, "If you saw the lady on the street you'd think she was a crack whore." Can you imagine such a thing happening to someone like Carolyn? Why is it that good women have such bad taste in men? Are they blind? Or aren't there enough good men like you to go around?

Des and I no longer talk about Him. She knows how I feel about her decision to be miserable with Brandon instead of happy with you. I make no apologies for how I feel. I'm the one who nursed her back to health after he took off on her with that Anita. I saw what a wreck he left behind. And I see her turning into that same wreck all over again. Her hands shook like crazy this afternoon when she was holding her coffee cup. And get this: As we were walking out of The Works she asked me if I'd heard from you. She brought you up, not me. So I told her you're going to be doing your own show out in L.A. with Miss Hawaii, and you'll never guess what happened next. She got this strange, dazed look on her face and then I swear she nearly passed out. Had to grab on to my arm or she would have pitched right over onto the pavement. She recovered quickly. In-sisted she'd merely stumbled. But I know a fainting spell when I see one. She's not well, Mitch. She's lost so much weight her uni-form is falling off of her. I told her to go see her doctor. She told me she had and that the doctor said she was fine. I don't believe her.

I know you are "over" Des but I also know she once meant the world to you. As a personal favor to me would you please give her a call and find out how she's doing? Maybe she'll tell you some-thing about her health that she won't tell me. And it will give you two a chance to discuss the professor's murder. Berger and Mitry used to be quite the crime-stopping duo here in Dorset, after all. Your insights into human behavior were always invaluable to her. Not that Des would ever admit that. But it so happens I've been around a few years and I know these things.

I do realize that this may be a bit awkward for you. I wouldn't ask you under any other circumstances. But I love her and I am worried sick about her.

Much love, Aunt Bella

p.s. I finally had to let Quirt out before he shredded all of the furniture. He has resumed prowling the island. Eats the dry food I leave out for him. Also the heads of numerous bunny rabbits. Life goes on.

To: Bella Tillis
From: Mitch Berger
Subject: Re: Unhappy Turn of Events

Dear Bella—Really sorry to hear about Richard. I didn't know him well but from everything Molly told me he seemed like a terrific guy. And I can't believe what's happened to her mother. When I first moved out to Big Sister I used to see Carolyn jogging through the Nature Preserve every morning. She'd always smile and wave to me. I remember that I kept thinking how weird it was for such a beautiful woman to be so friendly to a total stranger. My frame of reference was the city, where someone with her looks would simply stare right through me. You see, I hadn't figured out yet that Carolyn's behavior was the norm for Dorset. People smile at you there. Carolyn was part of my initiation to that otherworldly place.

I'll be sure to send Molly a note at Kimberly's. It sounds like her aunt's farm in Maine will be the best thing for her. She needs to get away from that mess. She and Carolyn both.

As to the resident trooper, ahem, where do I begin? For starters, you've totally fictionalized our crime-fighting exploits. Des never regarded me as anything more than an amateur goofball who kept blundering my way into her business. Really nice attempt at spin on your part, though. Have you thought about a career in politics? Hey, here's an idea: You could run for the U.S. Congress against Him. The voters need you, Bella. Congress needs you. Think about it.

Also, you've conveniently overlooked that she dumped me in a spectacularly heart-stomping fashion. So I will not be reaching out to her. Not about Richard's murder. Not about the state of her health. She's probably just dieting so she can fit into a thong bikini so as to please Him. Besides, her hands always shake when she drinks too much coffee. Tell her to drink less coffee. Tell her to eat more. Tell her to . . . Come to think of it, I don't care what you tell her.

Bella, I've met someone. She's a dance critic named Cecily Naughton. Cecily just moved here from London and we've hit it off big-time. Remember my former editor, Lacy Nickerson? You met her at the hospital in New London that time I got shot in the leg. Anyway, Lacy introduced the two of us. And before you even ask me, the answer is No, Cecily is not one of the chosen people. Though she is anointed. Her grandfather was the earl of somewhere. Not that she takes any of that peerage stuff seriously. She's a very smart, funny and opinionated woman. Also totally hot. We argue about our work a lot. We laugh a lot. What else can I tell you? Oh, I know—I haven't seen her since this morning and I already miss her.

Happily, she's arranged to be in L.A. while I'm out there. I sort of invited her to come, actually. She wants to check out a couple of experimental dance companies up in San Francisco. Then she's going to fly down to L.A. so we can spend some quality time together. I'm leaving on a flight first thing tomorrow morning. I expect to be at the Four Seasons for about ten days. I'll have my laptop. Feel free to e-mail me if you need me for any reason.

I'd rather you didn't say anything to Des about Cecily, if you don't mind. I simply wanted you to know I'm back on my feet and couldn't be happier. In fact, I'm practically giddy. Not that it's love or anything. Love doesn't just happen overnight. Not in real life, anyway. Only in movies that star Reese Witherspoon.

Seriously, I wouldn't worry about the master sergeant. She just forgets to eat when she's wrapped up in her work. She takes her job to heart. Sometimes too much. That's why she took up drawing. She'll be fine once she has a piece of graphite stick in her fingers again, which is something she knows perfectly well.

Want to know something? I came to a major realization today. Des and I didn't bring out the best in each other. We thought we did, but we were wrong. Brandon is the person who she belongs with. And now maybe I've found someone who is right for me, too. Things certainly seem to be turning out like they're supposed to. Who knows, maybe real life *is* just like the movies. *Fade out. Roll closing credits. . . .*

Love, Mitch

To: Mitch Berger
From: Bella Tillis
Subject: Re: Re: Unhappy Turn of Events

Dear Mr. Hot Shot New York Movie Critic—I am so pleased that you've met someone who you care about. I want nothing more than for you to be happy. I can't wait to meet your lovely Cecily.

Much love, Aunt Bella

p.s. Is Reese Witherspoon the one with the chin?

p.p.s. If I ever meet up with Lacy Nickerson again I intend to punch her in the nose.

CHAPTER 11

CAROLYN WAS LOOKING LIMP but a whole lot better. They'd gotten her into a shower. Her long blond hair was washed. And she was on an intravenous drip to bring her back from her malnourished condition. Her color had improved. So had her mental state. She seemed lucid and calm as she lay there in her bed. No restraints needed. For now, they were keeping her on a mild sedative.

She was in a semiprivate room in Middlesex Hospital, which was a half hour north of Dorset up in Middletown. Her roommate was in surgery, so right now Carolyn had it all to herself— not counting the tanned, weathered woman who was seated by the bed talking softly to her when Des arrived.

Megan Chichester of Blue Hill, Maine, immediately got up out of her chair and stuck out a hand.

"We meet at last," said Des, her own slim hand disappearing inside Megan's rough, calloused one.

"I came as fast as I could." Carolyn's sister was immediately on the defensive. "Not fast enough, I guess."

"There's no way you could have anticipated this. Don't blame yourself."

"She's right, Meggie," Carolyn said softly. "Please don't."

"Thank you both," Megan responded. "But I know what I know. And I don't think I'll ever be able to forgive myself." Megan was several years older than Carolyn. Mid-forties, maybe. Their faces had a similar bone structure. Those same high, terrific cheekbones. Otherwise, the two sisters looked nothing alike. Megan was shorter and stockier, her wavy dark brown hair streaked with silver. She wore a faded chambray shirt with the sleeves rolled up, jeans and work boots.

Des showed Carolyn her smile. "I've been sent here by Lieutenant Tedone to ask you a few follow-up questions. If you don't mind, that is."

"I don't mind. It helps to talk."

"I'd like to stay," said Megan, hovering over her sister protectively.

"That's absolutely not a problem."

Megan sat back down, farmer hands folded in her lap.

Des pulled up another chair and sat, Smokey hat over one knee. The room was on a high floor. She could see the Connecticut River outside the window. "How are you feeling today, Carolyn?"

"I'm not . . . exactly sure how to answer that," Carolyn said slowly. "I still feel like I'm not here. Not *me*. Haven't been me. Somebody else. Somebody wired and crazy. Or a-a total zombie. God, how do I *feel?*" She blinked at Des several times, then lowered her blue eyes to the clean white sheet covering her. "Like I want to crawl under this bed and stay there. I'm ashamed of myself. And *so* tired. I-I keep falling asleep thinking it's all just one big nightmare. But then I wake up and I remember it's not. It's all happening. It's really happening."

"We're going to get through this, sweetie," Megan said reassuringly. "I promise you we will."

"Richard is *dead!*" Carolyn cried out. "I thought we would always be together. I thought we were happy. We had each other. And Molly. And our work. Then one day he walks in and tells me there's someone else and he . . ." She let out a jagged sob. "Just like that it was over. Meggie, I know you two never exactly got along."

"That's not true."

Carolyn's eyes flashed at her. "It is so. You hated him. Don't pretend otherwise."

"I loved Richard," Megan insisted, keeping her voice gentle. "I just thought he could be a bit full of himself, that's all. Everything was always about *his* career. He treated yours like it was nothing more than a cute little hobby. Which I happened to find very condescending. But as long as you were happy together then I was happy for you."

Des soaked up this exchange with great interest. Megan Chichester was the only person she'd encountered so far who had a single bad word to say about Richard Procter. Had the negative feelings been mutual? "Carolyn, did Richard tell you who this other woman was?"

Carolyn gazed at her blankly. "Why do you need to know that?"

"Just trying to connect the dots. It's what they pay me to do."

"I asked him not to. I didn't want to know. Didn't want to keep running into her at the beauty parlor and the hardware store *knowing*. I simply told him to leave. And he did. This was . . . a few weeks ago. After that, I was so thrown that I did things I don't usually do. I-I can't explain why."

"You don't have to explain why," Megan said soothingly. "You went a little nutty. We all do that sometimes. That's what keeps us sane."

"Meggie, I went a *lot* nutty. Drank way too much. Brought strange men home with me. Got into dope. *Me* who never so much as smoked a joint before."

"She's not kidding about that," Megan told Des. "When we were kids Carolyn was always the goody-goody. I was the bad seed."

"Carolyn, what can you tell me about Clay Mundy?"

She stiffened slightly at the mention of his name. "He was . . . real sweet. Helpful, caring. A nice man. Or at least I thought he was. He's not. Nor is Hector. Those two made me do things that I would never, ever . . ." Carolyn broke off, shuddering violently. "They had friends who'd show up sometimes with deliveries. I did them, too. I had to. If I objected they'd hit me. Or burn me with cigarettes. Or tie me to the bedpost and do what they wanted no matter what. They kept me so stoned that I barely even knew what I was doing. I had no idea if it was day or night. Who they were. Who *I* was. But I couldn't make it stop. And after a while it all just seemed . . . normal. These nurses can shove me in that shower a million times, but I don't think I'll ever feel clean again for the rest of my . . ." Carolyn's eyes suddenly widened with fright. "What if I've picked up some horrible sexually transmitted disease?"

Megan reached over and stroked her forehead. "They're checking you for every little thing, sweetie. You're going to be fine. Don't you worry."

Carolyn breathed in and out, her calm slowly returning. "Clay's dope really pulled me in. I was swallowed up before I knew what hit me. I *wanted* to be swallowed up. Today . . . this is the first time my head's been close to clear in ages. I can actually tell the difference between right and wrong. But if you were to stick a blow pipe in front of me right now I'd lunge for it. Give me half a chance and I'll start up again as soon as I go home."

"That's why you're not going home," Megan told her.

"Meggie, I can't stay here forever."

"As soon as you feel stronger you'll start your counseling sessions. Those will continue even after you're discharged. And there are all kinds of support programs. And you've got me to look out for you."

"Is Clay . . . is he still there?"

"He's still residing in your home, yes," Des said. "He and Hector both."

"I don't want them there. I don't want them anywhere near Molly."

"Molly's safe. She's with Kimberly and Jen."

"And I'll tell the bastards to get out," Megan promised her.

"They won't listen to you."

"They'll listen to me," Des said. "And you have my word that neither man will be around Sour Cherry Lane for much longer."

"My sweet little baby girl," Carolyn sighed. "Her father's dead and her mother's a drugged out whore. God, what must she think of me?"

"She's concerned about you," Megan said. "But she's resilient and she's strong."

"And a lot of good people are looking out for her," Des said. "Not only the Beckwiths but Amber and Keith. Also Bella."

"And your friend Mitch, I bet," Carolyn said, nodding her head. "I know Molly adores him."

"Well, no. Mitch moved back to New York."

Carolyn looked at Des in disbelief. "I *knew* that. You two broke up months ago. Sorry, there are big chunks of things I keep forgetting."

"The doctor told you there might be short term memory lapses," Megan said. "But you're going to get better, sweetie. As soon as you feel up to it we'll head home to the farm and I'll put you to work out in the fresh air. You'll be your old self before you know it. Everything's going to be fine."

"If you say so," said Carolyn, unconvinced.

"How much do you know about Clay's business?" Des asked her.

"He never works at it very hard. Although he and Hector always have plenty of money. That's all I know."

"Those men who you said were making deliveries—deliveries of what?"

"Haven't the slightest idea. I wasn't very conscious of what went on outside of my bedroom."

"Do you remember when I came to your house to tell you that Richard had been hospitalized?"

"Maybe," she answered drowsily. "Not really."

"How about when Richard showed up there last week?"

"He wanted to come home. I didn't want to see him. Or him to see me. I told Clay to make him go away."

"Carolyn, what can you tell me about last night? Think hard, please. Any light you can shed will be a tremendous help. Did Richard show up there again? Did he knock on your door? Ask to see you?"

Carolyn's eyelids were starting to droop. "I don't remember anything like that. Richard knocking on the door. Or anybody else. Doesn't mean it didn't happen. I was so high that anybody could have been . . . They heated up a pizza."

"Clay and Hector?"

"They were in the kitchen playing cards. I was in bed with my iPod, blissing out on *Green*. I still love R.E.M. When I was in college they were the coolest band. So smart and hip."

"What else do you remember?"

"Hector," she replied, curling her lip in disgust. "He came in and did what he felt like. He smells really bad. I don't know, maybe I crashed after that. Until there was this huge commotion."

Des leaned forward slightly. "What kind of commotion?"

"You coming in to tell me that Richard was dead. Only I didn't believe you. I wanted to see him for myself. And there were police cars. And neighbors standing out there staring at me and . . ." She trailed off. "I wigged out, didn't I?"

"Just a little."

"Now I'm so tired," she murmured, her eyes falling shut. "I'm just so completely, totally tired."

A nurse bustled in to check Carolyn's vitals and change her IV bag. Des put her big hat back on and left the lady to it. Megan followed her out into the hospital corridor.

"May I ask you what else her doctor has told you?" Des said to her.

"That the emotional burden of Richard's death will make it even harder to wean her off of the meth. No surprise there." Megan jammed her hands in the back pockets of her jeans, rocking back and forth on her heels like an old-timey New England farmer. "He asked me if she's a strong person emotionally. I told him she is. But dear God, nobody's that strong."

"He discussed short term memory loss with you. How about the other possible side effects of prolonged meth use?"

"Such as . . . ?"

"Paranoia and rage. Episodes of violent behavior. We have a lot of criminal cases on file that fit such a pattern."

Megan glowered at her. "What are you saying—that you think Carolyn may have killed Richard herself and doesn't remember it?"

"I'm saying we can't rule anything out."

"I know my sister, okay? She's the gentlest soul on earth. She could never, ever do something like that. I don't care how stoned she was."

"We believe that two people were involved. The slasher and whoever helped him dispose of the body."

"She *wasn't* involved. And you'll never make me believe so."

"I don't mean to be harsh, Megan. I'm just trying to prepare you. Have you met Clay Mundy yet?"

"I have no interest in meeting him," she said, yawning hugely. And looking plenty weary herself.

"I take it you sat up all night with her."

"I did, yeah. I'm told there's a decent motel across the street. I'll get a room there until she's ready to leave."

"I was surprised it took you so long to get here yesterday from Blue Hill."

Now she eyed Des very guardedly. "What do you mean by that?"

"When I phoned your partner, Susan, she told me it's an eight to ten hour drive, depending on the traffic. You left there at noon and yet you didn't get here until midnight."

"That's all true. Except Susan didn't tell you that I was up at five A.M. putting in a solid six hours of chores before I left. My eyes started to get tired after a few hours on the road, so I pulled off at a rest stop outside of Ogunquit and took a nap for a couple of hours."

"That would be Ogunquit, Maine?"

"That's right. Now you're making it sound like *I'm* the one who killed Richard."

"Just connecting the dots, as I said before."

"And I didn't like it when you said it before," Megan blustered. "I'm not a dot. My sister's not a dot."

"I take it you and Richard had issues."

"Richard Procter was an overbearing, pompous jerk. I could barely tolerate the man. Is that what you mean by issues?"

"Did he have a problem with you?"

"Do you mean because I'm gay? As a matter of fact he did. He was not comfortable spending time with us at the farm. Didn't care for his precious Molly being around 'The Girls.' He was petrified that somehow Susan and I would indoctrinate Molly into the secret ya-ya sisterhood of queerdom. When we were here for Christmas he made it abundantly clear to us that he did not want to return to Blue Hill this summer."

"How did you feel about that?"

Megan shrugged her shoulders. "Sorry for Carolyn, mostly. Richard was a smart man. And a decent father, I suppose. But that doesn't mean he couldn't be a complete ass. Was I surprised when Carolyn told me he'd been sleeping with another woman? Not at all. Was I surprised that she told him to get out? You bet. And kind of proud of her, too. Carolyn can be something of a doormat. But she stood up for herself this time."

"Did you encourage her?"

"Maybe I did," Megan admitted. "She's my baby sister. I've looked out for her since she was in pigtails. But, believe me, I had no way of knowing the two of them would completely crash and burn like they did. I never saw it coming. If I had I would have been down here in a heartbeat. And if she'd wanted to take him back I would have made every effort to help, despite my own feelings for the man." Megan ran a hand over her face, stifling another yawn. "May I ask you something now?"

"Absolutely."

"How do I get Clay Mundy and that friend of his out of my sister's house?"

"We can help you there—when the time comes."

"When the time comes," she repeated. "What's that supposed to mean?"

"Right now, it's best if they stay where they are."

"Why?"

"Because they're suspects in an ongoing murder investigation. We want them right where we can find them. The status quo is the way to go—no matter how odious it may seem. Understand?"

"I'm a farmer. I understand pigs and goats. But you seem to care about what you're doing, so I'll give you the benefit of the doubt for now. Provided you're looking out for Molly."

"Molly's perfectly safe, I assure you."

The nurse came out of Carolyn's room. Megan excused herself and went back in to be with her. Des started down the hallway toward the elevator. As she passed the visitors' waiting room, she discovered Patricia Beckwith seated in there all alone reading Mitch's tattered copy of *Time and Again*. Dorset's meanest, richest widow sat very regally in her cardigan sweater and slacks, her back straight, shoulders squared, sensible shoes pressed close together on the floor.

"Why hello, Mrs. Beckwith," Des said, surprised to see her there.

"This is a fiendishly clever yarn," Patricia responded, glancing up from her book. "So inventive. And Mr. Finney's prose practically jumps from the page."

"I'm glad you're enjoying it. Is there something I can help you with?"

"Not that I am aware of. I've stopped by to see if there was anything *I* could do for Carolyn. When I discovered that you were in there with her I thought it best to give you your privacy. How is she feeling?"

"Down on herself. And plenty sick."

"Putting all of that poison in her system certainly didn't help."

"Never does. Did Fred Griswold run you up here? Because I can give you a lift back if you need one."

"It so happens I drove here myself," Patricia said proudly. "I simply could not abide being home with all of those troopers tromp, tromp, tromping around my family's land, bellowing to each other like wild boars. I felt trapped. Even violated, although I'm not certain why. I simply had to get away, so I got in my car and I drove. Would you believe this is the longest trip I've made in ten years? I was quite intimidated by Route Nine at the outset, I must confess. But once I became accustomed to my cruising speed I felt very comfortable. Although I must point out to you that absolutely no one in this state obeys the speed limit. I was doing a swift, steady fifty-five miles per hour and drivers were *flying* by me. My lord, how fast do they go?" she demanded. "Seventy-five? Eighty?"

"At least."

"And this is something that you're aware of?"

"It's not exactly a secret, ma'am."

"Well, why don't you enforce the speed limits?"

"We do the very best we can with limited resources."

"Yes, of course you do. I didn't mean to sound critical, dear. I was simply taken aback." Patricia hesitated, pursing her thin, dry lips uneasily. "The truth is I don't know why I'm here. I barely know Carolyn. It was Richard who I shared a bond with. I shall miss him terribly. And I wish to apologize to you with all of my heart."

"For what, ma'am?"

"You entrusted me with his care. I let you down. Let *him* down."

"None of this was your fault. I told you that last night."

"And I appreciate the sentiment. But I do not accept it. Frankly, I am overwhelmed by guilt, which I assure you is not a feeling with which I am accustomed. Nor is . . . this."

"What, Mrs. Beckwith?"

"Unburdening myself upon others. Don't believe in it. Never have. One's innermost reflections ought to remain one's own. This is why God invented the diary." Patricia reached for her handbag and got slowly to her feet, drawing herself up to her full, rigid height. "Do you think I may pay my respects now? I won't stay long."

"I don't see why not."

With great dignity the old woman left the waiting room and started down the corridor toward Carolyn's room. Des watched her go, thinking that Patricia Beckwith was not the coldhearted bitch everyone in town thought she was. But that was the reality of life in Dorset—once you got a rep it stuck to you. Des found herself wondering what Mitch would have to say to about this sensitive, caring and highly conflicted lady, probably while spraying a mouthful of his American Chop Suey across the dinner table. The doughboy never failed to wow Des with his keen insights into people. Maybe because his mind had been programmed so differently. Hers was the product of exhaustive professional training and old-school shoe leather experience. His a whacked-out kaleidoscope of human depravity, Hollywood style. Much as she hated to admit it, there were times when Des missed what he had to say. This was one of those times. So she tried putting herself in his Mephisto walking shoes, size chunky, and asked herself what he would see going on here that she wasn't.

And, damn it, she realized what it might be. Weird, yes. But staring right at her.

She'd been assuming that Patricia's attachment to Richard Procter was of the motherly variety. What if it wasn't? What if Patricia was the Other Woman who had destroyed the professor's happy home? Not your typical May-December romance, to be sure. But this was Dorset, ground zero for unusual love matches— as Des knew only too well. Was a torrid romance between Richard and a lady thirty-something years his senior a totally crazy idea? Maybe. Or maybe not. It would certainly explain why Patricia Beckwith was so wracked by guilt.

The nurse's station was right next to the elevator. Carolyn's nurse was parked there over a pile of charts. She was a stern-looking Asian woman in her fifties. Not real approachable.

Des approached her anyway. "How is Carolyn doing?"

"Mrs. Procter has been through a lot," she answered impatiently.

"That she has."

It wasn't long before the nurse realized that Des was lingering there. And looked up at her, frowning. "Is there something else, trooper?"

"There is, actually. And if I'm out of line please say so, but I was wondering if you could do me a small favor. . . ."

The call came through as Des was steering her Crown Vic back down to Dorset on Route 9, her hands wrapped tight around the wheel, mind turning over what the nurse had just told her:

Today her blood pressure was even higher—144 over 92. Not that this should have surprised her. Not when she'd come so close to blacking out at The Works when was she was with Bella. They'd been walking out to the parking lot. Bella was telling her about Mitch's new TV gig out in L.A. when, *wham,* there it was— the whole world a-rocking and a-rolling before her eyes. She'd recovered quickly, but Bella could tell something was wrong. Bella knew her.

So why can't she understand Brandon and me?

Maybe because no one else can understand what goes on between two other people. Those who seem to have nothing in common, like Amber and Keith, can't take their eyes off of each other. And yet the couples that seem to have it all together, like Carolyn and Richard, can unravel with the slightest tug of a thread.

The nurse had jotted down Des's blood pressure reading on a card and handed it to her. "Be sure to report this to your doctor when you speak with her."

"I understand these numbers are a bit borderline."

"They are *not* borderline, trooper. You may need to go on medication."

"I hate pills. Is there no other alternative?"

The nurse looked her up and down before she said, "Have you thought about a different line of work?"

This was where Des's head was when her cell phone rang. It was 5:30.

"You told me to call if I ever needed to tell you something or whatever. . . ." It was Jen Beckwith, trying real hard not to sound upset.

"Absolutely, Jen. What's up?"

"Probably nothing. I mean, maybe I'm just being paranoid."

"Jen, what is it?"

"I think Molly has gone in the house."

"What house?"

"*Her* house."

"I thought we all agreed that Molly was going to stay out of there."

"We did. We absolutely did."

"So how did . . . ?"

"I was in the kitchen getting dinner started. My mom's not home from work yet. So I'm rummaging around in the fridge, you know?" Jen's words were tumbling out fast now. "And Molly calls out to me from the living room that she has to go fetch this copy of *To Kill a Mockingbird* she's been reading. Like she has to return it tonight or it'll be overdue. That girl is so anal about library fines. So what if a dumb library book is overdue one day? What does that cost, a whole nickel?"

"Jen, did she tell you that she'd left the book *in* the house?"

"No way. I'd never have let her go. I thought she meant she left it up in her tree house. She promised me she'd be right back. Only she's been gone for half an hour now. Which is why I'm starting to worry."

"Can you tell me if Clay and Hector are home?" Des asked, keeping her voice calm.

"Their van's parked in the driveway. But I can't say for sure whether they're there. Maybe I *am* just being paranoid. The squirt could be chillin' in her tree house. Or maybe she went out to Bella's to feed the kitties. Except her basketball's still here, and she never travels any distance without it. She's working on her left-hand dribble."

"Jen, when is your mom due home?"

"Twenty minutes, maybe."

"I'd like you to stay put until she arrives. Please don't go over there by yourself. I'll check things out from my end and call you back in a few minutes, okay?"

Des hung up and speed-dialed Bella to see if Molly had shown up out there. Got Bella's machine. Oh, right, today was her yoga class at the senior center from 5:00 to 6:30. Then she and some of the other Q-tips usually went out for Chinese food together. So she wouldn't be home until at least 8:00. Damn. Next Des tried Bitsy Peck, who thank God *was* home. Asked her to check the barn for Molly. Bitsy promised she would. Called Des back a few minutes later to say that there was no sign of the girl. Or anyone.

She tried Jen again. "Has Molly come back yet?"

"No . . ." Jen answered warily. "But Hector's out on the porch now."

"What's he doing?"

"Just sitting there."

"Is your mom home?"

"She just called to say she won't be here until at least seven. Dr. Gardiner booked a last-minute appointment. Some old lady with back spasms."

"Jen, I'll be there in five minutes."

"What should *I* do? I can't sit here and twiddle my thumbs."

"I was just coming to that part. Go outside and start shooting baskets in the driveway like nothing's wrong. If Hector waves to you, wave back. And when I get there I want you to act like you were expecting me. Strictly a social call, got it?"

"Not really, but okay," the girl replied hesitantly. "Des, should I be scared?"

"Be aware. Be prepared. Don't ever be scared," she said as she ended the call.

Even though she was terrified herself. Positive that Clay and Hector had taken Molly hostage. Which was precisely the unforeseen circumstance she'd worried about when Cavanaugh had insisted upon holding off for another day. He wanted to see what Clay and Hector's next move would be. Well, they'd made it. Snatched up that little girl—because the opportunity had presented itself and because she was their last and best hope. They were staring at a murder charge. Sitting on a stash of meth. Surrounded by state troopers. And desperately in need of a bargaining chip. Now they had one.

Molly Procter's life in exchange for their freedom.

Des knew perfectly well what she was supposed to do next: Call her troop commander and fill him in. But she stopped herself because once she did she'd set off a full-scale siege scenario. And she did not want that. Not yet. Not when she thought she knew how to pry Molly out of there. The higher-ups would never, ever let her make her play once word got out about this.

Dorset was her town. That made this her mess. So there would be no such phone call. Not yet.

She always kept a gym bag full of spare clothing in the trunk. Needed to for all of those times she got drenched or splattered on the job. She pulled over onto the shoulder of Route 9, fetched it and climbed into the back seat. Stripped off her uniform. Changed into a pink polo shirt, jeans and running shoes. Then got back behind the wheel and resumed driving.

They still had the barricade set up on Old Shore Road at the turnoff for Turkey Neck. She passed through that, then through the second cordon where Turkey Neck met Sour Cherry. There was plenty of daylight left. Men were still out there combing the brush for the murder weapon.

"Thought I'd swing by to see how the little girl's doing," Des explained to the troopers on the barricades.

Which was fine by them. They didn't question what the resident trooper was doing there. As for Grisky and crew, well, they might wonder. Maybe go cellular about this unscheduled visit of hers. But by the time everyone had talked to everyone else she would have made her play.

Jen was dutifully shooting jumpers in the driveway, her face scrunched even tighter than usual. Hector was sitting out on the porch watching the trim young blonde dribble and shoot, dribble and shoot. Des had no doubt whatsoever that he was picturing Jen doing these things entirely naked.

Des pulled into Jen's driveway and got out, her unholstered Sig tucked into the rear waistband of her jeans, shirt untucked so as to conceal it. She waved hello to Hector, who raised a hand ever so slightly in response. Then she called out, "Hey, Jen, where's my girl?" Keeping her manner relaxed and casual. She was off duty. Not someone to be concerned about. "We're going to be late for the game."

"Molly's around . . . somewhere," Jen responded guardedly, chewing on her lower lip. "Haven't seen her in a while."

"Better find her or we'll miss the opening tip-off. Did she go home?" Des asked, nodding at Jen encouragingly.

"Maybe."

"Super, I'll grab her up." Des crossed the lane and climbed the Procters' porch steps, a big, friendly smile on her face. "Hey there, Hector. Could you tell Molly I'm here? I promised to take her to the basketball game tonight."

Hector sat there glowering at her. "What basketball game, lady? Ain't no basketball game now. It's summer."

"Which is when the girls come out to play."

"*What* girls?"

"The WNBA, Hector. Our very own Connecticut Sun are playing Charlotte tonight at the Mohegan Sun Arena. I've got courtside seats for Molly and me. Only we're going to be late. Where is she? Is she inside?" Des swept past him, pushed open the front door and bounded inside, hearing his howl of protest behind her. "Hey, Molly, are you ready to rumble?" she hollered, the floorboards of the old farmhouse creaking underfoot as she crossed the living room to the kitchen. "Let's go, girl! Molly . . . ?"

Molly was seated there at the kitchen table with her library book. She looked wide-eyed and terrified but okay—all except for those fresh red finger marks around her upper arms and neck. One of the bastards had grabbed her and squeezed her tight. Seething, Des shot a look over at Clay, who sat across the table from Molly smoking a cigarette and acting as genial as can be. The very model of folksy charm.

"Why, it's just the lady I was hoping to see," he said, treating Des to a crinkly-eyed smile.

"Is that a fact?" she said, smiling right back at him.

"Sure is. See, I've got me a whole batch of gutter installations scheduled for up in western Massachusetts," he explained, stubbing out his cigarette. "It means I'll be away for the next month or so. Me and Hector both. What with Carolyn's situation, I thought Molly and me better figure something out. We've grown real close these past few weeks, you know. So I was thinking if she wants to tag along we'd be more than happy to have her."

"That's very generous of you, Mr. Mundy," Des said. "Molly, we'll really have to scoot if we want to make the opening tip-off. You ready?"

Molly was too afraid to answer her. Or swallow. Or so much as blink. The girl was trembling with fear.

"What I was wondering," Clay went on, "was how long it'll be before they'll let us leave town. Because I'm going to fall behind schedule. And I sure could use the money."

"There's a murder investigation underway, Mr. Mundy. And the Major Crime Squad may need your help in apprehending the perpetrators. That's why they've asked everyone on the lane to stick around for the time being. You'll want to talk to Lieutenant Rico Tedone regarding this matter. It's his call. He may be cool with you splitting tomorrow morning. That's really not my thing. I'm strictly about local neighborhood issues. Plus I've punched out for the day. But I'll be happy to leave you his number." Des reached for the pad and pencil on the table. "Molly, why don't you go ahead and wait for me out in my ride? I'll be out just as soon as I write down this information for Mr. Mundy."

Molly's eyes darted toward the living room doorway. But she didn't move a muscle.

"Do you girls really have to rush off like this?" Clay protested.

"A promise is a promise," Des said, grinning at him. "Hey, would you like to come with us? It shouldn't be hard to scare up an extra ticket."

Clay shook his head at her regretfully. "Lady, I have been nothing but cooperative, know that?" He fished another cigarette out of his pack, looking around the cluttered table for a match. "Me and Hector both."

"And I appreciate it, Mr. Mundy."

"Is that right?" Clay got up out of his chair and got a book of matches in the drawer next to the sink, lazily lighting his cigarette. He tossed the matches back in the drawer, then yanked a Glock semiautomatic out of there and pointed it right at her. "So why are you treating me like a fool?"

Across the table, Molly let out a gasp.

"Let's just take it easy now." Des kept her voice low. "You're scaring the child. Please put the gun down."

"Not until I get some straight answers." Clay's manner had hardened. No more easygoing charmer. That particular act had left the building. "They haven't hauled me in for questioning yet. Now why is that? I'm the obvious suspect. Hell, I've got a big red X on my back. And yet a whole day's gone by and nobody has reinterviewed me. Or Hector. Not so much as a single follow-up inquiry. No search of the premises, nothing. I find that mighty damned peculiar. Don't you find that peculiar?"

"Mr. Mundy, if you've got a lost tricycle then I'm your girl. But I'm not involved in the investigation of Professor Procter's death. Now why don't you just put that gun down, okay?"

"They think they've got something on me, don't they?"

"Sir, I'm afraid I'm not following you."

"He *knows,* Trooper Des," Molly spoke up, her voice soft and quavery. "That I told you I was supposed to stay out of the root cellar or else. I-I didn't want to tell, honest. But he made me. I'm sorry. I'm really, really sorry."

"Don't be, Molly." Des's eyes never leaving that Glock. "You're going to be fine. Everything's fine. Isn't that right, Mr. Mundy?"

"Let me spell a little something out for you, lady," Clay responded coldly, his jaw clenched tight. "I've been on my own ever since my tight-ass stepfather kicked me out of the house when I was fourteen. I live by my wits. Play by my own rules. And not once has the law ever touched me. For damned sure not some village Barney Fife with tits such as yourself. I haven't spent a single night in lockup my whole life. Not anywhere. And I never will. Small spaces *get* to me, okay? I'd sooner die than get locked up in some cage. I *will* die if I have to—and take a few of you with me for good measure. That's a promise. But so far it's never come to that. Because I'm careful and smart and I know how to take care of business."

"Your business being seamless gutters, I understand."

"Don't get cute with me," he snarled. "Do you people actually think I don't know when I'm under surveillance? I *always* know. I can smell you from a mile off. I'll walk into a place, any place. For the sake of conversation, let's say it's McGee's diner down Old Shore Road. Everybody looks up at me as I come through the door, checking me out. Everybody except for this one guy with muscles who's sitting there over his coffee trying real hard *not* to look at me. That's when I know it's time to pick up and move on. Who thinks they're on to me? Is it the FBI or the DEA? Tell me, damn it!"

"Sure, I can do that," Des said. "If you'll do something for me."

"I'm the one holding the piece, in case you haven't noticed."

"And I'm the one who has the information you want."

Clay narrowed his eyes at her shrewdly. "What do you want from me?"

"The truth about Professor Proctor's death."

"How would I know? I had nothing to do with it. I'm trying to keep a low profile here. You honestly think I'd murder a guy and bring the law down on me? I'd have to be pretty damned stupid."

"Or just a hothead with a temper."

"It wasn't me who killed him.

"Liar mouth!" Molly cried out. "I *heard* you!"

Clay looked at her in annoyance. "What's this now?"

"The night you beat up Daddy in the driveway. You said if you ever saw him around here again you'd *cut* him!"

"Well, I didn't," he insisted. "Wasn't me."

"And I'd like to believe you," Des said, her eyes on that Glock. And her thoughts on the Sig stuffed in her rear waistband. "Do you know what sure would help convince me? If you'd let Molly go."

"I'm not holding her," he said easily. "We're just hanging together."

Des glanced over at the French doors that led out to the back deck. "You're saying she could walk right out that door if she wanted to?"

"Absolutely. She just doesn't want to."

"Is that right, Molly?"

The girl sat frozen at the table. "I'm fine right here, Des." Her voice barely a whisper.

"There, you see? She's fine. We're all fine. Now it's your turn, lady." Clay jabbed the air with the Glock. "Who thinks they're on to me?"

"It's a joint task force. And they don't 'think' it—they've known it ever since you left Atlanta. They're getting ready to shut down the entire Vargas drug trafficking operation." Des shoved her heavy horn-rimmed glasses up her nose and said, "You just described yourself to me as someone smart."

"So . . . ?"

"So let's say you have a big-league stash of ice down in that root cellar. If I were you I'd be trying to cut a sweetheart deal for myself right about now. Seriously, you are staring at a golden opportunity. Provide the Feds with detailed inside testimony and you'll be out in no time. Hell, they might even put you in the witness protection program. I heard them talking about it last night."

"Thanks for thinking of me. That's mighty generous." Clay kept the Glock trained right at her, giving her no opening to make a move. None. "But I'll take my chances south of the border. It won't be the first time Hector and me have had to disappear into the hills down there for a few months. That's how we've kept our records so clean. We know how to go native. Pay the right people off. The Feds don't. We'll be clearing out tonight. And you'll be helping us. You and Molly both. You're going to be our exit visas."

"Your hostages, you mean."

"We'll let you two go just as soon we cross the border. Then again . . ." He grinned at Des wolfishly. "Life is full of surprises. By the time we get there *you* may feel like going native with me."

"Dream on. If you want to hold me, fine. Why not let Molly go? You don't need us both."

"Not a chance. But maybe you'd like to see it for yourself."

"See what?"

Clay gestured to the trapdoor in the floor. "What's down there."

"You want to show it to me?"

"Absolutely." He groped around in the drawer behind him until his hand came out with a length of rope. "Put your hands behind you. Wrists together."

Des didn't budge, her mind racing. It was now or never if she was going to make a move for her Sig. But could she make it without endangering the girl? Or would she better off making a dive for his Glock? Yeah, that was it. Go for the Glock. Go for it. Go . . .

"Hands together *now*," Clay barked impatiently.

As Des stood poised there, ready to spring at him, it dawned upon her that she did not like how the kitchen floor had suddenly started rolling back and forth. Or the way Clay Mundy's face was swimming in and out of focus. . . . Oh, no, not now! No, *please*. . . . As she fought off the wave of dizziness, struggling to keep her wits, a cold splash of reality jarred her back to here and now: *I have no time for this. Molly's life is on the line*. Blinking, she saw Clay clearly once again. Only now he wasn't looking at her. His gaze was over her shoulder at the living room doorway. And now she was hearing the creak of a floorboard—Hector coming up behind her.

"Run, Molly! Get out!"

Molly darted for the glass French doors just as Des dove for Clay's gun, wrestling him for it. He got off one quick shot in Molly's direction, blowing out the glass as she ran out. Then a second, wild shot into the ceiling. Des could not tell whether Molly made it. Because by now Hector was all over her. Both men were— pummeling her, kicking her. Des gave as good as she got. Landed a hard right to Clay's nose that sent blood spurting. But then she felt a tremendous explosion inside of her head and this time there was no fighting it, no chance.

This time everything went black and stayed black.

CHAPTER 12

To: Mitch Berger
From: Bella Tillis
Subject: Local Emergency

Dear Mr. Big Shot New York Movie Critic—You need to come out here right away, *tattela*. Des is in the worst kind of trouble. I wouldn't ask you to come except you're the only one in the whole world who can help and this is a real life and death emergency. She needs you, Mitch. Come at once. Come directly here. Don't bother phoning or responding to this e-mail. Just come. If you don't, I promise that you will regret it for the rest of your life.

I'll explain everything when you get here. Please hurry.

Much love, Aunt Bella.

The slow, agonizing crawl of evening rush hour traffic finally began to pick up after Mitch made it past Stamford. It was 8:30 by now—more than two hours since he'd arrived home to pack for his trip and discovered Bella's strange e-mail.

He did try to phone her. But all he got was her machine. He'd hung up without leaving a message. Paced his apartment. Reread her e-mail again and again, searching for some hint as to what the hell was going on. A hidden kernel. A nuance. Something, anything. Got nowhere. Paced his apartment some more, boiling with frustration. Then abruptly grabbed the phone and switched to a later flight to L.A. tomorrow. Packed an overnight bag. Dumped some extra kibble in Clemmie's bowl, said good-bye and dashed out the door. He caught a cab down to a rental car place on West 81st Street off of Amsterdam, signed for a Chevy Impala and took off, scarfing down a takeaway supper as he crept his way slowly up the Henry Hudson Parkway to the Cross Bronx Expressway.

It was a warm, humid evening. He had the air conditioning cranked high and the Mets-Cubs game on the radio from Shea, Mets leading 4-1 in the bottom of the third. However, thunderstorms were likely to interrupt play at any time, according to Mitch's idol, the Weather Channel's ace storm tracker Jim Cantore. Who was never wrong. Mitch drove, sucking the last of his sweet papaya drink through a straw. The greasy wrappers on the passenger seat next to him all that remained of the three Gray's Papaya hot dogs he'd stuffed in his face before he'd reached the George Washington Bridge. Very first time he'd eaten anything so overtly unhealthy in weeks. But he'd had an uncontrollable yen. Stress, he supposed.

At a time like this a man needed a boost from his natural food group.

He drove, his mind drifting back to last night's adventures in bed with Cecily. How smooth her milky white skin had been. How uninhibited she was. How incredibly, freakishly limber. Their love-making had been boisterous, loud and an amazing amount of fun. It felt great to take his new, toned body out for a test run after so many months of celibacy. Cecily felt great.

As they were lying there in each other's arms, spent and ex-hausted, she'd murmured, "Now I expect you'll be wanting me to catch a cab home."

"Why would I want that?"

"Generally speaking, your prototypical male wants you out by two. Two-thirty at the latest. Can't sleep with a living, breathing, twitchy-legged female in his bed."

"I'm not your prototypical male."

"Do you mean to say you won't utterly freak you out if I spend the night?"

"Not at all. I happen to come from a long line of snugglers."

"This is most . . . unexpected."

"Unless you *want* to leave."

"Actually, what I want is a long, hot bubble bath."

"Right now?"

"If you care to join me I'll feed you strawberries dipped in hot fudge sauce."

"You make it hard to say no, Naughton."

"Making it hard is the general idea, Berger."

It all felt so right between them that when they were lolling in the tub together he impulsively suggested she spend some time with him out in L.A. And she impulsively said yes. He wasn't the least bit worried that they were moving too fast. They were just going with it. Letting it happen.

Except now, instead of jetting out to the coast in the morning, Mitch was steering a rental Chevy along I-95 through Westport. It was starting to drizzle. Back at Shea, the rain was coming down so hard that play had been halted. Mitch flicked off the radio and turned on the windshield wipers, recalling the first time he'd driven out to Dorset on another dark and stormy night one year ago. He'd never been to the place before. Barely even heard of it. It was Lacy who'd sent him there. Tossed him a Weekend Getaway assignment for the travel section—her way of forcing him to get his fat butt out of his apartment after Maisie died. As he drove along now, Mitch remembered that first time he set eyes on the little piece of paradise called Big Sister Island. The first time he'd seen the moldering wreck of a carriage house he would rent and eventually own. Finding the dead body in his tomato patch. Coming face to face with a tall, cool, supremely elegant homicide investigator named Desiree Mitry. She of the alluring light green eyes and breathtaking figure. A rescuer of feral cats who had a secret gift for drawing the victims whose killers she hunted down. It all seemed like much longer than a year ago. Maybe because it was so *over* between the two of them. And yet now he was heading right back out there to help her. Why? Because Bella asked him to? Or because he was the putz of the century? Why did he even care what happened to this woman who had stomped on his heart with her size 12 and a half AA lace-up boots?

He didn't know. But here he was, cruising his way north past New Haven and into the Land of the Quaint. Welcome to Connecticut's Gold Coast—Sachem Head, the Thimble Islands, Madison, Fenwick, Griswold Point and his very own Dorset.

He moved over to the far right lane as he took the Baldwin Bridge over the Connecticut River. Got off at the exit just on the other side of the river and started his way down Old Shore Road, rolling down his windows so he could inhale the rich aromas of the tidal marshes. By now it was past ten. He could hear helicopters circling low overhead. And when he passed Turkey Neck Road he noticed a police barricade had been set up there. TV news crew vans were nosed in together along the shoulder of the road. Mitch wondered what was up. And whether it had anything to do with Bella's e-mail. He flicked on his radio in search of local news. Couldn't find any. Settled for an oldies station that was playing "If 6 Was 9" by Hendrix as he eased the rental Chevy through the darkness of the Peck's Point Nature Preserve to the gate, where he used his card to raise the safety barrier and started his way *bumpety-bump-bump* over the narrow wooden causeway.

Home.

Hearing the water lapping against the rocks of his little beach. Smelling the fresh mown meadow grass. Seeing the welcoming lights of his snug little cottage. As he got out of the car, Mitch felt something thunk into his shin. It was Quirt's head. The cat had come running over to greet him. Now he was rubbing up against Mitch's leg and making that eerie, screechy noise that was what he did instead of purring.

Mitch picked him up. "Hey, big guy, don't tell me you're happy to see me."

Quirt licked him on the nose, which he never did. Then began to squirm and writhe in his arms, which he always did. Mitch let him in the house and stood there in the doorway looking around. Bella had moved the table over by the bay windows, which he didn't care for. His beloved sky blue Fender Stratocaster was parked just inside of the door. He'd chosen to leave his axe behind, and shouldn't have. He reached for it now and held it, loving the feel of it in his hands again.

Bella was in the kitchen. He could hear her charging around in there. Now she came into the living room with a cup of coffee in her hand and a scowl on her bunched fist of a face.

"Okay, I'm here," he said, setting down his guitar. "What's so urgent?"

Bella gaped at him in shock. "What are *you* doing here? Not that I'm not thrilled to see you. I just can't believe that you're . . . My God, so *skinny!*" She put down her coffee and threw him in a bear hug, her face colliding with his chest. "How did you get out here so fast? Was it already on the news in New York?"

"I don't know what you mean. I'm here because of your e-mail."

"What e-mail? I didn't send you any e-mail."

"You did so. You e-mailed me to come right away."

"No, I didn't."

"Bella, you said it was urgent."

"Mitch, I said no such thing. I may be crazy, but I'm not nuts."

"Well, if *you* didn't e-mail me then who did?"

"That was me," answered Molly Procter, who was standing in the kitchen doorway holding a glass of milk and a slab of Bella's marble cake. The freckle-faced little beanpole still wore that same bent pair of wire-framed glasses. And those dumb floppy socks of hers. And still seemed preternaturally wise and calm for her nine years. The only thing different about her were those angry red finger marks around her neck and arms. "I came out here and e-mailed Mitch while you were at yoga," she confessed to Bella, her rabbity nose twitching. "I read through some of your old e-mail exchanges so it would sound true."

Bella looked at the girl in bewilderment. "But, Molly, how were you even able to—?"

"You told me your password once. It's Morris, your husband's name. Because that's the one name you know you won't ever forget." To Mitch, Molly said, "Sorry if I scammed you, but a phone call wouldn't have worked. You'd have said no for sure. I knew this was the only way you'd come. And you just *had* to come."

"Why, Molly?" Mitch demanded.

"To save her," she replied, munching on her cake.

Mitch shook his head. "Okay, will someone *please* tell me what the hell's going on?"

And so Molly did. She told him about how Des had hollered at her to make a run for it. How she'd escaped out the kitchen door as Des fought Clay for his gun, which had gone off twice and shattered the glass but missed her. How she dashed around front to the lane, which was teeming with state troopers who'd heard the shots and wanted to know what was going on. How she ran right by them and straight into Jen's house to tell Jen's mother. "If I'd told the troopers myself they would have held me there," she explained. Then she'd dashed out the door of their house and run straight for Big Sister to e-mail him.

Bella picked up the story from there. She'd come home from dinner with her yoga mates to find Molly there. When Molly told her what had happened she phoned Des's friend Yolie Snipes. Yolie came right out to question Molly, then advised them that Molly may as well stay put on Big Sister for now. Sour Cherry had already been completely evacuated except for Emergency Services personnel.

"Mitch, the situation could not be worse for Des," Bella informed him, her face etched with concern. "Clay Mundy and Hector Villanueva are holding her hostage in the Procter house. They're armed, dangerous and desperate. They've already killed Molly's father."

"Clay kept telling Des that they didn't," Molly said. "But she doesn't believe him, and neither do I. They killed my dad."

"And now they're going to kill Des unless the authorities back off," Bella went on. "They want safe passage out of there. They intend to take Des with them. Once they're safely across the border in Mexico they say they'll release her."

"Like hell they will," Mitch said grimly. "Molly, where's your mom right now?"

"She's safe," Bella answered. "Des is the only one there with them."

"Okay, I get the picture. . . ." Mitch said. "But in the immortal words of Harry Longbaugh, better known as the Sundance Kid, *who are these guys?*"

Molly repeated what she'd heard Des tell Clay in the kitchen— that the Feds were convinced he and Hector were big-time drug traffickers who'd turned her home into a crystal meth stash house. The meth was hidden down in the root cellar, Molly believed, because Clay had ordered her never, ever to go down there. When she asked him why he'd smacked her so hard that her ear rang for a whole day.

Mitch was genuinely shaken to learn that Clay Mundy had struck this little girl. He went to Molly and hugged her. Or tried.

"Now is *not* the time to get all feely, Mitch," she scolded him. "Des needs us."

He released her, glancing over at Bella. "Not to be negative, but do we know for a fact that Des is still alive?"

"No, we don't," Bella had to admit. "No has spoken with her. Or seen her through any of the windows. The hostage negotiators keep asking Clay to put her on the phone, but he refuses to."

"She's alive," Molly said insistently.

"How do you know that?" Mitch asked her.

"Because she has to be."

"They don't know if she's wounded or she's tied up someplace or what," Bella said fretfully. "Which Yolie told us creates a very troubling, uh, what did she call it, sweetie?"

"A hold fire scenario," Molly answered promptly. "They've got this big huge SWAT team in place but right now it's a standoff."

Bella nodded. "Yolie said if it lasts much longer they may have to resort to bean bags."

"That means they fire a charge from a shotgun that won't kill anyone," Molly explained. "It stings and distracts the perpetrators while the SWAT guys storm the building."

"But it's very risky," Bella pointed out. "Because they don't know exactly where in the house Des is."

"Mitch, *I* know where she is," Molly said. "Just before Des went for the gun Clay was talking about showing her the stash of drugs in our root cellar. First, he wanted to tie her up with a rope. I swear that's what he did. Tied her up and threw her in the root cellar. That's why no on has seen her through the windows."

"Makes sense. What did Yolie say when you told her?"

Molly lowered her eyes. "I didn't."

"She sure didn't," Bella added disapprovingly. "This is all news to me."

"Why didn't you, Molly?"

"Because it's my fault Des is in trouble," the girl explained. "See, I accidentally left my library book over there. And it was due back. You have to return them on time. It's really important."

"It's not that important."

"It is, too, Mitch! And don't you ever say otherwise because you are totally wrong. When I went over there to get it Clay wouldn't let me leave. So Des got in the house with this totally lame story about us going to a Connecticut Sun game together. She put her life on the line for me. I can't let anything happen to her, Mitch. I just can't."

"So why didn't you tell Yolie where you think she might be?"

"I don't think it. I *know* it."

"I repeat, why didn't you?"

"For the same reason I didn't tell her that I also know how to sneak Des out of there right under Clay and Hector's noses."

"And this reason is . . . ?"

"Because you're the one who has to save her, Mitch. You two love each other. You belong together. Duh, don't you know that?"

"Molly, this is a serious life and death situation. We're talking about real life here, not some dumb old Hollywood . . ." Mitch caught himself, sighing inwardly.

Molly peered at him quizzically. "Not some dumb old Hollywood *what?*"

"Nothing. I was just about to say the very words that a certain green-eyed individual used to say to me at times like this. Allow me to appreciate the irony of the moment."

"Mitch, you have to decide. Are you going to save Des or aren't you?"

"Neither. I'm calling Yolie right now and telling her every-thing."

Molly rolled her eyes at him. "Oh, you are not. Come on, will you? We're wasting valuable time."

Mitch barged past Bella into the kitchen and dug around in the cupboard under the sink for the box of Cocoa Puffs he'd left hidden there behind the drain cleaner and furniture polish. Returned to the living room with it and plopped down in the easy chair, munching on a chocolaty good handful. That was one of the really great things about Cocoa Puffs—you never had to worry about them getting stale. "Okay, go ahead and tell me what you want to tell me. And I'll listen. But I'm making you no promises, understood?"

"Okay," Molly agreed. "But first you have to tell me something really important."

"Which is . . . ?"

"What in the heck did they do to your eyebrows?"

CHAPTER 13

DARKNESS.

Such total blackness that Des could not even tell whether her eyes were open or shut. Slowly, as she came back to the land of the living, the first thought to enter her semiconscious mind was that she'd gone blind. Must have. Until, that is, another explanation crept its way in: *There is something over my eyes.* Yes, that was it. She was in a hospital bed wearing thick protective bandages over them. Got herself into an awful accident of some kind. What kind? Had she been high-speed chasing someone? Did she flip her Crown Vic? Have to be airlifted out by Life Star helicopter? Had Mitch come to see her yet? Was he right here by her bedside? She couldn't remember. Started to reach a hand toward her bandaged eyes . . . and discovered she couldn't. Not without experiencing a spasm of pain in her shoulder so intense that she couldn't so much as move her hand. Either hand. Her wrists seemed to be joined tight behind her back. It was almost as if someone had cuffed them that way. Or bound them together with some sturdy . . .

And now she remembered.

Molly running for the French doors. Her diving for Clay's Glock as he opened fire. Wrestling him for it. Hector jumping her from behind. And then the explosion in her head that made everything go black. Hector must have cracked her over the head with something. And then they'd tied her up and dumped her here in this totally black place that smelled of damp earth and mold. The root cellar. Of course, they'd shoved her through the trapdoor into the root cellar beneath the kitchen.

But where was Molly?

As she lay there, blinded only by the darkness, Des took inventory of herself. She lay on her side in a fetal position, ankles bound together as tight as her wrists were. Something was stuffed in her mouth, she realized, her tongue probing it carefully. A rag of some kind. Her head ached something fierce, and the back of her neck felt wet. Her head wound must have bled. Her ribs throbbed where they'd kicked her. Arms seemed to be bare. The ground felt cold against them. Her fingers groped for the back of her shirt. It felt like a T-shirt or, no wait, a polo shirt. Right, she'd changed out of her uni before she got here. Which was when? How long had she been unconscious? How much time had passed since Molly made that dash for the door?

And where was Molly?

Had the little girl taken a bullet or gotten away? Was she safe? Was she lying dead somewhere? *Or* was Molly down here with her in this root cellar, bound and gagged same as she was? Des made a soft, inquiring noise through that rag in her mouth. More like whimper than anything else. Listened for a response. Heard nothing. Not so much as the sound of someone else breathing. She was alone down here.

Unless Molly was with her but was dead.

Slowly, Des tried to wriggle into a seated position. But she couldn't seem to make her body obey. Any sort of a movement made her head ache so badly that she began to feel really nauseated. Which was *so* not an option. Not with that damned rag stuffed in her mouth. . . . *I cannot throw up. I must not throw up. I will choke on my own vomit and die a horrible death like Mr. Jimi.* . . . She flopped back down to the damp earth, beads of sweat trickling down her forehead. Breathed slowly and evenly through her nose, in and out, in and out. Steadying herself until the nausea passed. But she would have to take it easy. Was showing all of the classic symptoms of a concussion, including that weird memory muddle when she'd first come to. Thinking *Mitch* would be there by her bedside. Whew, how ill was that?

She could hear sirens now. And cars approaching. Lots of cars. Brakes squealing. Doors slamming. There were rapid footsteps on the creaky kitchen floorboards directly over her head, followed by the murmur of angry voices. She did not hear a girl's voice. No Molly. Just the two men, Clay and Hector. She couldn't make out what they were saying. Only that they were arguing about something.

The gunshots, of course.

The troopers on the barricade had heard Clay open fire and now the cavalry was coming. Which meant she hadn't been out for more than twenty minutes. Also that Clay and Hector were in some deep, deep trouble. Armed SWAT teams would soon be boxing them in from every direction. As her fuzzy brain grabbed hold of just how utterly screwed those two were, something else dawned upon Des:

I am their hostage.

They hadn't dumped her down in this cellar to rot. She was their human bargaining chip. And Molly? Molly must be dead. Had to be dead. *Why else would they bother to keep me alive?* She'd gotten the poor girl killed. Should have called Rico as soon she'd heard from Jen. Shouldn't have gone in solo. But she had and Molly Procter, age nine, was gone.

Des lay there, grief-stricken and tormented by guilt. And yet also curiously aware that she'd be spared from having to cope with these awful feelings for long. Because she and Molly would be linked for eternity on this night. She was not going to get out of this alive either. It would not end well. She felt it. She *knew* it. Not because her life was passing before her eyes right now so much as because it was exposing itself to her. Allowing her, once and for all, to see the absolute truth of things with incredible clarity. Like the real reason for those dizzy spells. The elevated blood pressure and pulse rate. The constant clenching in her stomach. Abandoning the art that had given her life so much glorious purpose. Put it all together and it added up to fool. She knew that now. Knew what her own body had been trying to tell her all along:

I should have stayed with Mitch.

She'd convinced herself that she was happy with Brandon. He felt right. Their life together felt right. Hell, it was the life that she was supposed to lead. And Brandon was the man who she was supposed to be with, until death do us part. Except she'd been lying to herself these past three months. She hadn't taken Brandon back because she loved him. She'd done it because she was nothing more than a great big wuss. Brandon was the easy choice. The safe choice. Not to mention so handsome and accomplished that there wasn't a sister on the planet who wouldn't trade places with her in a heartbeat. None of which counted for a damned thing, she realized now—when it was too late to make it right. But at the very least she could admit the truth to herself as she lay here in the Procters' root cellar on this the last night of her short and unheroic life.

I should have stayed with Mitch.

Instead, she'd blocked out her feelings. Refused to recognize how happy she'd been with that tubby, schlubby Jewish man who'd spent most of his own life sitting in dark rooms staring at a wall. How desperately she'd missed him. Mitch Berger had been her soul mate. When they hooked up she finally became the woman who she'd always wanted to be. Someone who never had to hide a single feeling. Someone open, unafraid, confident, *herself*. Even now the doughboy was still inside of her. Just hearing from Bella that he'd be working in L.A. from now on with Miss

Hawaii had been enough to floor her. And yet when he'd handed her his heart, free and clear, she'd wimped out. She who wasn't afraid to walk into the line of fire.

God, what a mess I've made of everything.

And now she knew it. Now when she would never get the chance to tell Mitch how sorry she was. Because her time had run out. All Des had left were these last precious moments in this dark cellar where she could see things so very clearly. And maybe, before death came, take care of one final piece of personal business.

Des closed her eyes and she prayed.

CHAPTER 14

"Okay, we have to be really, really quiet now," Molly gasped in his ear as they neared the edge of the woods. "Got it?"

"Got it," Mitch whispered, his chest rising and falling from the dash they'd made across the Nature Preserve.

"We can't use our flashlight either—these woods are crawling with Feds. But I know the path home. Just follow me. And try to stay down, will you?"

Into the darkened woods they plunged, hunkered low like two woodchucks in sneakers. Molly a silent, sure-footed creature of the night as she led them along the invisible footpath, her damp little hand clutching his. Mitch bringing up the rear blindly and not at all nimbly. He stumbled repeatedly over fallen branches and exposed tree roots. Fell to the ground more than once. But he found Molly's hand and kept on going, nose to the dirt.

Thunder rumbled overhead. Off in the distance there was a flicker of lightning. The all-out summer downpour that ace storm tracker Jim Cantore had promised would soon arrive in Dorset. For now the night air remained warm, drizzly and dead calm. Mitch was drenched with sweat, mosquitoes feasting on him.

Molly had won out. He'd agreed to go along with her rescue plan. Hadn't called Yolie. Hadn't so much as thought about it. Des needed him. That was all that mattered. It meant everything in the world according to Mitch, which was to say the world according to MGM, RKO and the brothers Warner. When a woman from out of your romantic past needed you, you answered the call. So what if she'd broken your heart? If she was in danger you showed up. You didn't wonder if it was the right thing to do. You didn't hesitate. Did Cagney? Did Errol Flynn? Coop? The Duke? Hell no, pilgrim. Neither did Mitch Berger. Which explained why he was now dog-trotting his way through these woods with this strange, fearless little girl, armed only with a little flashlight that he couldn't use, a pair of wire cutters and Saul Mandelbaum's old Baby Terrier—the pocket-sized iron pry bar that his grandfather opened crates with back when he drove a produce truck to and from the Hunt's Point Market.

Here was how Molly had laid out her plan before they left:

"Our root cellar has four air vents, see?" she explained as she made a quick sketch on a notepad at the table. The vents resembled small windows in the farmhouse's foundation. Mitch's place had similar such vents. "They're covered on the outside with quarter-inch wire mesh to keep the little critters out. Under the wire there's this inch-thick plywood vent cover that gets screwed into place from inside the cellar. We put the covers in over the winter to keep our pipes from freezing. Once spring comes my dad takes them off or the kitchen gets all mildewy. Except he was so messed up this year he forgot. So the vent covers are still on, okay?" Molly paused to finish her glass of milk, licking her upper lip clean. Bella offered her more. She politely declined. "I bet Clay and Hector have never noticed them," she continued. "It's dark down there. And it's not their house. So why would they even care, right?"

"Right," Mitch said, standing over her with his eyes on the notepad.

"Anybody who's standing outside can see three of the vents." Molly ticked them off one by one with her pencil. "This one in front. And this one that faces the driveway. And this one over here by the chimney. So forget them. The troopers will spot you right away and blow the whistle." She grinned up at him. "But the *fourth* one faces the barn in back. *And* it's underneath the deck my dad put in when he installed those French doors. It comes out sixteen feet from the back of the house and it's raised twenty-eight inches off of the ground. That should give you okay head clearance. And the vent is twenty-two and a quarter inches wide by fourteen and three-eighths high."

"Um, okay, just exactly how do you know that?"

"Because I measured them for my dad when he was cutting new plywood covers. The old ones leaked. They're not all the same size, even though they look that way from a distance." Molly studied Mitch with a critical eye. "The old you might have had trouble squeezing through it. But now that you're Mr. Six-Pack Abs you shouldn't have any problem."

"And Des has gotten so skinny you could fit four of her through there," said Bella, parked there beside him with chubby hands on round hips.

"Molly, let me see if I've got this straight. . . ." Mitch said slowly. "I hike my way there through the woods in the dark past the FBI. I elude the SWAT teams that currently have the entire house surrounded. Slither my way under the back deck to the vent. Cut the wire mesh. Pry open the vent cover . . ."

"Which should be a snap," she interjected. "The frame's way punky with dry rot. My dad was planning to replace it."

"Then drop down into the root cellar and snatch up Des—if she's actually down there, and if she is she's still alive. The two of us escape the way I came in. Then the SWAT can go in and take Clay and Hector however they choose. Does that about cover it?"

Molly nodded. "Pretty much. Except for one teeny-tiny detail— I'm coming with you."

"Not a chance. It's one thing for me to risk my own life. I'm a grown-up. Or at least that's what my driver's license says. You're just a little girl."

"Mitch—?"

"It's too dangerous for you. I won't allow it. No way."

"Mitch, will you shut up and listen? You won't get within a hundred yards of the place without me. You'll never even make it through those woods. Besides, it's my father they killed and my mother they messed up. So stop being such an overprotective butthead, will you?"

"Fine," Mitch sighed. Because she was right about the woods part. "But once we reach the barn I'm on my own. I have to insist upon that. You will stay out of harm's way, understood?"

"Sure," Molly agreed. "Whatever you say."

Bella didn't try to talk them out of it. Just kissed each of them on the cheek, handed Mitch her flashlight and said, "I'm here if you need me, *tattela.*"

Which made it official: Bella Tillis, the pride of Brooklyn, U.S.A., widow of Morris, grandmother of eight and godmother to a million causes, was as big a fool for love as he was.

Congress. They absolutely needed her in Congress.

And now he and Molly were emerging from the deep forest darkness. Mitch could make out lights between the trees. The high beams of the state police vehicles that were parked out in the lane. The drizzle was becoming a light, steady rain. The rumble of thunder growing louder.

Molly halted there at the edge of the woods. They were down near the end of the lane—past Amber and Keith's place, and a safe distance away from the action. Staying low, the two of them scampered across the pavement and plunged into a different sort of rough terrain. This one a thorny, brambly thicket of wild berry bushes, barberry, privet and God knew what else. There was no path to follow here. Only dense, overgrown brush that fought back hard as they inched their way through it on their hands and knees, the thorns attacking their faces and bare arms. But for

192

Mitch there was no giving in to a few scratches. Not when Des needed him. Not when this fearless little girl wasn't hesitating to do what needed doing. So he pressed on.

Until finally they'd circled their way around behind the barn in back of Molly's house. It was very dark here. The barn stood between them and all of those lights out in the street. But they were close enough to the action that Mitch could hear the voices of the troopers now.

Molly took the six-inch Maglite from him and flicked it on, keeping its beam low as she searched and searched and . . . there it was, the old chicken wire fence she'd warned him about. All that remained of a vegetable garden from generations gone by. But still sturdy enough to block their way. Mitch pulled the wire cutters from his back pocket and snipped through it, then bent the edges back so they could pass on through.

The wind was starting to pick up, tossing the trees around. And the thunder was so powerful it shook the ground. Lightning crackled directly overhead, bright as daylight. Those helicopters were no longer circling around up there. They'd touched down ahead of the deluge. And now here it came. First Mitch heard it pound on the roof of the barn. Then he felt it pelting him, drenching him. His clothes stuck to him. But he didn't mind. He welcomed the cool, wet relief.

Quickly, they made their way along behind the barn, rain pouring down their necks. When they reached the side that was nearest to the back deck Molly poked her head out for a look—then retreated at once. Mitch had a look for himself. What he saw was two state troopers with shotguns staked out before him in the driveway, their backs to him, eyes glued on the house. Damn.

It meant they had to go with Plan B. His pint-sized partner was already working her way across to the other side of the barn—the

one that faced the backyard. Here, there would be nothing between them and the back deck other than the big old maple where
Molly had her tree house. No actual cover. Just forty feet or so of
open lawn. A much, much riskier play. Especially with all of this
lightning flashing away. The lights were turned off inside the
house so that Clay and Hector could move around in there unseen.
Not to mention get a better view of what was happening outside.
If either man were watching the yard he'd instantly see Mitch
making a dash for it. So would those two troopers on the other
side of the barn. Although Mitch was less concerned about them.
Their eyes were trained on those shattered glass kitchen doors, not
on the grass.

It was Mitch's only chance. He and Molly both knew it as they
huddled there together behind the trunk of the big tree, soaked,
scratched and bleeding.

He put his mouth to her ear and whispered. "I want you to wait
right here, okay?"

She whispered back, "No way. You need me to hold the light."

"Molly, that was *not* our deal."

"I tore up our old deal. This is our new one—so live with it."

"You'll make one hell of an agent someday, but right now
you're staying put. It's too dangerous."

Which was true. Trouble was, Mitch was talking to himself.
Molly was already slithering across the lawn on her belly toward
the house. Mitch shook his head and went after her, belly down in the
sopping wet grass. Hoping that Clay and Hector were watching
the street at this particular moment and not the yard. Hoping
those troopers kept watching the kitchen doors and not the yard.
Hoping the lightning would let up for one second. Just hoping . . .

They made it. The two of them were now tucked safely underneath the deck, rain trickling down on them through the gaps between the decking. The support joists down there made for

considerably less than the twenty-eight inches of head clearance Molly had promised him. But he was fine as long as he didn't try to do anything more than snake his way toward that air vent. Of more concern were those razor-sharp shards of broken glass from the French doors that had fallen into the mud beneath them. Also the rubble of rough-edged granite fieldstones strewn down there. But Molly, who was all exposed elbows and knees, didn't complain. So neither did he.

The fingers of her outstretched hand found the foundation of the house before them. Sniffling, Molly flicked on the Maglite, cupping its narrow beam with her hand to prevent the troopers from seeing it.

The vent was three feet to their left. When they'd wormed their way over to it Mitch found that it was just as she'd described it— quarter-inch wire mesh on the outside, a plywood cover underneath. It *seemed* big enough to squeeze through. Hey, it had to be.

The wire mesh was staple-gunned in place. It would take him all night to pry out those staples. Instead, Mitch got the wire cutters out of his back pocket. Stretched out on his side there in the mud, he snipped around the edge of the mesh. It was not a quiet job. But there was the wind and the thunder and the rain beating down. So he set off no alarm bells as he snip, snip, snipped away. A soaking wet Molly lay there beside him calmly holding the light as Mitch peeled the mesh back and folded it out of his way. Then he had to pause for a moment to catch his breath. His chest was heaving, sweat pouring from him along with the rain. Molly dug a damp tissue from the pocket of her shorts and dabbed at his forehead just like an operating room nurse. He smiled at her gratefully. If he ever had a daughter he wanted her to be just like Molly. Hell, he was even going to name his first girl Molly. Decided it right then and there.

She put her lips to his ear and whispered, "You've got one screw in each corner. They're an inch and a half long, if I remember right."

Nodding, Mitch exchanged his wire cutters for the Baby Terrier. Worked the thin edge of the pry bar between the vent cover and one corner of the frame and gave it a try. The frame was very soft, as promised. He lay there working the pry bar in and out, putting some muscle behind it now. It sure was a good thing he'd been logging time at the Equinox with Liza Birnbaum these past months. The old Mitch would have collapsed in an exhausted, quivering heap of man blubber by now.

The wood let out a groan of protest as it splintered away from the rusty screw. Mitch froze immediately. Molly flicked off the light. And they lay there in silence, listening. Hearing no voices, no footsteps. No response. No one had heard it.

The second screw came away easier. With an outstretched hand Mitch was now able to push the left side of the cover inward by a couple of inches, immediately releasing the moldy smell of the root cellar within. He went to work on the third screw, wedging the Baby Terrier into the punky frame, patiently prying the vent cover from it. And now the third screw came away and he was clutching the inch-thick plywood cover in both hands, working it back and forth until the final screw gave way and the cover came free. He turned it on its side and pulled it out through the vent opening, laying it on the ground next to him. Then he took the light from Molly and shined it downward at what appeared to be a four-foot drop to the cellar's dirt floor.

Briefly, Mitch thought he heard a faint moan coming from in there somewhere. But it was raining so hard on the decking overhead that he couldn't be sure. He put the Maglite in his mouth and plunged headfirst through the open vent. His head and shoulders made it easily. His hips and butt, well, not so much. He had to do some serious wriggling. Got himself snagged on the splintered wood, but Molly freed him. And he just did manage to squeeze through the opening, thankful for every single ounce he'd taken off.

The only trouble now was that he found himself teetering there on the vent frame. The top half of his body hanging in midair while his legs still flailed around out in the mud with Molly—who decided on her own that what he needed more than anything else was a good, firm shove. So she gave him one.

And that was when Mitch fell in.

CHAPTER 15

AM I TRIPPING?

That was Des's first thought. She was just plain imagining it. Had to be. She'd taken a big-time blow to the head. Wasn't totally with it. Was maybe even drifting in and out of consciousness. She had to expect this sort of thing to happen, didn't she?

Then came her second thought: Her ears were simply doing a number on her. Trussed up like she was in total darkness. Rumbles of thunder shaking the ground. That damned rag stuffed in her mouth. Little Molly very likely lying dead right there next to her. Her senses were spooked. Human nature to hear things that weren't really there.

So why am I still hearing it?

Actually, Des wasn't sure *what* she was hearing. Some kind of steady, determined little scratching noises. They seemed to be coming from somewhere down there in the root cellar with her. Could they be . . . ? Of course, *mice* were skittering their way along the foundation. She was hearing their little claws on the stones, that's it. Harmless little field mice. Not to worry. Unless, that is, they were *rats*. Please, God, please don't let them be rats. This is my final night on earth. I don't want the last thing I remember before I die to be rats all over me, gnawing on my nose and my lips and my . . .

Wait, now she heard a whole new sound. And it had zilch to do with rodents. This one was the sound a rusty nail makes when you're yanking it from a board with a claw hammer. Suddenly,

Des was blinded by a shaft of light. Her eyes blinking and watering as they adjusted ever so slowly to it. It wasn't even a bright light, really. Just the dim light of the night slanting across a narrow section of the dirt floor. She heard more noises, quicker and bolder. And now somebody yanked open one of the air vents, flooding the entire root cellar with half-light. Des could hear the sound of the rain coming down outside. She could even smell it as her eyes flicked wildly about, searching and searching.

She was alone down there. No sign of Molly anywhere in the small, bare, root cellar. Or anything else. If the meth was stashed down there they must have buried it.

Now a flashlight beam was pointing straight downward to the dirt floor. Gauging the distance maybe. She let out a moan, gasping as someone began to wriggle headfirst through the narrow open vent. Some fearless SWAT cowboy with more cojones than brains. Some daring, wonderful fool who placed no value on his own life. She wouldn't be surprised if it turned out to be Grisky. His operation. And his kind of grandstand play. No matter. If that bastard got her out here alive she'd kiss him. Hell, she'd *do* him. It would only take a minute and half of her time, after all. Yeah, it had to be Grisky. Only someone with his amount of advanced training could pull off a rescue operation like this with Clay and Hector right there above her in the house. The man must have been a Navy Seal before he joined the bureau. He was incredibly gutty and silent and sure as he made it through that opening, readying himself to drop soundlessly down to the dirt floor and . . .

And he landed with a thud.

Seriously, the man fell like a great big sack of potatoes. An "Oof" of air came out of him when he touched down. Des drew in her own breath, hearing rapid footsteps on the kitchen floorboards overhead. Had they heard him? Were they going to open the trapdoor and check on her?

No, please no. . . .

The footsteps retreated. They hadn't heard him. There was so much noise going on outside between Emergency Services personnel and the weather that he'd gotten away with it. Damn, he had balls *and* luck. And now her hero was crawling his way toward her. Checking her over from head to foot with his light. Then he turned it on himself so she could get a look at him and be reassured. Which was straight out of the rescue manual.

Except Des almost choked on that damned rag when saw whose boyish face was grinning at her. He'd been through hell getting here. Face, neck and arms all scratched and bloodied, streaked with mud. He was soaked to the skin in his Mr. Ralph Lauren polo shirt. But she was seeing *him* and her whole body knew it—that same old fluttering sensation from her tummy to her toes told her so.

He pulled the rag from her mouth and whispered, "Didn't expect to run into *you* here, thinny." His breath smelling of . . . was it pastrami?

She swallowed down huge, blessed gulps of air before her own lips found his ear, which smelled of some fancy new hair gel. Also cologne, she could have sworn. Which was positively *not* Mitch. "Am . . . I . . . tripping?" she gasped.

"If you're tripping, then we both are," he whispered in response.

"B-But what are you . . . ?"

"No big. I had a free evening so I thought I'd hop in the car and see what you were up to." Gently, he probed the back of her head with his fingers. "Hey, you've been bleeding."

"Concussion, maybe. I'm okay. Doughboy, what are you *doing* here?"

He took out his pocket knife and went to work on the ropes binding her wrists and ankles. "Helping out a neighbor."

"Neighbor?" She sat up as soon as her limbs were free, flexing them gratefully. "What neighbor?"

"Molly Procter."

"Molly's . . . ?" Des choked back a sob. "Clay didn't shoot her?"

"Not so you'd notice. But you can ask her yourself. She's waiting for us right outside that air vent."

"She's *here*?"

"Of course. How do you think I made it all this way without attracting any attention? Did you know she can actually see in the dark? I swear to God, that girl is part bat. Or *maybe* she's actually a girl vampire who—"

Des clamped her hand over his mouth. Sometimes it needed doing when he got his jabber on. "Please tell me the hundred percent truth about something, will you?" she whispered.

He nodded his head up and down mutely.

"Am I tripping?"

Chapter 16

"You're not tripping," he whispered after Des had finally agreed to remove her slender, clammy hand from his mouth. But, strangely enough, *he* was. Just being near to her, even in this darkness, Mitch could feel his skin tingling all over. Insane. It was totally insane.

"But what about . . . I mean, you and me. We're not . . ." Des shook her head, unable to string the words together.

No maybe about that concussion. She definitely needed to get looked at by a doctor right away.

"Listen, if Cary Grant can come to Ingrid Bergman's rescue in *Notorious* even after she's been schtupping Claude Rains left and right for months, then I'm man enough to come through for you."

Actually, Mitch was pretty proud of how adroitly he was handling himself. This was the first time he'd been face-to-face with the green-eyed monster since she'd stomped on his heart. And yet here he was being nothing but gallant. "The truth is that I still have feelings for you," he went on, determined to say what needed saying. "I guess I always will. You can't turn it on and off like a faucet. Besides, I figured I owed you one."

"For what?"

"All of the times you've saved my life. So now we're even. And everything's good between us, okay? Ready to get the hell out of here?"

"No need to stick around on my account."

Together, they crawled their way toward the air vent. Mitch

locked his fingers together to form a step and gave her a boost up and out with ease. She reached for Molly and embraced her. The girl buried her face in Des's collarbone, sobbing with relief.

Next it was his turn. He was able to hoist himself up to the air vent on his own, no problem. But getting out was a whole other plot. Des had to grab him under the armpits and pull and pull with all of her might. He'd forgotten how strong she was, concussion or not. Strong enough to yank him right through that opening.

And now all three of them lay there in the mud and broken glass under the deck, Molly wiping the tears from her eyes.

Mitch dug the wire cutters and Baby Terrier from his jeans and jammed them into Des's back pockets. "You found these down there," he whispered. "Got loose on your own. We were never here, okay?"

"Why?"

"Better this way. Much cleaner. Got it?"

She nodded that she did.

Now the three of them slithered out from the under the deck and back across the wet grass to the big maple. It was still raining out, though not with quite as much intensity as before. The thunder and lightning had passed over.

Once they were safely behind the barn Mitch pointed Des in the direction of those two state troopers in the driveway and gave her a quick shove. Then he and Molly dove back into the thorny thicket beyond the chicken wire fence and started their slow, hard journey back to Big Sister.

He could hear Des call out her name to the troopers. Hear them bark in response. Then came the urgent voices into walkie-talkies. Soon somebody with a bullhorn was ordering Clay Mundy and Hector Villanueva to come out with their hands up. Mitch and Molly had made it as far as the woods when all hell broke loose.

A lot of shooting. An insane amount of shooting. So much that it sounded to Mitch's ears like the bloody finale of *Bonnie and Clyde*.

The shooting was still going on back there when he and Molly cleared the woods and, hand-in-hand, dashed their way across the meadow for home.

CHAPTER 17

THE GLOVES CAME OFF once they found out she'd managed to free herself from the root cellar. With Des safely out of harm's way they gave Clay and Hector one last chance to come out with their hands up. Repeated it three times through a bullhorn, loud and clear. Clay and Hector refused to comply.

And then the shooting started.

No one was certain which of the two suspects was responsible for firing those first shots. Although Des thought she had a pretty fair idea. Didn't really matter though. The important thing was that the opening salvo absolutely, positively came from the house. The SWAT teams returned fire. Had no choice. Then they stormed the Procter cottage with overwhelming force. Clay Mundy and Hector Villanueva were given every opportunity to surrender. They would not.

When it was over, both men were pronounced dead at the scene from multiple gunshot wounds. There were no casualties suffered by any sworn personnel at the scene.

An internal State Police investigation into the raid on Sour Cherry Lane was launched the following morning. But there was very little heat behind the after-action inquiry. No bereaved loved ones coming forward to express outrage over Clay and Hector's violent deaths. No friends or business associates demanding answers. No one asking why they'd chosen to shoot it out like they had.

If anyone has asked her, Des would have told them: Clay had simply made good on his promise. He'd vowed to her that he would never, ever spend a single night in jail for as long as he lived. That night on Sour Cherry Lane, he made sure of it.

Grisky's team found the stash of ice down in the root cellar. Some 187 pounds of crystal meth buried in one-gallon plastic freezer bags under fresh dirt not four feet from where Des had lain bound and gagged. Also another twenty pounds of heroin. This information was not made public. The joint task force wasn't giving up on its quest to crush the Vargas drug cartel just because Clay and Hector were gone. Operation Burrito King lived on. So there was no mention in the media about the raid having anything to do with illegal drugs. Instead, the coverage focused entirely on the so-called "Triangle of Death"—Richard Procter, his estranged wife, Carolyn, and her lover, Clay Mundy. The official story line coming from the Major Crime Squad's homicide investigators was that Clay had knifed the professor in a fight over Carolyn. Hector had helped Clay dispose of the body. And when the state police closed in on them the desperate pair had set off a crisis by taking Dorset's resident trooper hostage.

For now, an FBI agent would remain stationed in the woods just in case someone associated with Clay and Hector moseyed along and tried to dig up their stash.

Brandon had been standing out in the middle of the lane looking utterly distraught when Des came staggering through the rain toward him, a big, strong trooper helping her along. Brandon ran to her and hugged her tight, kissing her, kissing her. And then here came Soave and Yolie, beaming with delight. All of them wanted to know how she got out. Des's ears were ringing. And her memory of the previous few minutes was a feverish stew of fantasy and reality. But somehow, she gave them what Mitch had fed her to say. That she'd managed to work the ropes loose. Found wire cutters and a pry bar down there. Jimmied open an air vent. Grabbed the nearest trooper. End of story.

It didn't fly for long, because when they searched the root cellar in the morning they found that her ropes had been cut with a knife, not loosened. And the vent cover pried open from the outside, not within. But for now no one showed any interest in pressing Des over this apparent discrepancy.

"It's all over."

That's what a relieved Brandon kept saying to her as the Jewett sisters were getting her settled in the back of the ambulance. The media people were shouting questions her way. She wasn't answering them. Wasn't up for any questions.

"It's all over."

He said it as they were being whisked away to the Shoreline Clinic together, his arm wrapped around her, making her feel safe and loved. He said it as she sat there on the examining table, an eleven-year-old doctor shining a bright light in her eyes and asking her to look up, down and sideways. The doctor told her what she already knew—that she had a concussion and needed it to take it slow for a few days.

"She'll take it slow," Brandon promised.

Otherwise, Des was fine. Shockingly so. Her blood pressure was a textbook 126 over 78, her resting pulse rate a steady 74. Des knew why. Hell, yes, she knew—because Mitch had come through for her. Risked his life to save hers. He cared. He still cared. . . . *"You can't turn it on and off like a faucet."* . . . As simple as that.

And hello, more than a tiny bit complicated. Not exactly helpful to discover that it was Mitch, not Brandon, who'd been in her heart as she lay there in that root cellar waiting to die. Des had already had her chance with Mitch and blown it. And now he'd given his own heart to someone else, according to Bella. A British dance critic-slash-bitch named Cecily. So it was too late for a do-over. Which Des accepted. Had to accept. Because it was what it was. Besides, Brandon was by her side right now being so support-ive and sweet. She belonged with Brandon. And she was going to make it work with Brandon. She was determined to make it work.

"We are taking the phone off the hook when we get home," he told her as the doctor was patching up her head wound. "You are going to sleep in tomorrow. And I am bringing you breakfast in bed."

She smiled at him, stroking his cheek gently. "Careful, baby, I could get used to being spoiled."

"Get used to it. Your man wants you to."

Brandon made good on his promise, too. He let her sleep sinfully late. And he really did serve her breakfast in bed—orange juice, ba-con, eggs and toast. Brandon had never been the greatest of cooks. But she forced down every greasy, lukewarm bite, yumming enthu-siastically as he hovered over her, plumping her pillows. She still had herself an awful headache, as well as that persistent ringing in her ears. But she felt sinfully decadent as she lay there sipping her sec-ond cup of coffee. And was genuinely touched by the way Brandon was fussing over her. He kept the local newspapers away from her. She wasn't ready for them. Instead, she leafed her way through the *New York Times* and *Boston Globe*, barely noticing the headlines. Nothing was taking place in the outside world that seemed to mat-ter to her.

Until, that is, one particular item in the *Globe* caught her eye. And held it.

As he left for work Brandon made her promise that she'd take it easy today. Des promised him she would. She was real convinc-ing, too.

But once he was out the door Des switched into action mode. Di-aled 411 for Moodus. Had herself a good, long talk with someone who she'd been wanting to speak with for a couple of days. Then she climbed into a fresh uniform, got in her cruiser and started back to Sour Cherry Lane with her head spinning. And not because of any damned concussion.

The thunderstorms of last night had passed over. The day was clear and bright, with puffy white clouds and a cool, fresh breeze blowing off of the Sound. Des rolled down her windows and savored it, knowing there wouldn't be many more days like this before the sweltering humidity of summer settled in.

The Procter house was a shattered, sodden wreck. There was broken glass everywhere. Virtually every pane of every window had gotten blown out in the firefight. The window frames and front door were in pieces. The weathered cedar shingles nothing more than splinters and shards.

Des rolled up to find all three generations of Beckwith women hard at work out on the front porch. Patricia, who had cared for Richard Procter a great deal. Kimberly, who had been ga-ga over him. And Jen, the born achiever, who never, ever smiled. Jen was helping her mother sweep the broken glass into a trash barrel. Patricia was taking a tape measure to the windows and jotting down her findings on a yellow legal pad.

Des got out of her Crown Vic and tipped her big hat at the regal old woman. "What do you intend to do now, ma'am?"

"Fix it up, naturally," Patricia answered. "Then re-let it. I was assured by a highly reputable contractor this morning that it's still structurally sound."

"And it has one heck of a fine root cellar, I happen to know."

Patricia paused from her measuring to cast a critical eye at Des. "You've been through quite an ordeal, young lady. I'm surprised to see you back at work so soon."

"I'm fine, ma'am."

"I'm told that Carolyn Procter has been informed of Clay Mundy's death," Patricia said. "Her sister, Megan, doesn't believe in shielding loved ones from bad news. A belief that I happen to share. I've never abided coddling."

"How did Carolyn take the news?"

"Like the strong, capable woman she truly is. She did not fall into hysterics or any other such nonsense, Megan said. Molly is spending the day with her at the hospital today. As soon as Carolyn's doctors feel she's ready, Megan intends to take them home to Maine. Permanently, it would appear."

"I hate to admit it," Jen said glumly. "But I'm going to miss the little squirt."

"Then we shall go to Maine and visit her," her grandmother responded, gazing cooly over at Kimberly. "All three of us, if that is acceptable to you."

"Really? I mean, sure. Sounds . . . great." Kimberly was visibly floored by her mother-in-law's invitation. Clearly, this signaled a major thawing of family relations. "I got me a week of vacation time coming in July. We could drive up. It'll be fun, won't it, honey?"

Jen blew a loose strand of blond ponytail away from her mouth. "If you say so."

Des stood there studying the girl, wondering if she'd ever figure out how to get her happy on. Or if her whole life would merely be filled with one grim, dogged achievement after another.

Now Amber and Keith came toodling down Sour Cherry for home in Keith's pickup, waving as they drove past. Des excused herself and strode down the lane after them.

They'd been out grocery shopping. Big, blond Keith yanked a forty-pound bag of birdseed from the back of the truck, hoisted it over his shoulder and started around to the backyard with it. Several bags of groceries remained behind. Amber, who was looking bug cute in a cropped knit top and tight jeans, muscled two of them out of there. Des grabbed two more.

"You would not *believe* the commotion we set off at the market," she chattered at Des as they made their way inside through the front door. "Absolutely everyone wanted to know everything about last night. They kept asking us a million questions. It's like we turned into overnight celebrities just because we to live across the lane. Can you believe it?"

"I can, actually. In fact, I had something I wanted to ask you myself."

They put their bags down on the kitchen table. It was an old-fashioned farmhouse kitchen, sunny, cheerful and spotless.

"Sure thing," Amber said. "What is it?"

"Did you wash the knife and put it back in your knife rack over there or did you bury it?"

Amber froze, gaping at her in wide-eyed shock. "*What* did you just say?"

Keith came in through the kitchen door now. All three of them were in there together.

"After you slashed Professor Procter's throat," Des said to them, "did you two hide the murder weapon in plain sight or did you bury it?"

He swallowed hard but did not respond. Just moved closer to his beloved bride, draping a beefy arm around her.

"Because if you *did* bury it," Des continued, "then my money's on that ton of cedar mulch piled out in the driveway. I'm guessing that the troopers never got around to digging it up. And they sure won't be bothering now. Why would they, right?" On their stunned silence she added, "I'm guessing your bloody clothes are under there, too."

"Please don't take this the wrong way, Des," Amber said quietly. "But are you still feeling the effects of that bump on your head?"

"Thanks for asking, but I feel fine. Plenty well enough to take care of business before I got here."

"Business?" Amber's big dark eyes bored in on hers. "What business?"

"Well, I had a nice chat on the phone with Professor Robert Sorin, who was Richard's closest friend on the Wesleyan faculty. You remember him, don't you, Amber? Lives up in Moodus? He sure remembers you. Professor Sorin has been away at an academic conference in Yellow Springs, Ohio. He got home late last night and was real shaken when he heard about Richard's death on the news. Given that his friend is no longer alive, Professor Sorin was willing to share with me something Richard told him a couple of months ago in the strictest confidence. Which was that he'd become romantically involved with a former student. A young Dorset woman who's now a grad student at Yale. And married. Kind of sounds like someone we know, doesn't she?"

Amber lowered those big dark eyes and stared down at the pink and yellow linoleum floor, wringing her hands.

Des kept going. "Keith, I also had a chance to read this morning's *Boston Globe* from front to back."

Keith raised his square chin at her challengingly. "So . . . ?"

"So the Red Sox trounced Toronto eight-zip the night Richard died. At no time during the game did the Sox ever trail. Yet when I showed up here in response to Amber's nine-one-one call *you* told me the Jays were killing them. You weren't watching that game on TV at all, were you? You were out in the lane slashing Richard's throat. Then the two of you carried him down to the river together and dumped him there, figuring he wouldn't wash up for days and days. And when he did that any and all suspicion would land on Clay Mundy and stay there. Then you cleaned yourselves up and hid the evidence, quick like bunnies. Which Molly never saw because she was too scared to climb down from her tree house until I got here. She didn't see anyone leaving the crime scene either. No one did. That's because you didn't have to

214

leave. You were already home. Still, you two were very careful. Amber, you called nine-one-one just in case one of your neighbors had heard Richard scream—figuring it would never occur to anyone that you were involved if *you* were the one who reported it. Especially the way Keith kept insisting he hadn't heard a thing." Des shook her head them disgustedly. "Clay was telling me the truth yesterday. He had nothing to do with Richard's death. Hell, Clay was no killer at all. A killer would have shot Molly dead the instant she started for that kitchen door. He just tried to scare her with a warning shot. The poor bastard didn't realize how gutsy she is. Not that I'm saying I feel the least bit sorry for him or Hector. They get no love from me. Those two sold dope that messed up thousands of people, a lot of them kids. They trashed Carolyn's life. Terrorized Molly. Tied me up and threw me in that root cellar. No, no, I will not be mourning them. But that doesn't mean I'm going to pin Richard's murder on them so his real killers can go free. No one deserves that. Do they, Keith?"

"Des, I honestly don't know what you're talking about," he said in a steady, earnest voice. "It's a total fabrication. Insane. And you can't prove any of it."

"Sure we can," she promised him. "*If* we have to. But I don't think it'll come to that. I know both of you and you're good, decent people who love each other very much. Most of the time, you can barely take your eyes off of each other. Yet right now you're afraid to so much as make eye contact. Would you like me to tell you why? Because you did something horrible together and you both know it. The guilt is already eating away at you. I know it's eating away at me."

"At you?" Amber frowned at her, puzzled. "Why you?"

"Because I should have seen this coming and headed it off. It was staring me right in the face, damn it. Richard *told* me what the deal was. Put it right out there when I found him out on Big

Sister that day. He kept muttering it over and over again: 'They both threw me out. They both threw me out.' I thought he was referring to Clay and Carolyn. My bad. He meant Carolyn and *you,* Amber. Both of the *women* in his life. When he took that after-dinner stroll from Mrs. Beckwith's he didn't head for his old place to see Carolyn or Molly. He showed up here to beg you to leave Keith. He was still crazy about you, wasn't he? Couldn't get you out of his system. It's like a very wise person said to me last night: You can't turn it on and off like a faucet."

Amber gazed at her searchingly for a long moment. "Keith and I . . . weren't married yet." Her voice was soft and trembly. "When Richard and I got involved, I mean."

"Do *not* say another word," Keith ordered her.

"Oh, screw that," Amber shot back. "I'm tired of keeping quiet. Keeping quiet has done nothing but send us straight to hell." She drew in a ragged breath and continued. "Keith and I got into this huge fight at Thanksgiving last year because I wanted to set our wedding date and he didn't. He wanted to wait a while longer. You know how scared off men can get."

"Sure," Des said. "Not like us."

"Things got so out of hand between the two of us that I threw him out. He moved back in with his brother Kevin. We were through, okay? It was *over* between us. Not for long. We patched things up over Christmas and Keith moved back in. We were married soon after that. But during those few weeks we were apart I was real lonely and hurting. Vulnerable, too, I guess. Richard knew right away that Keith wasn't around anymore. And one night he stopped by. Confessed that he'd been madly in love with me ever since I was a sophomore, barely nineteen. I'd never known how he felt. I mean, sure, he helped me get into Yale and found me this cottage and all. But I thought he was just interested in me as a promising young scholar. I realize now how incredibly naïve and stupid that sounds. An older man taking an interest in a female protégé—it *has* to be about sex, right?"

Des didn't answer. It wasn't really a question.

"But Richard was never like that. He'd never so much as hinted that he wanted me. Besides, he and Carolyn seemed so happy together. And he adored Molly. I-I was shocked when he told me. And flattered. And angry at Keith. And, let's face it, just a total fool. Because I let it happen, okay? It was all over in a couple of weeks as far as I was concerned. Had to be over. I'm not the sort of person who can sneak around with a married man in a succession of cheap motels scattered halfway across the state. He had Carolyn and Molly to think about. I had Keith." She gazed up at him, smiling sadly. "We were totally miserable those weeks we were apart. And so we got married and our lives returned to normal. I didn't tell him about Richard. And Richard didn't tell Carolyn about me. We agreed it would be better for everyone if we kept it a secret. We all need our secrets, right? No one tells their loved ones *everything*." Amber halted, her eyes shining. "But Richard wouldn't let go. He kept calling me on my cell phone. Saying he was going to leave Carolyn. That without me he had nothing to live for. I told him *no* a million times. He wouldn't listen to me. Just kept calling and calling. Sounding increasingly, I don't know, *unstrung* with every call. And then the crazy fool went and did it. He told Carolyn he was in love with someone else."

"Did he tell her it was you?"

Amber shook her head. "Richard had an intensely old-fashioned sense of honor. Behaving like a 'gentleman' meant everything to him. Carolyn's response was to throw him out, 'gentleman' or not. He moved into Bob Sorin's guest house, and that's when he really started to lose it. I could barely make sense out of what he was saying on the phone. And then one night he even showed up here. Knocked on that very door right there and begged me to take him back. Thank God Keith had volunteer fire department business and wasn't home. When I said no he fell to his knees and started to weep. Then he marched up the lane and stood out there in his own driveway begging Carolyn to take him back."

"This was the night he and Clay got into their fight?"

"It was," Amber confirmed. "I felt . . . I feel responsible."

"You weren't," Keith argued. "It was all his own doing. He should never have come sniffing around you in the first place. A professor is an authority figure. A guy in his position isn't supposed to hit on students."

"I wasn't his student anymore," Amber reminded him, a defensive edge creeping into her voice. "And I'm not a child. I'm twenty-three."

"Tell you what," Des interjected. "We can debate that point another time. Right now, let's talk about the night Richard died."

"He came back," Amber said hopelessly, her eyes puddling with tears. "We were in here washing our dinner dishes. There was a knock on that door. I opened it and there he was again, demanding that I take him back. Only this time Keith was . . . he was standing right here, Des. And Richard just kept on ranting anyway. I'll never, ever forget the look on Keith's face. I've never seen such disbelief. Or such total rage. He'd been drying our carving knife when Richard showed up. Had it in his hand. And he just chased after Richard and h-he—"

"I made that bastard pay," Keith blustered angrily. In fact, he was barely holding on to his composure even now. His face was red, eyes bulging, fists clenched. "And don't ask me if I'm sorry it happened, Des, because I'm not. I'd do it all over again. Amber's my wife. She's mine. He had no right to *demand* anything. He sure as hell had no right to put his hands on her. I don't care how many frigging postgraduate degrees he had. All I've got is a high school diploma, but I know right from wrong. And you don't come to another man's house and call out his wife. You just don't do that to a man. Not without paying for it. Christ, what was that smug bastard thinking?"

"He wasn't thinking," Des responded quietly. "Not clearly anyhow."

Despite the manly words coming out of his mouth Keith didn't come off like a man to her. More like a jealous, possessive little boy who had anger management issues. A boy whose eyes had started flicking furtively over at the back door. He was thinking about making a run for it.

Des tensed immediately, sincerely hoping he wouldn't. She didn't want to have to shoot someone she had once considered a friend.

To her great relief, Keith returned to his senses and sank slowly into one of the kitchen chairs. "He had no right," he repeated stubbornly. "Amber's mine. And just thinking about the two of them in bed together gets my blood boiling so bad I can barely . . ." He ran a thick hand over his face, sighing dejectedly. "I've ruined both our lives for good, haven't I?"

"And Richard's for damned sure," Des said. "Carolyn and Molly will never be the same. And then, of course, there's Clay and Hector. But we won't even go there."

"Des, I *do* wish I could take that moment back," he admitted. "But I can't. It happened. I lost control. We are talking about blind rage. More than that even. It was . . . I was *terrified*."

"Of what, Keith?"

"Losing her. I could feel my whole world—everything I live for and pray for—all going *poof* right before my eyes. You've got to understand something. I didn't have much going for me when I was growing up. I was a lousy student, a no-good athlete. Just a big, dumb oaf going nowhere. Kevin was the shining star of our family. Kevin had the brains, the personality, the get-up-and-go.

God, I wish I had a nickel for every time my parents said 'Why can't you be more like your brother?' And when it came to girls, forget it. I was so bashful I could barely open my mouth—until Amber came along." He gazed up at her lovingly, his eyes misting over. "I could say anything to Amber and she'd understand. Amber *believed* in me. She's the best thing that's happened to me in my whole life. I'd die without her. I guess that sounds pretty lame."

"Not to me it doesn't. But if you love her so much why did you panic about marrying her?"

"Because I didn't believe it. I was convinced she'd wake up on our honeymoon and realize she'd just made a terrible mistake. And want out. I couldn't believe my luck. Still can't. Someone as special as Amber wanting to be with *me*. So when I found out that she and Richard, that he'd *taken* her from me . . . I-I went nuts. Let my emotions get the best of me. That happens sometimes, especially after I've had a couple of beers. Not that I'm blaming Sam Adams. It's my own damned fault."

Des turned back to Amber. "And then you helped him dump Richard's body and hide the evidence."

"I owed him that much," Amber acknowledged, her voice cracking. "I'm the one who cheated. I-I let Richard love me. I should have just come clean about it when we got back together. But Keith was *so* happy. We both were. So I buried it deep inside and I hoped it would go away. Only it didn't. It was my fault, Des. I'm responsible for Richard's death, not Keith."

"So you phoned it in," Des said. "And when I showed here you two handed me a made-up story, hoping you could live happily ever after. Except it doesn't work that way, does it? You can't build your life on something rotten. You have to pay the price. It'll be better this way, hard as that is for you to imagine right now."

"What happens now?" Keith sounded more like a sorrowful little boy with each passing moment. "Are you going to arrest us?"

"No, Lieutenant Tedone and Sergeant Snipes will do that." Des heard them pull up outside right on time. She'd phoned them before she left home. Went to the front door now and let them in.

Then Des Mitry strode back up Sour Cherry Lane to tell the Sullivans' landlady, Patricia Beckwith, that she was going to have herself another vacancy.

Epilogue

To: Mitch Berger
From: Molly Procter
Subject: Hey

Greetings from way up here in beautiful Blue Hill, Maine, where it still goes down into the 40s at night even though, duh, it's July. It's pretty okay here on the farm. I miss Big Sister and all of Bella's kitties but Aunt Meggie has let me adopt a golden retriever puppy. He is big footed and sweet and kind of doofusy. I've named him Mitch. Hope you don't mind. And if you do, well, too bad. He already knows his name!

My mom is doing okay with her Work Farm Rehab, as she calls it. She's doesn't smile or laugh as much as she used to. But she looks much better, and puts in what Meggie's partner Susan calls "an honest day's work." Here in Maine, that's what passes for high praise, mister! Mom is even talking about starting a new Molly book, which would be great because we could use the money. Farmers are really poor. Did you know that?

She's not the only one who does "an honest day's work" around here. I'm now milking the goats like an old pro. We sell their milk to a cheese maker down the road. I also take care of the chickens and help tend the garden. Our veggie garden is huge. Everything is organic. Susan takes what we grow to a green market twice a week where chefs from all kinds of fancy restaurants in Portland and even Boston buy it.

You'd like it here, Mitch. Lots of really weird neighbors. A few kids my age. One really annoying boy named Connor who lives on the farm next to ours and just won't leave me alone. He has a crush on me that is so totally not mutual. I'm at least eight inches taller than he is. Seriously, I can drive to the hoop on him at will. But I let him score a bucket or two on me every once in a while just so he won't give up.

I still work on my game for one hour every day. Coach Geno has recruited girls from as far away as Alaska (check out Jessica Moore's bio if you don't believe me). So I'm not off of the UConn radar screen even if I am a million miles away. If there's talent out there, Geno will find it. And I'm the real deal. I know this.

We don't have a TV. Meggie and Susan don't believe in it. But I should be able to download your new show from your Web site. So be careful what you say. I'm going to be watching you, mister!

Anyway, I just wanted to say hi and tell you not to worry about me. I'm fine. I think about my dad an awful lot even though he's gone. But Meggie says that's an okay thing to do. He would want me to remember him, and I shouldn't fight it. So I'm not.

I think about you a lot, too. Can you come and see me some time? Alone? Don't bring what's-her-face with you, if you don't mind. Your English girlfriend. See, I still believe that you and Trooper Des are supposed to be together. I will believe this for as long as I live.

Your pal, Molly

p.s. It's only summer training camp and your Knicks already suck.

The early morning fog hung low over Santa Monica, totally obscuring the ultra-expensive view of the Pacific from Mitch's twelfth-floor balcony. In the heat of the day the dense fog would gradually morph into a gassy, sepia-tinted haze that smelled of rotten peaches. Just another spectacular day in paradise, Mitch reflected gloomily as he stood there in his complimentary Four Seasons terry cloth robe, sipping his coffee. He had yet another production meeting scheduled for this morning. This after huddling for hours and hours yesterday with the network suits—who had then taken him to dinner at some fashionable place in Malibu with Miss Hawaii and her Dodger soon-to-be husband. He felt bleary-eyed, sluggish and flabby today. Too many meetings. Too much rich food. He needed to hit the health club downstairs. Instead, he padded back inside his suite and started poring over his notes for today's meeting.

His bedside phone rang. It was the concierge calling from down in the lobby. "Mr. Berger, I'm sorry to disturb you so early but there's a young lady here at the front desk who says you're expecting her. A Miss Naughton?"

"I certainly am," Mitch exclaimed, brightening instantly. "Send her right up, please."

Cecily had finally made it down from San Francisco for a little full frontal pas de deux. Perfect timing on her part. Hurriedly, Mitch gathered up the newspapers and clothes that were strewn everywhere. The place was halfway presentable by the time he heard her tapping at the door.

"Welcome to L.A., luv!" he called out, flinging it open.

It wasn't Cecily.

Des Mitry stood out there in the hall, a leather shoulder bag thrown over one arm and an 18-by-24 inch drawing pad tucked under the other. She wore a pale yellow linen shirt, jeans and an exceedingly wary look.

"What are *you* doing here?" he demanded, staring at her in shock.

"I was on my way to Disneyland. Thought I'd pay you a visit. Bella told me where I could find you."

He shook his head at her, dumfounded. "Des, what is this?"

"Okay so there's something I wanted to say to you," she confessed. "I flew in on the red-eye to say it. May I come in or do I have to do it out here?"

Mitch let her in, eying her up and down. He hadn't gotten a real good look at her the night he rescued her from that root cellar. "You've gotten awfully skinny, you know."

"Back at you, relatively speaking."

"I've been working out with a trainer a little."

"You've been working out with a trainer a lot. I guess this means I don't call you doughboy anymore. What'll I . . . ?"

"You can make it Armando, if you'd like."

"Yeah, I'll get right on that."

"Can I order up some coffee or anything for you?"

"No, I'm fine," she said, standing there before him.

Yet again his skin started to tingle all over that way it did whenever he was near her. It never did that when he was around Cecily. Mitch didn't wonder why. He knew why. "Bella told me you'd given that up," he said, glancing at the drawing pad under her arm.

"I just started up again on the plane. Got me some crime scene photos of Richard Procter that I'm working from. It feels good, although the stewardess sure did give me some funny looks."

"I hear you nailed the Sullivans for killing him. Which I still can't believe."

"Believe it."

"Good job, master sergeant. I guess this means you don't need my help anymore."

"Not true. You're the one who cracked it."

"I did? How so?"

"It was something you said—about how you can't turn your feelings on and off like a faucet. Richard kept babbling some words at me on the beach that made no sense. Nor did his behavior. Not until you said that. Then the whole case fell right into place. Couldn't have done it without you. So give yourself a big pat on the back." She paused to clear her throat before she added, "It dawned on me that I never thanked you for saving my life."

"You flew all of the way out here to say thanks?"

"Some things you don't say over the phone."

"It was no big deal."

"It was a huge deal."

"Molly was the real hero."

Her face broke into a smile. "How is Molly?"

"I just got an e-mail from her. She's great. Des, have you got a place to stay while you're out here? I can call the concierge if you'd like."

"Not necessary. I'm flying right back. Just came to say what I came to say."

"How's your head?"

"Better. I've stopped answering phones that aren't ringing."

"And how about those fainting spells of yours?"

She bristled instantly. "Bella *told* you?"

"Naturally. She's worried about you."

Des turned his desk chair around and sat, her chest rising and falling. "Actually, that's something of an ongoing situation. It seems my blood pressure and resting pulse rate skew dangerously high when I'm with Brandon. I also lose my appetite for solid nourishment almost completely. Hence the slimming regimen. Long story short, Brandon is hazardous to my health."

Mitch responded with one simple word: "Bullshit."

227

"What did you just say to me?" she demanded, her pale green eyes widening.

"Brandon has nothing whatsoever to do with your health. Hell, he's a perfectly decent guy if your taste runs to chiseled, amazingly handsome alpha males. But it so happens that yours doesn't. The awful truth is that you made the biggest mistake of your life when you nuked our relationship—and you know it and now you have to live with it. *That* is what your body's been telling you."

"Mitch, are you purposely trying to make this difficult for me?"

"Why would I want to make it easy?"

"No reason," she said softly.

"Des, I appreciate you coming out here. It was a classy move. But you chose Brandon. And I'm with Cecily now. What's done is done."

"Things look a whole lot different in the light of day."

"Different how?"

"For starters, I've asked Brandon to find himself a new place to live, not to mention a new running mate. Someone more cut out to be a politician's wife than I am."

"What did Brandon say?"

"That he didn't understand."

"I don't think I do, either."

"The love isn't there," she said with a shrug of her shoulders. "He's not my man."

"How do you know that?"

"Because he didn't try to save me. If he was my man then wild horses couldn't have kept him away."

"Hold on a second. So the guy didn't go charging in there like the cavalry. That doesn't mean he doesn't love you. It just says to me that he isn't completely crazy."

"What, you're taking his side?"

"No, but I do think you're employing movie logic instead of real life logic. Which surprises me, quite frankly."

"You've rubbed off on me. What can I say? Except hold on because I'm just getting warmed up. For the past couple of weeks I've been thinking very seriously about transferring out of Dorset to a different town. Somewhere I could start over fresh without all of the emotional baggage. I've gotten so tired of everyone owning my private business. But this Sour Cherry experience has changed my mind. I'm finally beginning to understand those people. Or as much as anyone can who isn't actually one of them. I'm doing good work there. I can make a difference. So I'm staying."

"Good, I'm glad to hear it."

"Are you really?"

"Of course. Why wouldn't I be?"

"No reason," she said quickly, her eyes darting away from his. "How's everything going with your new TV venture?"

"Okay, I guess."

"You don't sound real pumped."

"No, I am. And the network is real excited. We just have some creative differences to iron out."

"Creative differences? Exactly what does that mean?"

"It means I want to be creative and they want something different."

She nodded her head. "And it's their network so you have to toe the line. Sure, I get you."

"Actually, it's not like that. Nobody has said the word *No* to me. It's more like we're speaking a different language. Whenever I talk about the stories I want to do everybody's eyes start to glaze over. It reminds me of when I had this idea a while back for an epic Hollywood novel. Sort of a *What Makes Sammy Run?* meets *The Godfather* meets *The Big Lebowski*."

"You never told me that."

"I never wrote it."

"Why not, Mitch?"

"Because every time I told people about it their eyes would glaze over." Mitch paced his way out to the terrace and back again. "Can I tell you something crazy?"

She looked up at him and said, "You can tell me anything."

"I don't care about being rich and famous. This isn't me. Before you knocked on my door I was seriously thinking about chucking this whole deal and going with Lacy's new e-zine instead. Cecily wants me to. She thinks this whole move is a big mistake."

"Are you planning to mention her a lot?"

"I haven't set an exact number yet. I'll keep you posted. My point is I'd be able to write whatever I want. Spend time on Big Sister again. Walk on the beach. Putter in my garden. Play my music and . . . Did I just say something funny?"

"Why, no. Not at all."

"Being back there the other night made me realize how much I miss the place. I was happy there. Of course, it would mean a lot less money coming in."

"On the plus side, you could let your eyebrows grow back."

"There is *nothing* wrong with my eyebrows."

"Whatever you say, Armando."

"I'd have to ask Bella to find another place."

"She can bunk with me again. Although she'll need to establish her own address soon."

"Why is that?"

"You're going to love this—she's talking about running for Congress against Brandon. Where on earth would she get a fool notion like that?"

"I can't imagine. You said you were just getting warmed up. Is there anything else that you flew out here to tell me?"

"Ask you. And I have no right ask it. Not after everything I put you through. But I need to know the answer."

"To what?"

"You once told me that elephants and Jewish men never forget."

"Yeah, that sounds like me."

She swallowed hard and said, "Do you forgive?"

He gazed at her, getting lost in her eyes for a long moment. "It's too late, Des. What we had together in Dorset, that was something magical. But we can never get it back. It's gone for good. You're wasting your time here. I'm sorry."

"So am I," she said, her voice heavy with regret. "But, hey, thanks for an honest answer."

His bedside phone rang, startling them both. It was the concierge again. "I'm terribly sorry, Mr. Berger, but there seems to be some confusion. There's *another* young lady down here who claims to be Miss Naughton."

"It's true, she is. They're sisters. Very long story. Would you . . . Oh, hell, I'll be right down." Mitch hung up, grabbed a Mets T-shirt from the dresser and dashed into the bathroom. Shucked his robe. Put on the shirt and the jeans that were hanging from the back of the door. Found his Pumas on the bedroom floor. Stepped into them and started out the door.

"Mitch, where are you going?" Des called after him.

"Downstairs to break up with Cecily. Des, I just tried lying to you and I can't. I won't. The truth is that I'm very good at forgiving. Forgiving is one of the things I do best. And I'm still so in love with you that I haven't been able to breathe since you walked in this room. I'll love you until the day I die. Hell, I'll love you even after they've put me in the pine box and covered me over with dirt and grass and-and . . ." He came up for air, his hand gripping the door handle. "You'll still be here when I get back, won't you?"

"I guess Disneyland can wait. Mind if I call room service?"

"Not at all. What are you in the mood for?"

"The lumberjack special—with extra pancakes. I'm absolutely starving all of the sudden. In fact, I don't think I've ever been so hungry in my whole life."